Spirit Guide

Angela K. Crandall

Copyright © 2016
Angela K. Crandall

Angelada books
ISBN-13: 978-0692814970
ISBN-10: 0692814973
Kindle Edition
ASIN-BO6WP5QV65

First Edition

Cover design by Angela K. Crandall and Toni Kerr.

.

Special thanks to:

Toni Kerr for helping me design my book cover. My mother for pressing me never to give up on my writing. Friends and family for their encouragement and support.

Chapter 1

(Saturday, March 27th)

(Starla)

My palms were sweaty. I felt like I was on fire. The dance was tonight. Jensen, Molly and I had just finished up a big test for Myth class weeks ago. It seemed like, eons really. I stopped jogging and leaned up against a tree surveying the park. I'd like to say this is where it all started, but it began the night I came home from Denny's, so I'll save you the details. My name is Starla; I am a half Kitsune fox and half human. My best friend Molly exposed what she feels is her deepest, darkest secret. Then I found out I'm in love with my best friend.

I started to giggle. Your life is not a movie, I told myself twisting around to see Ranger Mike. He'd run up behind me.

"Hey, are you and Jensen, going to the dance tonight?" he asked.

I pushed myself into a standing position. "I wouldn't miss this dance for the world. I need some semblance of order after all the chaos that went down," I replied.

He crossed his arms, taking a quick look around the park. "I understand, too much. Nayla has been asking about you. I know she said she'd let you off the hook for a while. Nerves are dancing all over the place with the bandits in our seclusions chambers. Jones has been in and out on occasions. Rascal is pretty upset that he'll need to testify in the trial. You can see why she is anxious to get started on your training."

I kicked the sand beneath my feet with my shoes, "I have a month and a half before I'm let out for the summer. How's Cal? Has she asked about me?"

1

"Eva won't let her out of her sight. Nayla mentioned, you and Cal will be training together. She can't quite figure out how to stay in one form. You know she keeps transcending back and forth. We aren't sure why at this point," he muttered.

"Oh, that's extreme! While I'm here, can you do me a favor?" I asked.

"Um, maybe what is it?"

"Mom and I would like to have Cal over for breakfast soon. Could you ask Eva? She loved mom's pancakes. I'm kind of busy, and I don't have her digits. Eva can join us. If it makes her more comfortable, in human form, of course," I chuckled.

"Sure. Where are you off to, after this?"

"Molly and I are going to get our hair done. She wants it to be a surprise for Maine," I said, then smiled. My heart belonged to Jensen, yet I couldn't stop being ecstatic about Maine and Molly. She'd waited so long to be happy.

"Oh, you already have your dresses?"

"Yes. I'm going to wear this fantastic flowing iridescent rainbow-dress. Molly's actually, jealous. She said she saw it first! I won the debate, however. She's found one similar to it. I had a notion it fit her personality better."

He grinned, "Her folks are letting her go, with Maine then?"

I let out a long sigh and placed my hands on my hips, "Molly's mom is a strong lady. After our encounter at Thunderhead Bay, they had a lengthy discussion concerning unconditional love. Either Mr. Fretner accepted his daughter with the ground rules her mother laid out or..."

"She'd kick him out?"

I nodded.

"Wow, a Christen woman doing that? Something you don't hear about every day."

"Tabitha is one of a kind. Anyway, I've got to rush," I said.

2

"Tell Molly I said hello, and Jensen?"

"I won't be seeing him until the dance. Kind of like pre-dance jitters! Maybe that's why I'm so energetic today! Bye!" I waved running off the trail towards town.

I pushed my way into the beauty parlor in full swing. Almost, all the chairs were occupied by customers. In the back, only one sink remained opened for use shampooing. Rita stood at the register ringing up a customer. I swung my long tresses behind me up into a ponytail. I should have done it earlier to avoid all the hair flying in my face as I ran. Tapping my jean pocket, I made sure my wallet still resided there before greeting Rita.

I approached the desk, "I'm here for our ten O'clock appointment."

"Oh, hello Starla," she said, then smiled at me. "Molly called and is running late. She said not to worry. Her mom had a last minute errand."

"Sure," I shrugged. "How's business been?"

"Rather, steady," she said, picking up the pen next to her. She then wrote something down in her notebook on the counter. "I'm just confirming your appointment here. I've had some dye jobs here and there, pedicures, and brow waxing. Hmm, no one's asked for any wild hair colors lately." She looked up from her book, "you and Molly are set up with Iris today."

"Thanks," I said, turning away to take a seat.

"Wait, you're appointment was made for the works package right?"

I motioned with my hands to the top of my head, "Yes, Shampoo me, deep condition me, and a whip it on top."

"Starla, you are a hoot, go sit. Molly should be here soon," she chuckled.

I gave her my best grin and sauntered over to the sitting area. Ah, magazines galore! I picked one up to leaf through as I waited. I checked out the pictures. I'd started to make collages with them recently and hung some on my bedroom wall. Mom said it was rather creative. Maybe Rita would let me have a few, or at least give them to me instead of throwing them out.

"You're looking at magazines again? Ever since Thunderhead Bay you've been doing those."

I set it aside. "Molly, I didn't even hear the bell ding. I had hoped that Rita might let me have one or two of these. Mom's not letting me near her stack til she finishes reading the ones the library was going to discard. These are new!"

Molly flopped down in the chair beside me.

"Why the long face?" I asked, setting aside *Glamour*. I nudged her with my shoulder.

"Dad wants to meet Maine," she grumbled adjusting her purse on her lap.

"Well, it's a little late for that now. Maine and Jensen's plans were to pick us up at the apartment. Then we would meet Owl at the dance. I'm pretty sure he's coming alone."

Molly managed a forced grin. "Owl is going stag? I thought he had his eye on someone."

"Did you see him checking anyone out recently? We haven't hung out together since the test. I've yet to attend any clan meetings either," I added.

"No, he doesn't seem like the sort of guy who'd go to the dance alone," she commented.

"No, he's with us as a group. So do we need to stop by the house so your dad can meet Maine? How should we handle this?" I rummaged through my purse to find my chap stick, got it! Grape glam and slid some on my lips. I offered some to Molly.

"No, thanks," she said, waving her hand. "Do you especially feel the need to experience my dad flipping out?"

"He'll be fine. As long as you don't do anything drastic. You don't plan on making out in front of him, do you?" I drawled out.

Molly rolled her eyes, "Only you'd consider that," she laughed. It definitely would upset him. I'd better stick to hand holding." She winked at me.

"So you're saying..."

"I'm not saying anything. Besides, this is our first official date. Is Jensen excited about your up do?"

"He isn't aware that beautifying myself is on the list of to do's." I adjusted myself in the seat. My butt was starting to hurt. I'd be glad to sit down in the comfortable beautician chair.

"My butt hurts," I muttered.

Molly muffled a laugh into her shirt, and Iris strutted our way. Today, she wore a long flowing hippie dress and had her bright red hair pulled back in a bun. Red huh? I liked it. The last time I saw her, it had been black with purple streaks. If I did that, mom might freak!

"Ladies, I can only prep one of you now. Who wants to be shampooed and conditioned first? Or if you prefer Rita will be available soon.

"I'll hang around. You go first. I need to contemplate adding a bit of color to my hair, say a few streaks of pink, no maybe purple!"

"You should go for it. It's our night to let loose besides it washes out right?" questioned Molly. She got up from her seat.

Iris beamed, "It's your choice semi-permanent, or Permanent, follow me," she said. Molly placed her purse over her shoulder, proceeding to the shampooing area. She sat down and let Iris wash her hair. I picked up a magazine and leafed through it.

Would Jensen be prepping for the dance? He'd told me days ago, he'd planned something special. He wouldn't even give me a hint! I'd begun the guessing game in my head. Limo, private party, a dinner at Olive Garden? He wouldn't dare take us to Denny's, would he? I'd be going back to work Monday.

Rita tugged at my hair, "Starla, daydreaming as usual?"

I set down Cosmo, and stood up, "Besides my up-do, I'd like to get some purple streaks."

"I can manage that, and semi-permanent is all I have in stock. Follow me. We'll get started."

An hour or two later, Molly and I were staring at our new selves.

Iris smiled, "There you go, do you girls love it or what?" She swiveled Molly towards me in her chair. A smile spread a crossed my face. She had gone with a few streaks of red throughout her blondish-brown hair. It had been styled with a few ringlets to accent her pretty face. "You look breathtaking! Maine will be impressed. She'll fawn over you," I exclaimed.

"Me, look at you!'

I'd decided on two long braids which Rita had pinned to the side of my head. One streak of purple dressed up each braid, and several highlighted streaks ran through my long curly tresses that fell framing my face.

"I did go a bit overboard, but mom will get over it," I replied.

"I take it you girls are ecstatic about your new hair styles?" asked Iris.

Rita had returned to the desk to ring up our orders.

"Ecstatic doesn't even describe my emotional state," exclaimed Molly, standing up from the chair. She removed her frock handing it to Iris.

"No words could describe what you just did for us. Thank you," I said and unfastened my smock. After, handing it to Iris, I casually crept up to the counter. Molly was busy explaining that Maine and Jensen would be picking us up for the dance in a few hours.

"How much do I owe you?"

Rita leaned on the counter observing Molly, "Your mom came in yesterday. She didn't want you, or Molly to worry about the bill. It's taken care of."

"Then tips," I said, pulling two tens out of my wallet.

Rita put up her hand and shook her head.

"You have to take tips, or you'll be insulting us girls. We're extremely grateful. If you'd only seen us a few weeks ago, you'd understand why," I explained.

"Alright then, if you insist. I'll make sure Iris gets her half," she answered.

I turned away from the counter, then remembered the magazines.

"Oh, Rita, before I leave, can you save me some magazines instead of tossing them? I've been working on some art projects."

"Sure, I'll give them to your mom the next time she stops in," she answered.

Molly skipped up to me, "Ready to go?"

"Yeah, lets," I said linking my arm in hers.

We exited the parlor, and my face fell into a frown. Cal, she should be experiencing this too. How far had she fallen behind in life due to her captors? What had she felt, gone through, experienced?

It wasn't that I didn't adore the friend walking beside me, but I worried about another.

She too had a lot going on. I didn't know a lot about what had happened while she was being held hostage. We hadn't spoken since the rescue.

"Starla, you OK?"

I stopped and gulped back a few tears. I still had to do my makeup back at the house. "It's Cal. Eva's been keeping her from leaving the park. I realize they want to protect her and slowly integrate her back into the community and clan. It's her choice if she chooses to come back to this part of her life. I can't help but think she should be having these experiences with us," I stammered.

"You're a good friend," Molly said, pulling out a tissue, and handed it to me.

"Thanks," I said, wiping my eyes before my tears hit the ground.

Chapter 2

(Dan)

Sitting on the couch in the living room, I allowed my hands to rest on each side of her neck. I gently massaged the knots. Moving closer, I continued down her back. She leaned against me, allowing me to apply more pressure. It wasn't easy to restrain myself. Every part of me wanted to place my arms around her. A few times we'd hugged goodbye since Starla's return from the mission. I'd held on a little too long, but she never mentioned it. Each day that passed, I'd wanted to be back in our home together. Now the bandits were captured, and the trial would take place in a week, I needed my wife by my side.

"Ah, Thank you, honey," said Tri turning towards me. I took her hands in mine, but couldn't meet her eyes. She moved in closer, leaning her forehead against mine. Then looked up into my eyes. I couldn't turn away.

"I need to be with you, but I don't know," she choked.

"How much longer, I mean, how much more time do you need?" I whispered.

"Megan keeps asking when you'll be home. That part truly gets to me, but it's not that simple."

"What's the problem?" I mumbled.

"I need to know how I'll be received by the clan," she admitted.

Softly I stroked her cheek, "I don't think they'll reject you. Nayla has taken to Starla. They refer to her as Starla Ariana. Did she tell you that?"

"Hmmm," she nuzzled closer to me, letting her chin rest on my shoulder. "I'm not going to jump into this all at once."

9

"It has to be gradual," she insisted. "What's going on with Eva (Kristin) and Cal? If I could meet with them outside of Hunters Park, perhaps I'd feel more comfortable."

I put my arms around her and pulled her close giving in to myself. Sighing, I ran my hands along her back. "I'll discuss contact with the clan. Mike said Starla had asked about Cal this morning. It might be good to invite her and Eva, over for pancakes. Cal mentioned wanting them following her rescue."

Tri pulled away from me. There was a puzzled look on her face. "Will Cavin allow it?"

"If he believes it will bring you back to us he'll agree to almost anything," I answered. Tri pushed me aside. I moved back and gave her breathing room.

"The trial. When it starts, how will it affect Starla and Jensen's relationship? Will it?" she asked.

"She'll be training with Nayla while most of it is going on. That's the plan unless anything changes. They'll both be busy. It's not like we'll keep them apart on purpose. Now, discussing the trial could be an issue. Nayla needs Starla to concentrate on who she is going to become."

Tri reached for a pillow and pulled it close to her. "I cannot have my daughter taken from me. She told me she would be allowed both lives. Make it clear to them that she must be able to function in this world. I won't allow her to disconnect from everything she knows for the clan's protection."

I took Tri's arm tenderly and softly caressed it with my fingers. "They won't. You have to learn to trust them again. The bandits screwed it up for us, everyone. The instant we captured them and contained them, we got our lives back. Now we have to seek justice for Rascal's son and those they killed in the massacres. The only way we can do that is, with a trial. Starla's training plays a part in this. I don't know how.Nayla has the answers to that."

10

Tri nodded at me. Then set the pillow down beside her on the sofa. "Starla and Molly should be back soon. You can stay if you want. I'll make us coffee."

"Sounds good, I'd rather not discuss any of the plans for her training til after tonight. Let her have one evening stress-free from the pressure she'll soon be under."

"This is happening too rapidly. Nayla promised her down time. This isn't, what we initially signed-up for. I'd hoped it could wait til the semester was over," responded Tri standing up from the couch.

"I know. It's not what I wanted either. I'll do everything, I can in order to make sure she finishes her classes. If we're fortunate, we'll have this wrapped up in a week or less. We'll have to call Starla Ariana in for some of the trial. Right now Cavin is trying to coordinate with Nayla on this," I said as we stepped into the kitchen. Before she could protest, I walked up to the cupboard and pulled out the coffee can. I began measuring it out into the coffee maker observing my wife situate herself at the dinner table. She smoothed out the wrinkled tablecloth several times before I set two steaming hot mugs down.

"Creamer?"

"Yeah, I'll get it. I forget you don't take it black," I responded. Then opened the fridge door, and rummaged around till I found it pushed behind the orange juice. I shut the door. Then slide it next to her along with a spoon I'd grabbed off the countertop.

"Thanks," she replied, stirring it into the mug.

We had just sat down and had begun sipping our drinks when we heard a click, click clock. The door to the kitchen from the back opened and in walked Starla.

Chapter 3

(Starla)

"Hey," I hollered opening the back door. Stepping into the room my eyes fell on my father seated next to my mom at the dining room table. She was distraught. I pushed the door shut behind me. The coffee smell wafted into my nostrils. I grabbed a cup from the cupboard and poured myself some before joining them at the table.

"Mom, you Ok?" I asked, reaching out for her hand. She took it, squeezed, then pulled her hand away.

"Your dad and I were discussing a few things. It would be nice, for Cal and Eva to come over for pancakes soon. Dad mentioned Cal wouldn't shut up about them. It's about time they let her loose for a few hours."

Sipping my black gruel I nodded. "This needs creamer," I complained. Mom pushed some over to me, and I poured it into my drink. "It's weird. Today, after Molly and I had our hair styled, my stomach tightened in the realization that Cal wasn't going to the dance with us. After all, these obstacles that occurred leading up to this moment. I realized if she hadn't been, taken she'd almost certainly be a part of my crowd. It's daunting, how I took for granted, what I've had. If I'd only known." I frowned.

"Don't, Cal will be back. You two will catch up, and reconnect. It'll take time for sure. Your ties, however, are not forever severed. Focus on tonight," suggested my father. He gently placed a kiss on my mother's forehead.

"Alright," I agreed. Something was definitely, bothering mom. I downed the rest of my coffee and then got up, washing out my mug in the sink.

"No one is going to comment on my purple hair?" I asked, placing my cup in the rack to dry. "Usually, I'd get all kinds of parental sass about being an adult," I commented turning towards them.

My mother sauntered up to me and placed her hands on my shoulders. "Soon, you'll have many more responsibilities to bear. For now, I want you to indulge in frivolous fun. Besides, I'm sure Don will do enough ranting once your back at the diner," she gloated.

"Fudge, I never gave that a second thought."

My dad chuckled. "Don't worry, and if he gives you hell just ask him about the time he got beard hair in someone's scrambled eggs! He started wearing a beard net that looked ridiculous until he finally gave in and shaved it off. I'm sure he has worse things to deal with than a waitress with purple hair," he acknowledged.

"Thanks, dad," I said, walking over to him. His arms reached out and pulled me into a hug.

"Always my Star, Starla."

I pulled away. "Remember dad, I am a grown up," I said and punched his shoulder.

My mom strolled over to the table, picking up dad's empty coffee cup. Then put the creamer back into the refrigerator. "You two, come on, play nice. I'm going to pick up Megan at Carol's. Then I'd like to get pictures of you and your friends before you leave. Is Jensen bringing Molly?"

"He was going to bring Maine and meet Molly and me here. That was until Mr. Fretner decided he needed to meet Maine before the dance," I said rolling my eyes.

"So you and Jensen want to be her back up?" asked my dad.

"She needs us in case it doesn't go well. We're not going to beat him down or push our own ideals on him.

"I'm hopeful that when he sees them together, it will open his heart to accept who his daughter is," I declared.

"Fair enough, be careful," my dad advised.

"Mrs. Fretner is rational. As for Mr. Fretner, I've never gotten good vibes from that man," my mother added, as my father neared the kitchen exit.

"Where's Fritz?"

"Around here somewhere, he's probably chewing on that bone your sister gave him this morning. Now your father has to go back to do some work for Cavin. Me, I'm going to reclaim your sister."

"Mom, you realize she and Carol, are attached at the hip. It's a tween thing," I sighed.

"I'm just glad she hasn't got a boyfriend yet. For now, it's only you and Jensen I need to be concerned about," she retorted.

"Bye Mom, Dad," I said, waving them off. After they had shut the door behind them, I turned to the hallway to head upstairs.

I shut the door to my room, letting my hand fall on the grainy door. My eyes caught sight of the poster above my bed of a red fox. Mom had bought it for me soon after the mission. She'd said it looked a lot like me. I wasn't sure, but it did make me feel akin to my clan. I crawled over to my bed and pulled myself up onto it. Afterward, I sat cross-legged in meditation form. Maybe I could conjure up my spirit guide fox. If not, perhaps speak to Cal. I closed my eyes, imagining the field of wild corn, or hay, desiring escape. Not once had I been permitted to transform since the mission. Drifting off into my own mental world, I ran, in my desired body.

I'd gone pretty far out into the nothingness until out of the air a fox jumped in front of me. At first, I thought it was her, Amare my spirit guide. No, Nayla. She paced around me in a circle not allowing me to pass into the next field beyond.

"You're not supposed to be here," she warned.

"I can't take it anymore. I have to adjust. Plus, you never told me not to meditate. You can't expect me to hide this part of myself til you're ready to use it," I nagged.

Nayla nudged me, "It's not about controlling you. In a few weeks, you'll be training. When you illuminate yourself here, you're vulnerable to other entities. You could open a portal for them to enter into. If you're not careful, they could invade this sacred place."

"What? People and creatures can just enter my mind!" I exclaimed.

"Shh, settle," she whispered soothing me. "You just need to be taught how to keep them out. Guard your thoughts when you're meditating. If you're calling for someone, you must be able to identify them on the cusp of their entrance. You have to know how to lure the approved spirits into your space. That's all. Now I need you to go back. Get ready for the dance. Enjoy yourself Starla. Let Jensen sweep you off your feet. Just be, for once relax! Cal is fine," she ordered.

"You knew, about my thoughts, my feelings today?" I cowered back, ready not merely to run, but to open my eyes. I expected that here I could feel tranquility before the butterflies in my chest, Jensen at my side, and Molly. It would be the first time I met Maine.

"Hey. It will be, fine. I'm only cautioning you. It's my job to shield you from harm. After tonight, if you yearn to run in fox form come see me. OK? We'll start training. Just get me a schedule to work around. You were supposed to have downtime," she instructed me.

"I have to keep advancing into this role. Simply put, I cannot just disengage from what you've taught me so far. These few weeks I've been running in the park, concentrating on Jone's class, finishing up my math and lit class. My brain feels like this growing orb about ready to burst!"

"So have fun tonight. Besides, Dan told me you still have a few weeks left of classes."

She was right. One week each of Math and lit, then I had to make it till May 1st for Jones, really retiring from college.

"No, don't give Tri something else to hold over my head Starla, not now. Please," Nayla pleaded. I could hear in her voice the desire for pity.

"I never meant to place you in the middle. This static situation with your mom is making it difficult. Currently, we're trying to gain back her trust. That's all I can convey to you for now. Please let us take care of you. Now go," she hissed.

My eyes fluttered open. I rubbed my sweaty palms on the bedspread. Ah, still a human. Strange, that had not gone over as I'd expected. Heck, I hadn't planned on meeting Nayla there. Jumping up from my bed, I slide onto the floor towards the dresser. Once I reached it, I proceeded to pull out my nylons to go with my dress. I laid them on my bed. Then pulled my princess attire for the evening out of my closet. I slammed it shut, and stood in front of the mirror admiring myself with my dress held up against me. For a second, I was in awe imagining Jensen's face light up as he saw me in it.

Chapter 4

(Dan)

The training grounds appeared barren. This is where he wanted us to meet, wasn't it? I checked my watch and discovered it wasn't quite three O'clock. Starla would already be primping for the dance. It almost felt like she was going to prom all over again, not that I had been there. Missed moments in Starla's life now swept over me like a rain cloud. Had I been a good father? Was I protecting her? Had it been worth it?

"Ah contemplating the good father card again, I suppose," said Kaya strolling out of the dining hut. "We were just finishing a late lunch. Have you eaten?" she asked, taking my arm.

"I had coffee with Tri. I guess I could eat if it's not too much trouble. Wasn't Cavin supposed to meet me here? Is everything alright?"

"Let's go into the dining hall. We'll discuss the issues boggling our minds at this point. Nayla is trying to stall them so that Starla Ariana can finish up her math and lit classes."

I nodded. We continued on our way to the building. Kaya opened the door for me, and I followed. We passed the meditation room, hall of pictures, and entered the dining room. Cavin, Lance, Shellena, and Nayla sat at a round table with a few plates of food left. It appeared as if the rest had been cleaned up.

"Are the kits gone for the day?" Kaya inquired as we took our seats.

"They left to go hunting. Eva and Star are with them currently," Cavin stated.

"Help yourself to something to eat Dan," said Kaya, pushing over a plate with a few turkey sandwiches on it.

17

I took two of them, and then filled a glass with some water from a pitcher on the table. "How are things with our prisoners? Are they behaving themselves?" I began to munch on the sandwich in front of me and tried not to eat too quickly.

Nayla hopped up onto the chair beside me, "Gavin keeps trying to harm himself. Sika is a mess. He's been attempting spells that have only backfired, causing himself harm. We've made sure there is nothing in their cells. The Gladiator, he's not saying or doing much. Odd, since he's the toughest one of the group. Minder has been staying with Nuria and Cal. She's been helpful at keeping the lot of them from destroying our current hold setup."

"Has anyone heard anything from Rascal? This trial to take place is about his son," I stated, setting down my water glass now empty.

"He's been by to see Nuria a few times. He hasn't had any contact with the bandits concerning Martin. We thought it best not to rile up the captives til the actual trial. He's pretty much in agreement with this decision," answered Cavin.

"Good idea," Lance spoke up.

"You've both been awfully quiet on this matter. What are your concerns?" Kaya directed, at Lance and Shellena.

"Once on trial how are we going to get them to talk? We can't force them by implementing spells. It's against the code unless we're in battle," Shellena noted.

"Bargaining often works, If they give up who killed Martin they'll receive immunity from death and banishment," Nayla suggested.

"That's way too simple and easy," shouted Shellena. "You cannot let them off the hook without giving them a sentence. Wake up, River Rogue! All that they did to Star's family, our ancestors. We can't let them live!"

"Shellena, we do not execute. If we did, we'd be bringing ourselves to their level," Cavin interjected. "The dilemma we're facing is what should we do after the hearing."

"We cannot keep them as our prisoners. Starla suggested she wanted to go after these scientists. Perhaps they would be of some help with that. If so, they may be useful to keep around," Nayla admitted.

"These creatures are not exactly the agreeable type. Shellena and Lance. You have the ability to control others. Manipulation is it something you'd consider doing," I questioned.

Shellena let out a long sigh, "It's not an ability we mess with given that it's easy to get caught up in the vanity of it."

"What she means is we're sometimes driven, by needs. It can easily be misused. I'd consider it only if there are no other options," Lance muttered.

"So, Cavin, who do you, have in mind from our tribe, or neighboring clan to handle the questioning? You know we do need a lawyer," I blurted.

Kaya took Cavin's hand, and they both directed their eyes at me.

"Oh no, I am no lawyer. I'm an investigator or better yet a detective, not an attorney," I affirmed.

"It may be, but I cannot see Mike questioning these monsters. The wolves across the way may be able to sit in as a jury. I don't expect you'd want to involve the human community. Tri is reluctant still to join us?" Cavin inquired.

I ran my hands over the table cloth smoothing it out a bit and exhaled. "Tri is hesitant to re-connect with us. Cavin, what am I suppose to do? I just want to go home and be with my family." I struggled to keep the tears away. Nayla nudged my hand, and I gently pushed her nose away from me.

"Did she give you any demands? Wives usually ask for things or make suggestions. What did she say, when you spoke?" asked Kaya.

"She wants you to let Cal and Eva (Kristine) out of their seclusion so they can join us for pancakes," I admitted.

Shellena laughed, "Is that all?"

"It's about earning her trust again. That's all I could gather from our conversation. I'm not sure what she's afraid of. The bandits are in our custody. Step by step she's letting me in, but the floodgates have yet to open," I replied.

"What do you mean by that?" Lance complained.

"She's not in one-hundred percent. Not with the clan, nor with our relationship. I can tell she'd like to be, but as I said she's afraid of something. One is of losing Starla, to being a guardian. I've had to reassure her that she's safe here."

"That's logical," Cavin commented.

"Well, I should go get the hunters. Star and Eva could use a break. Nuria, Minder, and Cal are off at her cabin if you want to stop by there. I'm sure Cal will be thrilled to get out of hibernating for a day," Kaya remarked.

"Where's Eva staying? Cal and her, they aren't, connecting?" I countered.

"No one is feuding. Cal's lived with Nuria for a long time now. Eva understands, and they're getting on well. Now go!" Kaya ordered him.

I got up from my seat and noticed Shellena and Lance clearing off the table. "We'll see you later, Dan. You did get enough to eat?" asked Shellena.

"Yes. Thank you," I replied, stuffing my hands in my pockets.

I strolled back to my car from the training area. I hadn't been planning on a trip out to Nuria's today. I'd hoped to get to see Starla all dressed up. *Jensen!* I put my hand up to my forehead. He should have been present for our meeting.

I'd have to fill him in later. I'd told the boy he would be aiding with the trial. Now I wasn't sure it had been the best idea. It seemed like a good plan at the time. We'd just captured the bandits; Tri was finally starting to see me as part of our family again. Megan was optimistic about her mother and our future together. It was her eyes that gave it all away, beaming every time I showed up or stepped into the room. Tri I sensed wanted us together, but was conflicted by her own issues regarding the clan, or was it me? I shook it off, reminding myself that she allowed my affections towards her this afternoon.

My car was the last one left in the parking lot. Earlier, after I'd arrived, I'd seen a few people picnicking. I guess they supposed it was safe during the day. I unlocked my car door, opened it, and sat down. If I timed it right, I could make it back by six. That would be just in time to see Starla and her friends head out to the dance. If not, Tri would take pictures. I'd yet to see those of her prom. I turned the key in the ignition. Then flipped on the radio to the oldies pulling out of the parkway. Should I have phoned them first? Did they even have a cell phone? I shrugged it off. I'd better just get.

Chapter 5

(Starla)

The door to my room creaked open. "Starla," my sister said, peering in.

"Hey, how was your day with Carol?" I picked up my purse off of the dresser. Then turned to face her leaning against my bureau.

"It was OK. We scoped out some new items at the mall. I found a cute pair of earrings at Claire's. Then we hit up the food court. Let me tell you, a few of the boys hanging out by Taco Bell were pretty adorable. Eighth graders," she added, then grinned. She reminded me of the Cheshire cat from *Alice in wonderland*.

"Do you suppose any of them are worth getting to know?" I asked, standing up straight. I walked over to the bed and sat down.

"Maybe, I'd hang out with one or two of them first."

"What about that boy, Chaz? The one I met at the *Great Expectations* film. Do you still like him?"

Megan flopped down beside me on the bed. "He's decided to go out with this chic, Shell. I'm not sure how long they'll last, though." Megan rolled her eyes. "She's been playing him. He gives her gifts, takes her out on the town, and treats her to the movies. Everyone sees it but him." She confirmed, "It's OK, I have Carol. We're considering joining the drama club next year anyhow. It could be fun. Plus, I'd get to know some pretty sweet guys."

"Why not now, what's holding you both back?"

"It doesn't start til 9th grade unless we can find someone to run it. I'm trying to get through my classes with honors."

I stood up from the bed getting ready to head downstairs to meet Jenson. I gathered my purse and picked up my keys sitting on the nightstand. "You're more of a geek than I am," I teased.

She pouted a bit as we left my room.

"I know, I'm helping you with that terrible math class, remember?"

"Yes, and I cannot wait til it's over!"

She chuckled at that while we made our way down the stairs to the landing.

"What are you and Jenson, going to do, after the dance?"

"He has a surprise planned. I'm not sure if it's after the dance or before it. I suspected a limo or perhaps we're all going out for dinner before. He's kept me guessing. I'm not much of a girlie girl, but tonight I feel truly beautiful," I said, spinning around in my dress.

Megan grabbed my hand pulling me into a hug. Then quickly let go. "Just don't step on his feet while your dancing," she giggled. Then placed her hand on my shoulder.

I pushed back the curtains on the door to peer out the window. Nope, no sign of anyone yet. I let the curtains fall back. Megan took her hand off of my shoulder. I turned to face her.

"It's too early, didn't Jenson say he'd pick you up around eight? It's only seven-fifteen," said my mother, stepping out of the kitchen into the hallway. "Why don't I get a photo of you and your sister before they arrive? I'll grab my camera. One second, I'll be back.

My mother hurried out of the hallway into the living room.

"I have my cell phone. She could have used it to take a picture of us," I stated.

"Mom's old school. You should know that by now."

"You're right," I admitted, resting against the door.

"Where's dad?"

"Oh, he's off doing errands for Cavin, or trying to find a way to convince mom to go back to the clan," I speculated.

"We wouldn't have to live in a cabin nearby if it happened. Would we? I'm not a woodsy person," Megan confessed.

"Probably not," I answered. Then rolled my eyes. Sisters.

My mom rushed back into the hall. "OK, I found the camera. Are you two ready to strike a pose?"

My sister and I muffled laughter at my mother's pop culture reference. I should learn how to vogue. It was the one dance move I knew I couldn't mess up. It was also a catchy tune!

Chapter 6

(Dan)

Nuria's cabin was just up ahead. I traveled down the dirt road lined with pine trees and turned into the driveway. Then pulled in parking the car. I got out, slamming the door rather loudly. It didn't look as if anyone was home. Still, I stepped onto the porch. In the window to the left side of the door, Cal and Nuria sat cross-legged on the floor leafing through some books. Nuria looked up, then waved. Cal saw me, stood up and raced to the door. I stood back as it swung open. She popped her head out.

"Hi stranger," she greeted me. "Do you want to come in, or we could sit on the porch," she suggested. "Nuria is just setting aside the books we're going over. I'm trying to catch up on some studies."

"Are you not attending the local school? Ah, what grade are you suppose to be in any way?" I asked, scratching my head.

Nuria came up behind Cal. She opened the door a bit wider. "Come in. You must be getting chilled. Cal, did you invite our guest inside?"

"I thought we could sit on the porch," Cal complained.

"It's still winter, and it doesn't appear as if Dan has dressed for the weather," Nuria scolded. "Come on in. I'll get you a cup of coffee. What is it you're here inquiring about? I wasn't expecting to see you until the trial," she acknowledged, shutting the door behind me.

I took off my coat, handing it to her. She hung it on a rack near the entrance. Cal headed over to the gray couch and sat down.

"I was just asking Cal about school? Is she attending?"

"We're working on getting her caught up. She's taken a few tests, online." Nuria pointed to her computer on the desk in the corner.

"There are efficient tutorials so we can determine what levels she's at in each subject. It will be a year or two before she's caught up. Better to do it here around family. Don't you think?"

"I suppose. You've fixed the place up," I observed, surveying the main room. Nuria had new lovely red curtains on the front window. A dining table sat back near the wall, next to her hidden bedroom.

"Minder helped me touch it up a bit. Do you like the new table?"

"Nice touch," I added.

She pulled me out a seat at the table. I sat relaxing in the wooden chair. They really had made a home out of this little cabin, I thought.

"Give me a minute."

Nuria turned, scurrying over to a cupboard on the right side of the table. She hunched down, reached in and pulled out a coffee maker. Then grabbed filters and a bag of ground beans. She juggled them in her hands. Then set them down on the counter, and grabbed the plug pushing it into an outlet. She stood up to face me, "I'm going to be doing some renovations. Now that I plan on living here permanently, I'll add a small kitchen. I don't see how I could live without it now that Cal is here, and Minder."

I nodded, "Are you and Rascal speaking, or-"

Nuria blushed. She put the filter in the coffee maker and measured the grounds placing them inside. "I'll be right back," she said, dodging my question. She took the coffee pot and headed to the bathroom.

"Did I say something wrong?"

"She gets flustered when you ask about Rascal," said Cal. She turned back to her book she'd been studying.

I played with the sugar packets in a container on the table for a bit. Then choose out a few before picking up two small cups of vanilla creamer.

"Cal, if it's alright would you like to have pancakes with Starla and Tri tomorrow?"

Her face lit up, "I would love that! I'm not sure, though, if I can. I mean, it is sort of, short notice," she replied.

"Short notice for what?" asked Nuria, stepping back into the room.

"Tri and I thought, if it was OK, Cal might come over for breakfast tomorrow," I offered. "I would be there with Tri, Starla, and Megan. She'd be safe. You're welcome to join us, and Minder."

"Mom and I were going to have breakfast here tomorrow, but she could come too, couldn't she?"

"Of course," Dan chuckled.

Nuria took two cups off of a shelf setting them down on the table. "Perhaps we should get out of this stuffy cabin. We've been spending most of our time here. When in the morning, would you want us to arrive?"

"Oh, say ten-ish. Starla will be out late tonight at this dance of hers."

The coffee finished brewing, and Nuria poured it into our mugs.

"Cal, do you want to join us?" she asked, turning towards her.

Cal set down her book on the coffee table. "Sure. I'd like my coffee with cream, though."

"Of course. After Dan leaves, we'll finish the equations you were working on," suggested Nuria.

"Mmm hmm," she answered, shuffling over to join us. Cal plopped down beside me. She grabbed creamer adding it, to her drink. "Are you going to tell him about Rascal or what?" Cal pressed as she stirred.

Nuria settled into her seat, sipping her coffee. I waited for her to respond.

"Running off, wasn't the proper thing to do," she confessed. "We haven't fully mended our relationship. We're on the right track, but how do you tell your boyfriend your girlfriend's a werewolf? It's why I ran off every time there was a full moon. In spite of that, I finally convinced him it's vital he's present during the trial. Cal and Starla will begin training soon. I didn't know they would be learning side by side. It was Nayla's idea."

Cal set aside her coffee. "Yeah, it's not something you advertise. The first time you changed, I thought I was going to have a heart attack! I'd only been among the bandits for a few weeks. It seems like ages ago, now I'm home. Other than that, I'm super excited about training with Starla. Minder reminds me of the huge responsibility that comes with knowledge."

"She's right, make sure you pay attention to her. I'll want updates as you both progress," I addressed Cal. Then looked back to Nuria, "Rascal will understand. He's dealt with supernatural things among his Indian tribe as well as the fox clan."

"Perhaps," she admitted, staring into her coffee cup.

"How's Eva?"

"She's doing just fine," Nuria replied, tapping the side of her mug.

I glanced down at my watch, 6:15. "Shoot, I should be going. Starla will be leaving for the dance soon. I'd like to get a few pictures with her," I stammered.

"It's fine, go. We'll see you at breakfast. I'll just get instructions from Mike. He knows where Tri lives, right?"

"Here," I pulled out my detective card and used the pen sitting on the table to write the address.

"Thanks, now go, we'll see you later."

"Later," I said, waving goodbye to them.

Chapter 7

(Starla)

Mom finished taking several pictures of Megan and me in different poses. The best one of us was of her and me, curtsying to each other wearing funny expressions on our faces. Dad would love that one! I smirked to myself, then pulled the curtain back from the window. I'd been waiting in the entrance for Jensen and Maine for ten minutes now. Megan had run upstairs to do some studying.

"Starla, they'll be here. Besides, your dad just called. He's on his way to see you before the dance. Now, I know Molly's at home. Let's hope all goes well with Mr. Fretner, meeting Maine. Hopefully, you can get copies of her pictures. I'm sure her folks will take some."

"Okay, Mom," I replied letting the curtain fall back into place.

"You have your cell phone. Right? In case you need to call me?" she asked.

"Of course, if we go out to any after parties I'll call. If I need to, I can crash at Molly's. I'm pretty sure we'll take Maine home afterward unless they're OK with her staying there. If I'm also, staying. Still, Mr. Fretner is pretty stern. I sense Tabitha would agree with him on that one."

"Maybe, it's hard to tell. Besides, it's not like they would do anything with you there. Would they?" asked Mom.

"Probably not, Molly's shy," I confirmed, shrugging it off. "Have you heard anything from Cal or Eva?"

"Not yet, I suggested, she and Eva stop by for breakfast eventually."

"Oh, could I ask my friends to join us? That is if you don't suppose Eva would mind?"

"Well, I'm not sure concerning the current situation. Molly and Jenson are fine, but Maine isn't in the loop of our secret circle," she reminded me.

This is my life. My existence, I thought. Irritated, that my mom would so quickly write off Maine meeting Cal. This would be my first time meeting her face to face. I planned on getting to know her and including her in many of our group activities. I hadn't considered being a part of the clan would mean shutting her out of my life. Then what about Molly? She was an accepted member. It wouldn't be fair to her, to have to hide who I was from Maine. A sudden knock at the door startled me. I jumped back, almost falling onto the floor!

"It's your dad," said my mom. She helped me to steady myself. Then opened the door.

"I almost thought I'd miss you," he explained. Then stepped into the entrance hall. Mom shut the door behind him. He took off his jacket and hung it on the coat rack. "I see Jenson has yet to arrive?"

"Yes, he appears to be a tad late," I said, stepping over to my father. "Dad, did you talk to Eva? How's Cal?"

"I went over there this afternoon. Mike mentioned to me you spoke to him about having them over. Minder, Nuria, Eva, and Cal will be joining us around 10 a.m tomorrow. I have one request. It's to be a family meeting. Ah ah! I don't want you to think I'm discrediting the assistance your friends gave us on our last mission. Presently things are sensitive. Molly and Jenson would be fine, but I don't want Maine to feel sideswiped. Once things move along, perhaps the laws and rules will change. I don't want you to work yourself up over this. I know how agitated and angry you get when you believe you're not allowed to forge your own path," he noted.

I wanted to pound my foot into the tile floor. Instead, I kept myself composed taking in deep breaths and exhaling them out. *You are an adult, living at home. Therefore, you still have to live under their regulations.* I reminded myself.

"Dad, I'll be here in the morning for breakfast with everyone. I'm not sure what Jenson, has planned for us tonight. I may not be home until dawn," I stated.

Then glanced at my mother to see her reaction, but she only smiled at me. Then picked up the camera, she'd set on the table near the entrance.

"Here, we should take photos. Jenson ought to be here any second," she declared.

I put my arm around my dad's waist. Then gave my best cheesy grin. "OK, it's time for a silly picture," I said, giving my father bunny ears. They were more like side peace signs since I'm shorter than him.

Mom chuckled, "You both seem to be having a grand time, however, your chariot awaits!"

Jenson opened the door and then took my hand, placing a purple corsage on my wrist. He gazed up at me. "Um, Maine's at Molly's already. We'll meet them there. Something about her parents wanting to meet theirs. Molly called me earlier," he said.

"Oh, OK, it's fine," I mumbled, reaching out to hug him. He pulled me close for a few minutes and then gradually let me go.

"I couldn't get a limo. My grandpa lent me his old 1979 Volkswagen Super Beetle Convertible." He grinned pointing towards it. "Isn't she just beautiful? Black isn't a bad color either. Less chance of getting pulled over by the cops!" He bragged.

I muffled a laugh. My Jenson always concerned about being pulled over. I took his hand, standing in the open doorway.

It's a classic," I said and meant it; I placed my arm around his shoulders. Then pulled him closer, "should we get going?" I asked. My dad turned to Jenson, "Photos first if you don't mind?"

"Sure, Can you make me a copy?"

"Of course," he answered, taking the camera from my mother. He took several shots of us and managed to rig it, so all four of us were in one. "Take the camera, make sure to get pictures at Molly's." I nodded to my mom. Then hugged her goodbye. "You two go have fun," she said, shutting the door behind us. Dad had already headed for the kitchen. Mom must have promised to heat him up leftover spaghetti.

"Do you know how things are going with Molly? Has she checked in with you?" I asked as we made our way to the parked car.

"Everything is fine. No news is good news."

I stopped, leaning against the passenger side of the car. My hand curled around the handle to open it when Jenson bent down kissing me softly on the lips. He stepped back, and I turned to open the door.

"No, let me," he offered, pulling it open. I sat down. He leaned into the car studying my face. "I wouldn't worry. We'll see what's happening. If need be, we'll officially rescue them from pandemonium."

Jensen got in the driver's seat. He buckled his safety belt and grinned at me. "You ready?"

"Yes, now turn up the music!"

"I'll turn it on, but not up to loud. This car is my grandfather's. I promised him I'd take good care of it. If I do, then someday it will be mine."

"Your grandpa must be a cool guy," I acknowledged.

"He is, and he'd be in awe of you," Jenson replied.

Chapter 8

(Dan)

"Thank you for this," I said. Then sat down at the table. Tri put a warm plate of spaghetti in front of me. I scooped up several noodles and began to eat.

"You're welcome. It's good to see you still have that appetite." She smiled. "It's a bit hard to believe we've made it this far," she commented, pulling up a seat beside me.

"What do you mean?" I asked.

"With Starla and the clan. I'm still skeptical about our situation, but so far Cavin seems to have it under control. You know, from what you've told me about Thunderhead Bay. Has he changed since I'd lived there?"

"Cavin," I said, shaking my head. "He's still pretty much running the show. Every now and again Kaya puts him in his place. Starla dug into him a bit during the last mission. She's a lot like you were at her age."

"I bet the quirky sense of self, and sass. When you spoke with Eva, what did she have to say?"

"I didn't, Cal is currently staying with Nuria. I found it all a bit strange. She claimed Cal's used to being with her. Eva was going to join them for breakfast tomorrow at the cabin. Minder is also living there," I explained.

"And that is because..."

"From what I gathered Nuria's helping her with her studies. She needs time to adjust to a regular routine. If Eva was upset by this, she would have argued that Cal ought to live with her. I assume there's a reason for this."

"I suppose your right," Tri admitted.

We sat in silence for a few minutes as I finished up my food. Then I took a long drink of my water and set it down."Delicious as always," I confessed, wiping my mouth with the paper napkin."

"Do you care to stay and help with the dishes?"

"I'll wash them, if you dry them and put them away. About tomorrow I invited Cal, Eva, Nuria, and Minder for breakfast. Now, when you see Minder, please don't stare. She's a hybrid wolf-vampire. If she does show up, I'm not exactly sure how we're going to keep it on the down low."

Tri chuckled, "Do you think you're one of the kids, using that term, down low?"

"Hey, it's cool slang," I answered.

"I can tell you've been hanging out with the clan. Have you been training the new kits?"

"Kaya has a bit. Lance was chiding Starla about it during the training for the investigation. She didn't like it much." I got up from the table and pushed in my chair. Then started to pick up the dishes. I slightly brushed Tri's shoulders while I passed her. Standing at the sink, I started the water, letting it fill. Unexpectedly, Tri wrapped her arms around my midsection pulling me close.

"I miss you," she murmured into my back.

"Me too," I responded, turning around to hold her. I rubbed her back and let her nuzzle my chest. I felt her begin to pull away. She gazed up at me.

"I just sense, it's too soon for you to move back in," she sighed, her hand resting on my chest.

I nodded, "I understand. I'll just finish up the dishes," I said, pulling away. "Did you want me to leave after, or?"

"Could you stay? Maybe we could watch some TV, or play dominoes with Megan. She's up in her room studying."

"Why not, if they need me at the station they'll call me." I picked the towel up, off the counter.

Tri leaned into where I stood, turning off the water. Then took her hand and pushed her long strawberry blonde hair behind here ears.

"I'm glad you never got it cut," I added.

"Oh, my hair? I prefer it long. It doesn't mean, I hadn't considered it," she reminded me.

Megan peeked around the doorway into the kitchen. Tri and I were hip to hip almost touching. She skipped into the room and put her arms around us.

"When are you, coming home dad?" she asked. Tri went to hand me the plate she'd just washed, but it fell from her hands, shattering on the floor. We jumped back unharmed. I looked at Tri and thought maybe too soon isn't soon at all.

Chapter 9

(Starla)

When we arrived at Molly's the blue Victorian home seemed empty. Maybe Maine's folks parked in the back alley. I'd hoped Mr. Fretner hadn't scared them away.

"It's OK, I'm sure everything is all right," Jenson reassured me.

We made our way up to the spacious porch. A wooden oak door with a brass knocker stood before us. I noted to the left a warm, soft glow coming from the window of the living area. Then the swing that hung beyond that for warms days with iced tea.

"Haven't you ever been here?" asked Jenson.

"Yes, but that swing wasn't here." I lifted the knocker and knocked three times. Jenson held my hand while we waited.

"What do you suppose they're doing in there, a prayer session maybe?"

"What makes you say that?" asked Jensen.

"You never know Molly's parents, especially Mr. Fretner..."

"What do you know about Maine? Her folks might--"

The door to the house swung open. "Hey, we're just out back, taking a few photos," Molly sniffed.

"Are you crying?" I asked.

"No, it's just allergies," she answered, letting Jenson and I enter.

Molly led us into the kitchen.

"Why aren't we just, walking out back?" I inquired, standing aside. Molly opened the refrigerator. She grabbed three orange sodas out of it. Then slammed it shut using her foot.

"Maine's out back with my folks. After a few snapshots they began a heated discussion," she informed us.

"About?" I asked, taking my soda from her, and handing Jenson, his.

"Maine and I, of course, what else," she complained pushing open the back door.

A girl with long blonde hair stood off to the side with her arms crossed. Molly strolled over to her handing her the soda.

"Maine, this is Starla, and Jenson," she said introducing us.

"Hey, so what's going on?" I asked.

Maine pointed to the other side of the deck.

"The girls need ground rules," shouted Mr. Fretner. He sat in a lounge chair in an impassioned debate.

"No, these girls are adults," stated a woman a bit taller, blonder, and thinner than Maine.

I observed Tabitha off to the side while Mr. Fretner and who I perceived was Maine's mother ranted at him; her husband stood farther away near the back fence.

"Enough," snapped Tabitha. "This is supposed to be a happy time. If Maine and Molly want to stay the night together, it's their call. Yes. I may be a radical liberated christen, but if this makes our daughters happy. Then we should support their relationship," she demanded.

"Wow, way to go, Tabitha!" I muttered under my breath. Maine and Molly looked horrified at her outburst. I took my camera out of my messenger bag. Mrs. Fretner saw it.

"Starla, Jenson," she cooed waltzing over to us. "Sorry, you had to witness that. Why don't we take some pictures? I see you've brought your camera."

I wanted to roll my eyes at her. Tabitha while strong when it came to standing up for her daughter, still treated us as if we were in high school. Let's just get this over with, I thought. Molly, Maine, and Jenson looked as if they were thinking the same thing.

"Here," I said, handing it to her.

"Now, why don't you all gather around and get close. There you go, a few serious photos, and then fun ones, OK?"

We gathered near and posed for the camera. Molly seemed to cheer up a tad. I sensed Mr. Fretner wouldn't be around much longer if he didn't watch his step. Was I psychic too? After several photos, Mrs. Fretner handed me my camera back.

"Molly, whatever you choose to do is your choice," she said, patting her on the back. "Maine, take care of her and keep her safe," ordered Mrs. Fretner. Then she looked back at her daughter. "Don't worry about your dad. He's struggling with you growing up and, this. He loves you."

"Mom, we need to go," Molly said, taking Maine's hand. "I'm not going to say goodbye to him," she pointed to her dad still jawing away.

"OK," said Mrs. Fretner shrugging it off.

"I'll be right back," Maine told Molly. She left wandering over to the side of the fence where her mother stood.

"So you guys are going to stay the night where?" asked Jensen.

Molly laughed, "Just over at the lodge. It's not what they imagine. We're not rushing anything. I... We... just want to be together," Molly stammered blushing.

"I understand," I said, hugging Jenson's arm.

"We should get going," Jenson fretted glancing at his watch.

I finished my orange drink and handed it to Molly, who set it on a table nearby.

"We'll go. See, Maine's on her way back. Then you and Starla can get all cozy. If you want, I'll drive. If it's ok with Jenson," Molly smirked.

"Fine by me," he said.

Loud dance music erupted out of the gymnasium doors. Jenson and I skipped arm in arm along the hallway. I leaned into him a bit, enjoying his touch.

"Look at those two," he said, pointing to Molly and Maine ahead of us, walking hand in hand. They were glowing.

"It makes me smile Jenson, aren't you happy for them?" I tugged on his hand a bit pulling him near.

"I am," he replied, kissing my cheek softly. "What about us? Are we still on that trial basis?" he whispered in my ear.

"Hmmm," I sighed.

"Too soon?"

I pulled him off to the side while Maine and Molly approached the gym doors.

"Are you guys coming?" she asked.

"We'll meet you in there, give us a minute," I answered.

Molly nodded in response. She and Maine disappeared into the gymnasium.

"It hasn't been, that long since you sat down in the diner to talk to me about your feelings. I'd been denying mine for you for too long," I said, gazing into his eyes. "At the same instant, it isn't easy to just let myself fall without fear." My heart pounded in my ears and goosebumps crawled up my back.

"I'm anxious about the trial, and my training. I've felt the connection with my clan, growing stronger. If I let you in; I have to know you'll stay. So far it's been wonderful, scary, and exhilarating." I felt his arms envelope around me.

"Hey, we'll take it slow, I don't plan on going anywhere," he said, moving back a bit to admire me. "Besides, you would kick my butt if I broke your heart," he teased.

I slapped his shoulder playfully. "I'm not sure about me, but Nayla or Owl might," I added.

"We'd better get in there. You do want to dance, right?"

"Of course, I do," I admitted pulling him towards the gym doors as they opened.

"Get in here, Molly and Maine are heating up the dance floor!" hollered Owl.

"What? I didn't know Molly could dance?" I blurted dragging Jenson into the gym.

It wasn't Molly that knew how to dance. It was Maine. She was guiding Molly step by step. It looked like a mixture of hip-hop and salsa. Oh, what now? Were they, voguing? Or break dancing?

"Come on you two! Join us," she shouted over the loud classic rock. Molly, who is usually hesitant in social situations, was letting loose. Why not? It is my night. After this who knows what might happen.

"Now you two stand apart," directed Maine. "Here's how you do the 1, 2, step. You've heard the song right?"

I shook my head no.

"You've got to get out more," suggested Maine. "Now, drop it like it's hot," she ordered.

"Huh?" I asked.

"Starla only knows how to stand and sway," Owl teased, as he strutted up to me.

I glowered at him. "Really Owl, I do know a bit more than that," I replied. Then attempted voguing. I imitated what I'd seen on a late night show once. Jenson joined in, and then everyone else, including Maine, and Molly. By the time we had finished, I was out of breath.

I'd fiercely vogue'd my heart out! I took Jenson by the hand, leading him away from the group so we could be alone.

We stood in the middle of the gym, and he placed his hands on my waist. I let mine, linger around his shoulders. We started to dance.

"Is vogue your only dance move?" he asked.

"I can tango a tad," I chuckled.

"Tango, I like that," he said, giving me a suggestive look.

"Slow Down Mister," I reminded him.

"Only teasing," he responded. A slow song had just started up. I saw Molly and Maine close, but still reluctant to hold each other to near.

"She'll get there, comfortable with herself," Jenson whispered in my ear. I rested my chin on his shoulder.

"I just--"

"Care too much, I know, me too," he said staring into my eyes. I moved my chin from his shoulder to lean my forehead against his. Gradually the space between us disappeared. Our lips met resulting in a warm kiss. I pulled back and nuzzled into his chest. I could slow dance like this forever, I reflected.

Abruptly Jenson jolted back removing his hand from my arm. "Starla, your birthmark is vibrating!" He held me at arm's length astonished.

"No, not now," I groaned, turning to the side to see Molly snuggled in Maine's arms. They continued to slow dance.

"Do you envy them?" he asked.

"Right now, I do. This was, supposed to be my last hurrah until training began. Why can't they call my cell like regular people?" I whined. Jenson's hand traveled from my shoulders into my palms. He squeezed them in his.

"I'll go tell Molly we have to take off. Maybe Maine's folks can pick her up or we could come back," he suggested.

42

I gently pulled my hands out of his. Then turned towards the gym doors. "No, I'll go. If I'm not back in an hour or so call me."

"Your cell, isn't it in my car?"

"Nope, I've got it right here," I said, pulling it out of the pocket hidden in the seam of my dress.

"What do I tell them? I can't cover for you for over an hour," he insisted.

"You have too. Maine can't know what's going on! My dad already told us this," I insisted. Vibrations from my birthmark grew stronger. I feared I'd transform right there if I didn't take off. "I have to go," I pressed trying not to make a scene. The music changed to a fast dance beat. The crowd around us started dancing to a Dj version of YMCA. I pushed past Jenson and rushed out of the gym.

"Starla, wait," he called after me. I just kept running.

Once outside I stopped in the courtyard to catch my breath. The snow reached my ankles. I shivered, I'd left my coat behind in Jenson's car. So much for planning, I reflected. OK, maybe I should call Nayla, duh! Man, I was so wrapped up in the excitement of the night.

"Nayla, can you hear me? What's going on? Is this urgent? Is Cal hurt, Eva, What is it?" I waited for a response. In the distance, a figure shuffled towards me carrying something. I turned ready to bolt again when I heard a familiar voice.

"Starla, Jenson wanted you to have your coat!" Owl raced up to me out of breath. "Dang, you're fast! Just like a fox," he commented. Then started to laugh, "Pun intended too!"

I grabbed the coat from him. Then put it on. I had no time for games or shenanigans.

"Why do you look so angry?" he asked.

"I have to get to Hunters Park. I don't know what's happening. My birthmark went wacko giving off vibrations. I tried calling Nayla, but she hasn't answered me."

"I'll come with you," he suggested.

I shot him an angry look.

"If it's about the bandits, I need to be there. I want justice for Du-Vance. And if this is escalating I prefer to know the status of our defense," he shouted.

"Shhh," said Nayla, poking her head out of a nearby bush. "Come on you two. We need to get to the station it's urgent! Sika attacked Minder. She's pretty banged up, but she'll live. Cavin is an emotional wreck. It could have been Kaya; she's been bringing them their meals. Minder's too stubborn for her own good. Come on. I'll tell you more when we get there," she snapped.

Chapter 10

(Dan)

"Tri, maybe you should sit down. I'll clean up this mess and finish the dishes."

Megan sat on the kitchen counter with a smirk on her face. "Mom, I don't know why you're so shocked. I've noticed you both ogling each other. A cuddle here and there. Starla and I know you love each other," she blurted. Then started picking up the clean dishes on the counter, putting them away.

Tri handed me the broom and dust pan. Megan stood off to the side while I swept up the mess. "Your mom still thinks it's too soon for us to rush into anything. We've been trying to play it cool around you girls. When I come home, we want to make sure it's for good. We feel we still have issues to work out," I responded.

"What is there to work out if you care for one another? You're still married. It's not like you two ever got a divorce," she lectured.

Tri sighed, "Maybe she's right? We've been acting like lovesick teenagers," she pointed out.

I dumped the broken pieces of the plate into the trash. Was she caving? After all, the talk about being unsure? Then again women change their minds all the time. I didn't dare tell her that. I thought for a moment before reacting. Then answered her, "Perhaps, but you have to work out the personal issues and problems you have with your family. I can't move back in not knowing where you stand. I'm their allie. I need you by my side one hundred percent."

I could tell my wife was trying to keep her cool in front of Megan. She'd crossed her arms, glaring at me for a few moments. Then pulled out a chair from the kitchen table. She sat down, pulling her legs onto the chair then crossed them, laying her hands in her lap.

"No pressure there, this is why he can't move back right now," she stressed, staring at Megan. "I'm not sure how to gradually assimilate back into that world. Nor how much a part of it, I want to be. Nevertheless, Starla has made her own decision. I respect that, your sister is an adult. It's been difficult for me to acknowledge. After your dad asked her to help with the Du-Vance case. I decided I had to face this."

"I thought after Thunderhead Bay it'd be over," she commented, stretching out from her former position in the chair. "Then there she was joining the clan," she said, throwing up her hands. "I accept that. I'll see Eva my best friend tomorrow for the first time in years. It's going to take time, patience, and a lot of understanding."

Tri stood up and pushed the chair against the table. "I'll find my way back, but it's not going to be my entire life. I've worked too hard to make my own outside this confusion."

I only nodded. What else could I say?

"I'm going to go do my homework," Megan offered, backing up out of the kitchen. She grabbed her backpack and headed upstairs.

"I'm I-- didn't' mean to upset her," I stammered.

Tri put her hand on her forehead.

"She just wants us back together, wants you to be happy," I added.

"I'm aware of that. We need to make sure we're all on the same page. If I choose not to be involved in all the investigations, drama, and affairs of the clan." Tri stopped.

"What is it?"

She lifted up her sleeve, "Oh, no! They can't be calling me!" Tri slammed her fists on the table. "Dan, did you put them up to this," she hollered.

"I swear, I had nothing to do with it!" I retaliated. She got up, and I followed her out into the hall. She snatched her keys off the side table clipping them to her jeans. Then grabbed her coat quickly putting it on.

"I'd ask you to come, but someone has to stay here with Megan," she sputtered.

"Why don't you stay. I'll go instead."

She rolled her eyes at me, "If this is it, then I have to be there."

"It, it! Do you know something, I don't! You're not even in contact with the clan," I argued. She hung her coat back up and threw her keys down on the table. They slide across it, then hit the wall.

"Go! Just go," she cried.

I left, shutting the door behind me. This wasn't good. I'd thought, I'd been making strides with Tri. I hoped they knew, what they had just done. I'd told Cavin several times, contact me. Never for any reason contact Tri. Unless it had to do with Starla, being in danger.

Chapter 11

(Starla)

Once we'd arrived at the Ranger's station Owl and I took our seats at the big conference table. Mike sat across from us. This time, there were no donuts.

"Call your mom," the ranger ordered me.

"What about, the clan?"

"They'll be here, don't fret. I'm worried your mom is going to freak out over what Nayla did," he said eyeing her.

"What, I thought she'd want to be here," Nayla mused. "I simply sent out the signal. She can either choose to ignore it or join us," she purred.

"Chances are my mom's having a heart attack," I retaliated.

"I like your mother. She needs to get back in the game."

I ignored her for the moment, reaching into my dress to retrieve my phone. I pulled it out, flipped it open, then dialed. I listened to it ring till she picked up.

"Hey, are you OK? Has your dad contacted you yet?" asked my mom.

"For now, I'm fine. It seems there's been a problem with the bandits. They tried to escape, and Minder was injured. Is dad still there?"

"No, he left a while ago, after my tattoo vibrated. It made me furious. I was not expecting contact. I'd been getting ready to leave when I realized someone had to stay here with Megan. Your dad said he'd go."

"Are you going to be OK? I know your upset Mom."

She sighed. "Yes. I'm OK, only disappointed. I wanted you to have one amazing night with friends before the trial. The commotion appears to be starting all over again," she complained.

"Mom, it's alright. It was fun for the half hour I was there," I gushed, laying it on thick. "I'll get through this, Owls here. We're meeting Jenson back at the dance before midnight."

"Do you think the conference will be over by then?" she asked.

I saw my dad; Minder, Cavin, and Kaya enter the Ranger's station. They quietly took seats around the table. Kaya sat next to me and laid a hand on my shoulder. I smiled at her. Then looked away as I answered my mom, "I hope so, if not I can always demand it."

My mom laughed nervously on the other end of the phone. "I suggest you do that, Hun. What then?"

"We'll get a bite to eat somewhere. Afterward, I'll have Jenson drop me off at home. I can crash til tomorrow. If the breakfast meeting is still on the agenda," I hinted, drumming my fingers on the table.

"Make sure you give Nayla the evil eye for me."

"I've already made sure she knows you're not happy with her. I have to go... everyone is here now."

"Be careful, if you need anything call me," she advised.

"I will." I closed my phone, then slipped it into the hidden pocket in my dress. Cavin began to clear his throat. He looked over at me. Then nodded to Kaya. She stood up to address us.

"First, I want to apologize to you, Starla Araina for having to interrupt your dance tonight. Where's Jenson?" she asked, looking around the room.

"Back at the dance, he's waiting for me. He'd been hesitant about leaving. I knew, if I wanted to get here in human form, I couldn't wait for him. He sent Owl after me, seeing as I had no coat. That's why he's here and not Jenson," I answered.

Kaya nodded, then motioned for Minder to take the floor.

"I should have known better than to assume I could get an answer out of Sika. Wanting to avoid the trial I went to Kaya. Then suggested I take the food to the prisoners. Once I was there, Gavin and Gladiator appeared handcuffed. Sika sat in the back corner of the cell. He seemed coy and ready to rumble. I slid into the chamber. Afterward, I began to interrogate him. At first, he played dumb saying that Martin Du-Vance wasn't part of the plan. They had only intended to lure us in, using Nuria and Cal after their capture. The plan was to attack us on our way to save our friends from the entity they'd hired. Only then would they take us down, and destroy us. Sika claimed he didn't know anything about a peace treaty Martin had arranged. During this explanation, he'd managed to fit his hands through the cuffs. He must have been avoiding meals. It couldn't have been a spell, given that, we have the place charmed. Jones made sure of that," she chirped.

What Jones? I knew he was a protector, of some sort, but this!

"Your arm, black eye, he did that to you!" I blurted.

"Yes, I'm humiliated," she groaned, placing her furry hand on her forehead. "I didn't heed the warnings Cavin gave me earlier in the week. He told me to take it easy in training. If I, didn't I'd drain my powers. So when I went to trip Sika, I missed. Then attempted to grab his hands pushing them behind him to bring him to the ground. He moved fast maneuvering away from me. I didn't see him slide his hand underneath me and grab my leg. He pulled me to the ground, shoving his elbow in my face," she grimaced.

"Definitely a nasty shiner," Owl commented.

"I'm not the helpless female type. I like to be in control myself. This time, though I don't know what I would have done if Shellena and Lance hadn't shown up. They were beginning a hunt when they saw me. Sika was holding me down.

Lance busted the lock and stunned him with his venom. During that time Shellena kept the others from escaping," she confessed.

"When you were confined did you get any new information out of him?" I wondered out loud.

"He claimed the entity he hired to keep Cal and Nuria trapped killed Martin. I don't believe him. One thing I do know is we are not going to conjure that thing back up!" exclaimed Minder.

We all nodded in agreement.

"The difficulty is attempting to prove which of the bandits, killed Rascal's boy," added Minder.

"If they won't talk, we'll simply have to exile them," suggested Cavin.

"If it comes to that then the case will be over before it starts," argued my father.

Nayla hopped onto the table and began her usual pacing. She looked as if she were about to have a fit. "NO, if they claim the entity killed Martin then we get them to help us locate the scientists. Cavin something had to create that demon! It didn't just arise out of the sky and appear out of nowhere. It may have been conjured yet the question remaining is who created it?"

"Let's not assume the entity was developed by the same scientists the bandits were twisted by," scolded Cavin.

"It sounds far-fetched, but maybe it's possible," Owl intercepted.

I laughed. "Anything is possible. No matter what happens, we have to decide how to handle the prisoners we have in custody," I spoke up. "Also, do not forget the bandits hired it!"

"OK, Starla Araina," my father answered.

"Sika is the dilemma. He holds the most power. He's also still in love with me," admitted Minder.

"It's not so much that he's in love with you, but the idea of controlling you. Gavin and Gladiator hang on to his every word.

Every leader has his or her puppets. They are his. Sika makes them promises of who knows what, and they follow his lead. Maybe we should offer them a deal," purposed Kaya.

Cavin's face contorted into an angry glare. He raised his hand to silence us. "I do not look at you as my servants, but as my people. I do recognize your evaluation of what Sika is doing. Living creatures have the ability to manipulate and control others. Authority can go to one's head, making an individual evil. It's a choice. I've chosen to lead this clan. I admire those who stand by not only me but beside each other. The trial will take place in a week's time. We'll find out if Sika is telling the truth. In the meantime, Starla Araina, you and Cal will start your training. I'll ask the clan next to us to guard the chamber after sunset. Dan, I'd like you to contact Rascal. Let's see if his tribe can offer any suggestions or protection."

"What about my classes, my job at Denny's?"

"We'll work around that. Starla Araina, tell your mother I'm sorry. We do want her back. It wasn't right for us to intrude," Cavin admitted. He jumped down from the chair he sat on.

"Is that it for tonight?" asked Mike.

"There's nothing more to add," Kaya announced.

Nayla hopped down from the spot she'd inhabited on the table top. She walked over and nudged my hand. I gave her a few pats on the head, stood up and knelt down beside her. She coyly smiled, revealing her teeth. I inched back a bit unsure of what she was about to do. Then she let out a loud laugh.

"What's wrong with you Nayla," demanded Kaya, as she strolled over to us. Owl and everyone else seemed to be getting ready to depart. The ranger was closely watching us.

"Nothing, I just wanted to see her jump. I'm in a mischievous mood.

"Now, Starla Araina, I will contact you for training, be ready," she commanded. Then disappeared in a mist before us.

"Something's up," observed Mike. "She's been a lot more sassier and spiteful recently."

"We're all worked up," pointed out Cavin. "Let's not jump to any conclusions," he responded. I nodded and got up from where I was kneeling. Owl took my coat off the back of my chair.

"Let's go," he suggested.

I glimpsed over at my father, "Dad?"

"It's alright, you, and Owl head back to the dance. Enjoy as much of the night as possible. I have a hunch it's only going to escalate from here."

Kaya floated in her beautiful human form over to the lodge door. She opened it for Owl and I. "Don't let Nayla get to you. If anything's wrong, I'll detect it," she reassured me.

"OK, she might just be mad at my mom. I get the gist they were close at one time?" I inquired.

"Perhaps," she said as the door shut behind us.

Chapter 12

(Dan)

"What was that Kaya? Why is Nayla so on edge? It can't be that Tri isn't here right now. She's segregated herself from the clan for years! Why would it irritate her now?"

Kaya shut the door behind Owl and Starla shaking her head. Then looked back at the group of us. "I'm as confused as you are, regarding her actions. Nayla has not been the same since our return from Thunderhead Bay. It wasn't too noticeable at first. It just appeared as if something had gotten under her skin. She isn't possessed. Star performed a spell to confirm it."

"Well, we should keep an eye on her. Everyone is on red alert now. Tri has a strong backbone. Nayla desires her here because she would be valuable. We shouldn't pressure her. The more we do, the less likely she'll be joining us. You have to give her time to recognize that with Starla Araina being her daughter; she'll forever be connected to this life," I stated.

"She'll come around," assured Cavin. He sat down beside Kaya gently stroking her furry back.

"How come Shellena and Lance weren't here tonight?" I asked.

Minder stood up from her seat. "They stayed behind to keep the bandits in check. They don't trust Sika. He's the biggest threat. Gladiator might have some intelligence, but Gavin is just a moron." Minder rolled her eyes and drummed her fingers on the table. "The minions merely follow orders," she confirmed.

"You don't think they'd ever go against Sika?" I asked.

Minder shrugged her shoulders. "It could happen, but they sure didn't struggle to help me when he held me down. They laughed right along with him," she commented.

"Cavin, should I help Minder back to the cabin now?" interrupted Kaya. She started to stand up.

"No, Minder should stay with us til she's healed. Nuria's with Cal. She'll be fine for one night."

"Alright," she confirmed, sitting back down.

Minder smirked, "I guess. If it reassures you of my safety."

"In the morning, I'll relieve Shellena and Lance. Kaya is there anything else to discuss before we call it a night?" asked Cavin.

Kaya exhaled, "Mike you've been quiet concerning these matters. Do you have any other suggestions besides the idea's mentioned?"

He cleared his throat. "Throughout the trial, we need to be leery of attempted escapes. I suggest armed guards not only guarding our buildings when inhabited, but also surrounding the prisoner's chamber at all times. Jones will be necessary for our security. If the entity did kill Du-Vance and it was created by the scientists. It would mean the bandits know of their location. Gavin and the Gladiator are the weakest links. Sika could have killed Minder. He's warning us that getting further information will not come effortlessly. Ultimately, my job is to protect Hunters Park and its visitors. Other than that, if you need my assistance, I'm always here. I always have been," Mike affirmed.

Cavin trotted away from Kaya proceeding to the door. Before he opened it, he turned around. "Let's all meet Monday. I'll have Nayla contact Starla Ariana about training. Dan, I may have to have you interrogate Sika. Shellena and Lance should be present to keep an eye on any funny business. This meetings adjourned. I wish you the best as you leave. Be careful, out there," he advised.

Chapter 13

(Starla)

Owl propped open the gymnasium door. A soft melody drifted out into the hall. The dance was winding down for the evening. Thank goodness I'd had time to relax on the walk back. Owl took my mind off of things by talking to me about the work he'd been doing for his native tribe.

"You ready? We only have an hour left," he said.

"Oh, yes. Of course! I'd like one more slow dance with Jenson. Who do you have eyes for these days?"

"No one in particular. Ladies first, " he said, motioning for me to enter.

The disco lights danced against the walls. I felt the music vibrating the entire gym. My gaze fell on Maine and Molly sitting at a table with Jenson. We made our way over to where they sat sipping tropical punch. A smile formed on my lips. Jenson had set a place for Owl and me.

"Jenson said something came up. Is everything alright?" Molly asked.

"Yes, it's taken care of for now."

Jenson stood up and pulled out the seat for me. I sat down next to him. Owl sat beside Maine.

"I was disappointed there weren't any doughnuts this time."

"Donuts?" asked Maine.

"Mike at Hunters Park. He usually has them when I meet with him. Oops..."

"Starla helps the ranger, who runs the park. She keeps an eye out for loiters and punks," Molly joked.

"No. Really, it was a situation where someone was hurt. We had to find out if there was a way to prevent it from happening again," Owl explained.

"I was worried about you. Why didn't you call?" Jenson asked.

"Sorry, I assumed you knew, I was safe. If I wasn't, I would have contacted you," I answered.

"Everything's, OK, though?"

"For now," I replied. "Let's just enjoy the rest of our evening," I said, resting my head on his shoulder. He put his arm around me giving me a little squeeze, then gently kissed my cheek.

"Are you ready to dance?" He offered me his hand, and we stood up.

"See you guys later?" Molly asked.

I nodded to my friends at the table. Then turned to Jenson. He lifted his hand up to my face and brushed the hair out of my eyes. We lingered there in awe of one another for a moment. The butterflies in my stomach would not cease their fluttering. I leaned into him and with my friends watching, I planted one right on his lips. Then pulling him away from the table I led him out onto the dance floor. I found us a nice open spot where the only person's feet I would have to worry about tripping over would be mine or his.

"I was the one who asked you to dance, and you took the lead," he admitted.

"Hmm, you know you've got yourself involved with a tough, independent woman," I replied, letting my hands drape over his back.

"I did, didn't I," he mused.

We swayed back and forth to "Time After Time" an old school classic. I did adore Cyndi Lauper. I pulled him closer worried that the clock would strike midnight.

"What do you want to do after this," he murmured in my ear.

"A picnic under the stars would be nice. Do you know of any place besides Hunters Park?"

"Not around here. There is the school near the Seven-Eleven. Do you know it?" he asked.

"Yes, I can never get enough of their Slurpees. I also worship the hot dogs and nachos," I confided.

"Well then, do you want to go?"

"We should go check on Molly and Maine. They'll need us to take them to the lodge," I reminded him.

"Sorry I was lost in our moment," he admitted.

"Good pick-up line," I teased him, playfully punching him in the arm. We separated. He took my hand. I spotted Molly and Maine, heading over to the punch bowl. Off to the side, Owl danced with a pretty brunette I hadn't noticed before. Huh, maybe she was a transfer student? Jenson gently tugged my arm.

"They do look pretty cozy, don't they?"

"Yeah, who is she?"

"I'm sure if it's serious, we'll find out," he replied, batting his eyes at me.

"Now you're being silly," I responded, amused at his remark.

Molly and Maine walked up to us with drinks in their hands.

"So how much longer do you two... want to stay?" asked Maine.

"Ah, we were thinking of taking off. Starla and I talked about going to get some food at Seven-Eleven. Then heading out to star gaze at the school nearby."

Maine rested her head on Molly's shoulder, "Sounds romantic, don't you think Moll?"

"It does," Molly sighed, putting her arm around Maine loosely.

"Should we drop you two off at the lodge, or..."

"Sure. I... We don't want to intrude on your alone time," said Maine gesturing to herself and Molly. "Earlier I was concerned. You left the dance so suddenly without Jenson. Then Molly told me, you've had a lot going on, with college and family."

"It's been pretty crazy. I'm grateful to have a first-class support group to get me through the rough patches."

"I bet. I'm just going to grab our coats, Molly." Maine inhaled her punch and then handed her the empty cup. "Thanks, I'll be right back."

"So how's it been going?" I asked.

Molly blushed. "Butterflies, sparks, and thank goodness only a few glares and stares," she confided. "I wish you two could have spent more time with us. I'd like you both to get to know, Maine."

"I know, clan stuff," I whispered.

"Kind of figured that. If you need me for anything, especially the healing part I'm your girl," said Molly.

"Whose girl, I thought you were mine," intercepted Maine. She'd come back with their coats.

"Sorry, awkward. I was just telling Starla if she needed me due to family stuff I'm here for her."

"That goes for both of us," Maine chimed in. She helped Molly with her coat, then put her own on. "You're not going to let your girl, go out in that frigid weather, without her jacket are you?" asked Maine.

"No, he's not," answered Owl. "I grabbed these off the chair where you left them. I had to dance with Melina. I couldn't help it. She's amazing on the floor, smart, sassy, and loves to read," he smirked.

Jenson and I burst out laughing.

"Well, she is," he persisted.

"Owl that's why we were laughing. Good luck, and thanks for bringing us our coats," I told him.

"You're welcome," he replied, waltzing off as they announced the last dance.

"Alone, at last," said Jenson. He laid out the blanket underneath an old oak tree. We'd picked up our smorgasbord of goodies and were ready to devour a massive amount of nachos.

"I'd be ecstatic about us being alone too, but I'm famished," I said, sitting down. Jenson set down our nachos and the two chili dogs we'd purchased joining me on the blanket.

"Now, no monkey business mister," I warned him.

"Are you going to fill me in what happened tonight? I would have asked earlier, but..."

I took several large bites of my chili dog washing it down with the cherry Slurpee. After wiping my face with a napkin, I replied. "Nayla signaled me because Minder was attacked. She'd convinced Kaya to let her feed the bandits. She was planning to interrogate Sika. She thought maybe we could avoid the trial."

"Did it work?" he asked, between bites of food.

"No, and Nayla was acting unusual. When I got there, I found out she'd signaled mom. Of course, she totally freaked. Dad came instead. They'd been at the house when she got the buzz," I explained.

"Training, when does it start?"

"Next week sometime, but it could be sooner," I replied.

60

"Here or I'll end up finishing them," he said, giving me the few nachos that remained.

"Thanks, no more clan talk, OK? Let's just savor the rest of the evening."

"Sure thing," he replied, tousling my hair. I pushed him back, and he stopped. Then started picking up the remainder of our late night snack. I tossed the trash into the bag and handed it to Jenson. He set it aside without a word taking me in his arms. I leaned back to look up at the sky. It was perfect, millions of tiny lights sparkled above us.

"You good?"

"No, I'm perfect," I answered.

Chapter 14

(Sunday, March 28)

(Dan)

I pulled up to the curb and parked my car. It was rather bright out. The sun hit the snow reflecting back at me. I shielded my eyes taking the keys out of the ignition. Maybe I should have called before showing up. I looked down at my watch. No, it was ten fifteen-ish. Opening the car door, I noticed Megan, milling about on the front stoop. She looked tired and grumpy. Tri must have let her stay up late watching movies or television.

Once she saw me, she raced down the sidewalk. I pushed the car door open, then got out slamming it shut behind me.

"Hey dad," said Megan grabbing my arm.

"Hi there, is your sister up yet?"

"I tried to get her up. You know Starla, always wanting five more minutes." Megan rolled her eyes. "Jenson dropped her off a little after two this morning."

"I see. Did you and mom stay up watching movies all night?"

She shook her head no, and we strolled towards the apartment entrance.

"I woke up when she came home. Mom and I watched a few Hitchcock films. I fell asleep after that "Vanishing Lady" one. It was weird," she said, scrunching up her face. We walked up the steps to the entrance. I reached for the door handle, but Megan grabbed it first and held it open for me to enter.

"Dad, let me get your coat. I'll hang it up for you," she offered.

I gave it to her, then stood off to the side. She hung it up, then shut the door behind us.

"Go ahead," she said, motioning towards the kitchen. "I'll go get Starla, up." She turned to walk upstairs.

"No, you won't. I'm already here!" Starla peaked her head out of the kitchen doorway. A smile spread a crossed her face.

"Oh, come here! Besides the interruption, how was your date last night?" She stood there silent. "Well?" I pressed.

"That's kind of, personal. If you have to know... Dad, we're good. We had a nice time. Just me, Jenson and some yummy nachos. A quick ride around town before heading back home. It's not as if we had anywhere to go," she replied.

I could feel my face turning a beet red. Starla turned away from me entering the kitchen. Megan giggled at the astonishment on my face. Jenson and yummy nachos do-not put a friendly-image into a father's mind. I shook it off. The smell of freshly baked Lemon muffins sifted into my nostrils. I had forgotten about those. Tri always made them with real lemon zest, scrapped off of the lemons and squeezed some of the juice into the batter. There would be orange juice, coffee, and perhaps a mixed fruit salad. That is if she was feeling energetic. I turned off dad mode and entered.

Megan followed me. She pulled out a seat at the table where Minder was setting down a basket of muffins. I went to grab one. She slapped my hand aside with her human-like paw. I pulled my hand away, taking a seat next to Megan. She didn't appear afraid of Minder. Tri must have introduced them upon her arrival.

"How have you been since the attack?" I asked her.

"I'm doing alright. There is a slight limp on my left leg. It should heal soon. Cavin put ointment on it last night. Afterward, Kaya said a prayer to the gods."

I nodded, "Glad to hear it wasn't as bad as it appeared."

"Thank you. Um, by the way, Nuria, and Cal might be late. I left them with Nayla. They were discussing training. Cal's a bit unsure about it. Are you excited, Starla?"

"Of course! I only want to know what I'll be learning."

"Well, I wouldn't be surprised if Nayla shows up with them. You know Tri. She's been going on and on about how we need you," Minder gushed.

"I know, I'm not happy about it. I filled you in this morning on why before the girls got up."

Tri walked over placing a pot of coffee on the table, then grabbed the fruit bowl from the counter. She handed it to me, and I set it down.

"OK, that should do it. Now we just require Nuria, Cal, and Eva," I added.

Tri was just about to sit down when a loud banging came from the back entrance. Fritz bolted out of the laundry room. Then proceeded to bark and jump at the door.

"It's Cal! I got this," said Starla. She hopped up from where she sat rushing to the door. "Fritz, get out of the way," she said, gently pushing him aside. Then opened the door for them. Cal gave Starla a quick hug. Then spotted Fritz. "You have a dog. I love doggies." She bent down, and Fritz began his examination. As this went on Nuria, and Eva made their way to the table.

"How's everything? Did the meeting go as planned?" I asked. I could hear the girls whispering about the dog. Megan had gotten up to chat with them.

"Fine, Nayla was concerned regarding when training should start. Cal just started her studies, and Starla is finishing the semester. So you see she is taking into consideration other things, besides clan concerns," stated Nuria raising an eyebrow.

"I would hope so," Tri replied, pouring the coffee for each of us. I took the cup from her adding in the cream. Not bad, I thought placing it back on the table.

"Can you pass me the fruit," asked Minder.

"Sure," I said, reaching a crossed the table.

"No pancakes," asked Cal as she sat down.

"Sorry, I forgot about them. Please come eat, we have affairs to discuss," Tri insisted.

I finished handing the fruit mix to Minder, and she handed it back.

"Who's having an affair?" Megan asked intrigued. She sat back down beside me. Then took the fruit bowl out of my hand dishing herself some up onto her plate. Afterward passing it to Starla, who declined. Instead, she reached over and took a muffin out of the basket.

"No one. The affair is Cal and Starla's instruction." Minder paused. Starla had begun to nibble on her muffin. I grabbed one myself almost knocking over my coffee. Oops.

"Cal, has Nayla discussed with you your duty to Starla?" asked Eva.

"Wh--Wh-at? You have a duty to me, but how?" Starla interrupted.

"Nayla told me we're connected. Our moms are best friends. They've had each other's backs for years. When Tri, your mom was a part of the clan, they shared a gift that tied them together. When they're united, they can protect one another. You know how witches can create a safe circle. It's something like that. It requires us both," said Cal.

"You're my best friend. It doesn't make you my slave. You don't owe me anything," said Starla.

"No, but we owe it to each other. If it can protect us, it will help you as a guardian, defend our clan," replied Cal.

I shifted in my seat and gulped down some more coffee. Then looked at Starla. Megan pushed around the fruit on her plate. Minder started drumming her fingers on the table as usual. Eva got up, removing a few of the plates pushed aside.

"Do you want to be tethered to me for life? What does it entail? You don't have to follow me everywhere I go. Do you? Not that I wouldn't want you to attend college with me," Starla suggested.

Eva turned around facing her. "Your rambling. You both only tether to each other during combat. Which I'm sure you won't be engaging in anytime soon."

"That's true Eva, but why is Nayla so gun ho about getting started? Why not wait til the semester is over for Starla. And Cal is closer to finishing her education?" Tri asked.

"Because, Nayla is Nayla. She's paranoid. She has this gut feeling that something is going to go down, during the trial," Eva answered.

"Which means we should prepare for the worst. It will put her at ease and allow us breathing room." I paused for a minute. Then wondered why Jensen wasn't here. "Starla, why isn't Jensen here?"

"Dad, Mom would never let him stay over."

"Don't get smart with me. He should be here."

"Dan, he had to return the VW bug to his grandfather this morning. I spoke with him last night. Starla was exhausted from the fiasco with the clan. I wasn't going to keep her waiting while he and I talked. You can meet later," suggested Tri.

"You're right. I'll contact Owl too," I noted.

"Cal, and I want to catch up. Can we nix this clan stuff for now?" Starla asked.

"Go ahead. We'll clean this up. Your dad and I need to talk. Oh, and Megan, please do your homework. You promised me if I let you stay up last night you'd finish those math problems."

"OK, but it won't take long. Remember, I helped Starla with her homework."

"Stop bragging," shouted Starla from the hall.

I laughed, shaking my head, "How do they ever get along?"

"I don't know, they just do," Tri replied.

Chapter 15

(Starla)

Cal and I hurried up the stairs, stopping once we'd reached the top. I put my hand on the railing. Then started down the hall.

"This hallway is rather narrow," she observed. "Which room is your's?"

"It's on the right, like five feet from here. Megan's down the hall a ways. I can usually sense when she's about to invade my space," I replied.

"Ah, Okay" Cal answered.

"Here we are," I said, opening the door to my room. I stared at the messy bed. I hadn't bothered to make it this morning. What had I been thinking?

"This is it, my room. Please ignore the chaos."

"It's cool. Pretty bare for a room. I do like your poster of Buffy," she commented.

"Yeah, she's sort of my hero," I replied, tidying up my bed so we could sit. Cal, however, began to explore starting with my bookshelf.

"So," she drawled rifling through my collection. "What have you been up to, you know before you saved me?"

I sat crossed legged on my bed. She picked up my copy of *Little women* and started reading the back cover.

"Just the usual. I had college orientation and finally got to meet Molly and Jensen. We were friends online first. Sometimes I contemplate if someone set that up." I shrugged. "Then, of course, Shellena and Lance came to visit me. Did I know who the hell they were at the time? No, no one ever told me anything back then. It all came at once. I mean, how did you find out? Did your mom tell you? Where's your dad?" I stopped mid sentence. Maybe the bandits had gotten him. I hadn't heard Cal, or Eva, mention her father at all.

Cal set the book back down on my shelf. She came over to the bed.

"Scoot, let me sit. K?" She giggled a bit, then got serious. She laid her hands in her lap and then looked up at me. "To be honest, I'm not sure where my dad is? You know when I wandered away that day? Mom and I had gone to visit him at his office before it happened and he wasn't there. They'd had an argument earlier that day. I've been trying to recall what it was about for a long time. I had-- a while since I was with Minder. It wasn't bad you know." She sighed, "just a lot of manipulation to make me think the clan was evil. Even though I knew about our clan, I hadn't met anyone there. Not really. I was a baby when Cavin fawned over me. He said you and I would do great things. Mom recently confided it to me. I've always known I was half fox at least. She warned me not to tell you. She said we needed to be kept safe. I'm not sure how she kept me quiet. Do you remember the day we both were goofing around? You almost found out! Mom nearly had a heart attack when I told her. She said I could never encourage you to let that part of yourself come out again. We were little. I still ponder how I understood half that crap back then."

I pushed myself against the headboard and leaned back. "You OK? Being back and all?" Then I scoffed, "That entity was pretty crazy. I thought he'd kill Nayla. I have a lot to learn."

"We both do, Nuria was more help than any of us."

"Yes, but without all of us, I don't think we would have escaped," I admitted.

"After Shellena and Lance visited, did your mom tell you?" she asked.

"It was complicated. I didn't even tell my mom I turned. They knew it would happen. I'd find out eventually."

"What about Megan?" she asked, leaning over closer to me.

"Mom says she has different gifts. That now and then, a Kitsune fox and humans, have a child with no abilities to transform. Megan's super smart. That's why she brags so much about Math. She must get it from my dad."

"Yep, super smart, detective," she replied.

"What happened when you were with the bandits?"

"What do you want to know?" asked Cal.

"Did they exhibit any weirdness or odd behavior? Did you ever hear them making plans to kill Du-Vance? If so, you need to speak up about it. You know, Jensen's supposed to be helping my dad. He hasn't included him in anything yet." I got up off the bed and walked over to my closet. Opening it, I grabbed my green coat.

"Are we going somewhere?" asked Cal.

"I thought maybe we'd head over to the park. I want to interrogate the bandits."

"First, let me answer your question. Sit, and after that, we'll see if Cavin will allow it."

"OK, dish, but I wasn't going to ask permission," I said joining her back on the bed. I threw my coat down beside me. "I don't suppose they would let us interrogate them, after what happened to Minder? We should just do it."

"Starla, you've always been pretty wild. Although, you usually don't break rules. When I was with the Bandits, they were careful about what they mentioned around me. They manipulated me into believing the clan had planned to sacrifice me to the gods. I'd never met anyone from our group besides your family. I hadn't a clue what happened at gatherings. Thus, it was terrifying to hear it from strangers."

"I can't imagine what it must have been like for you. During the investigation, I read that the bandits were caught and questioned, after you were captured. How did they do that, if you were with them? Did they keep you locked up somewhere?"

Cal played with her shoe laces, then rubbed the sole of her shoe before answering me. "They had to go into town for food, supplies and such. Often they would leave me with Minder. The detectives questioned her separately. I only know because she and Sika got in a fight over it. He was afraid she'd break down and give them information. Why do you want to know? It doesn't matter does it?" she asked, clenching her shoe.

"I guess not," I answered.

She let go of her right shoe and pushed her feet off the bed, letting them dangle over the side. "Listen, when Nuria met up with Minder she was guarded. I wasn't sure if she would even help us. Minder was freaked out. Sika had been trying to talk her into another attack. It had something, to do with the scientists. It wasn't legal. There was late night chatter regarding the creation of explosives, ending their lives for what they had done to them. I never found out if they even knew where these people were! I don't know what they had intended for our group. I'm sure it wasn't good," she said, shaking her head.

"Well, Cavin will want to hear about this! Cal, we have to tell him!" I said, standing up.

Cal ignored me and got up from the bed. She headed to the door, then stopped halfway there and turned around facing me.

"Can I borrow your copy of *Little Women*?"

"Of course, you can," I answered.

She walked over, grabbing it off of the shelf. "Thanks, I haven't made it to the library yet."

"You're welcome," I replied, as I approached the door. "Are we going to do anything about what happened?" I asked, placing my hand on the handle ready to exit.

"I'm not ready, to confront them. You,-- you weren't forced to live with them," she stammered. "It wasn't bad at first. They treated me as a part of their tribe. Then several weeks past. I asked about seeing my mom again. Then you, or when I could go back home. I tried to run away, but Sika caught me. Towards the end of our time there he started abusing Minder. He asked her why she was protecting me, the enemy. I gathered, they thought they could use me as a bargaining chip." She shuddered. "Minder protected me from Gladiator, and Gavin a few times. She didn't want to be a part of the group anymore. Gladiator and Gavin took orders from Sika due to fear. They're scared of him. They immediately do what he asks. As far as Du-Vance, if they killed him, I don't know."

Chapter 16

(Dan)

I placed the last dish from breakfast in the dish rack to dry. Then sat down to discuss what had been weighing on my mind. "So, Tri, It would be helpful if you'd consider coming to a clan meeting. I'm not insisting you join us permanently."

"Why not?" Eva interrupted. "The bandits are in our custody now. Cal's back home, and there is nothing we can do about Lang or Du-Vance. Those cards, have been played."

Minder rolled her eyes at Eva. "While that's true, we still need to be leery of Sika. I won't be going alone to confront him again. His actions confirmed the need for the trial. There's no way we will get any information out of them without force or threats. I'm not sure which Cavin plans on using. Let's hope he has a plan of action, other than a discussion."

Tri nodded. "I have to agree with you on that. What happened during the time you were with Sika? Did you see him attack anyone from the tribe? Do you know anything about Du-Vance's death?"

"Dang girl. You said you didn't want to get involved," I chided.

"Dan, I do care about our daughter, Cal, and the clan. I'm just apprehensive of it, overriding my entire life again. The only reason I'd become involved would be for the protection of our daughter. And yours, Eva," she said, nodding to her.

Eva pulled Tri into a side hug. "I'd appreciate it if you would do that, for us. Cal and Starla are connected. You know what that means." Eva let her hand fall onto the table. Then grabbed her drink. She sipped her leftover cold coffee.

"What does it mean?" asked Nuria.

Tri put her hand to her forehead. Then began to rub it in circles. " Eva and I may have to demonstrate to our children how to protect each other. Starla and Cal are linked."

"Do you suppose that's why Nayla was acting so off at the emergency gathering?" asked Minder.

"Most likely, she could teach them herself. It is more useful to have guardians of the past or ones who used to be active, help guide them in the process of discovery," stated Tri.

"Dan, did you know about this?" asked Nuria.

"Personally, I doubted, I could convince Tri, to come back to the tribe at all. Have I convinced you?"

Tri pushed her chair away from the table standing up. "I'll come to one meeting to discuss the possibility of assisting. Don't expect me to be a part of the trial. I'm doing this for Starla and Cal. I know how important it is for her to solve this Du-Vance mystery. I support her decision to be a guardian. For now, I'm only her mother. After the training and the trial, I'll make my decision as to if I'll rejoin the tribe."

"Fair enough. Nuria, do you and Cal want to stick around for a bit or do you have plans for the day?" I asked.

"Maybe I should tell them what is going to happen in the next couple of weeks," suggested Eva.

I shook my head. She was really, going to push Tri's buttons with this one. She'd started doing just that towards the end of Tri's era with our tribe.

My wife stifled a foxy throaty grunt. "We'll get to that after the meeting. It will all occur soon enough. Dan, let me know when Nayla wants Eva and me there for the first session, and, or meeting. You know, which, ever comes first."

"Ok, so should I leave now?" I asked, backing away from the table.

Nuria gave a quick laugh. Then put her hand to her mouth to stop herself. "Sorry," she said, holding up her hand.

"Should I go get the girls?" asked Tri.

"If you don't mind, I'd like to stay for a bit," said Eva. "Nuria if it's OK, I'll bring Cal to the cottage afterward."

"Sure, that's fine," she gave in.

"Excuse me," I said and pushed my chair away from the table. I stood up and walked over to my wife. "I hope you're OK with all this. It is a lot to take on."

"It's for Starla," she said, taking my hand in hers.

"I have to meet with Owl and Rascal today. Jenson is also a factor. I can't keep leaving him out of this."

"He'd be pretty upset if you did," said Tri.

"Yeah, she adores that boy," I replied.

Tri leaned in and gave me a quick kiss. "Now, go!" she said, pushing me away.

"Nuria, Minder, do you want to tag along?" I asked heading towards the back door.

"I'm going back to start a lesson plan for Cal. Minder you can go if you want."

"Nah, but I have to get going. I'll see ya later."

"Yep," said Eva.

I held the door open for Nuria and Minder. Then waved goodbye to Tri and shut the door behind us.

Chapter 17

(Starla)

A cold wind rushed past me at the bottom of the stairs. I paused to look over my shoulder. Nothing. Could Nayla be spying on us? I shrugged it off. Cal and I turned away from the front door, taking a right into the hall, then another right into the kitchen. Mom and Eva sat at the table drinking coffee. I grabbed two cups out of the dish rack and filled mine up. Then added the cream and sugar I'd taken off of the counter. Did Cal drink coffee? They were chatting about maintaining a garden of all things.

"You want some?" I asked Cal, holding up a cup. She shook her head and then went to sit down next to her mom. I turned sideways at the counter so I could see what was happening at the kitchen table. Then took the creamer pouring it in my coffee. I stirred.

"Hey, where's Nuria?" asked Cal.

"She's working on your lesson plan for tomorrow. Minder had to leave. She didn't give a reason, and Dan's on his way to chat with Rascal. He mentioned contacting Jenson. What have you girls been up to?"

Cal held up the copy of *Little Women* I'd given her. Then set it on the table.

"Ah, a classic! That's a good choice. You could do a book report on that or even a research paper on the author," Eva suggested.

"I guess if it counts towards school it would be worth it. I'd rather write a book report than complete a math lesson," she replied.

I laughed, "We have one thing in common there. I can't stand it! I never can seem to figure out algebra." I took the spoon out of my coffee cup placing it in the sink. Then gripped my coffee cup and took a few sips.

"It's not that I don't excel in it, but the time it takes to work out the problems using the long hand method. Nuria insists on it! I'm not sure when I'll ever use it. Especially if I'm going to be primarily in the clan," she stated.

I nodded to her and then joined them at the table.

My mom chuckled. "Well, you may have to use it when they harvest the crops. They still do that, don't they?"

"Kaya has a small garden. Everyone is responsible for a particular crop. You know corn is one of our staples. We hunt too, for small game such as rabbits."

Eating a rabbit? I'm not sure I could stomach such a thing, I thought. Eva rambled on.

"Did you two have a discussion concerning what happened when you were missing?" she asked, drumming her fingers alongside her cup.

"Bits and pieces," replied Cal.

"You can't just keep holding it back honey."

Cal's face got red. She got up pushing her chair away from the table.

"We're not leaving yet. Please sit back down," Eva urged.

"Starla, can you get me that coffee now?" she asked.

I went to stand up, but my mom interrupted me.

"Let me," offered Tri. She moved to the counter and began to prepare Cal's drink.

I turned to face Eva. "We should be doing something. Cal, did you tell her what you told me?"

"She knows all about the god sacrifice thing. The massacre at River Rogue. Gosh, the bandits wouldn't shut up about it! How it was such a victory for them. I don't even want to recall the details. It was awfully gruesome."

"That's not what's important. It's what you said they'd planned." I gave Cal a stern look. Then turned to gaze at my mother, then Eva. "The bandits wanted to seek revenge against the scientists," I blurted.

My mom raised her eyebrows. The cup in her hands shook. Gently she steadied herself before placing it next to Cal.

"Starla, you spoke of going after them yourself," replied Tri, sitting back down.

"Yes, Mom, but not to kill them," I insisted. Jez! I'd startled her with my statement, yet she seemed against the whole idea.

"This trial is about Du-Vance, not the scientists," Tri replied.

"Then why did dad say, he wanted Jenson on an assignment to locate them?" I asked.

"Considering the circumstances, it's a side project. He figured it would keep Jenson busy. Most likely he'll be doing research first. Then when the clan plans on initiating a retrieval or combat, against them, if needed, everyone will know. Right now, we must find out what happened to Du-Vance. I'm not sure what we'll do if we don't come up with any answers. Cal are you sure you haven't forgotten, anything? That you remember everything, that happened while you were in their custody?" asked my mom.

"For real! You think I would keep it from you, if I had the answers?" she replied.

"No, but when a child goes through a traumatic experience he or she doesn't always recall what occurred. I did have to take psychology for my basics in college. Have you been meditating at all on this?" asked my mom.

Cal turned to me and rolled her eyes."Meditation is a bit hokey, don't you agree?" She fiddled with her heart necklace. Cavin must have given it back to her.

"I used meditation to find you. It's helped me solve cases. I wouldn't call it hokey. It could give you perspective on what happened to you. I bet Nayla will have us use it in training."

"Isn't it boring, sitting with your eyes closed?" asked Cal.

"No, you concentrate on a place, a person, or a memory. You pull out images from it. If you focus on what you know, then there are times when you can uncover the unseen."

"Nah, I don't believe you," she replied.

"Say you have a dream. You know there was a fox in it, but not who he or she is. You can pinpoint details of him or her. You may end up visiting the spirit of the animal, or hybrid if the fox is part human. It's a different experience for each of us, I suppose."

"You astral traveled, didn't you?"

"I,... I have. You know this. When I came to save you and said I'd be back."

"This is great! Mom, you didn't tell me she knows how," exclaimed Cal.

"I only am aware of how to astral travel, using reflection. I can't touch people without my body present. My mental powers are goofy. I did manage to get through the Thunderhead Bay ordeal. You can't just, poof, jump out of your body, can you?"

"Not that I know of," Eva confirmed.

"You could teach me," suggested Cal.

"That's not such a sizzling idea. The last time I meditated, Nayla invaded. She crashed my party, fearing an entity of some type might get in. She'd never warned me before. I promised her I wouldn't attempt it without notifying her at least. She requested I wait til training. Then she'll teach us how to block unwanted spirits from entering our sacred space," I replied.

"When did this happen," asked my mom.

"Yesterday, I came home from having my hair done. I wanted to contact Cal. I... I was upset she wasn't going to be at the dance with me and Jenson," I said, my voice shaking in an unsteady manner. "She should have been able to, but the bandits ruined it. If you only hadn't been captured. All the things that could have been, for you, for me, our friendship," I stopped mid sentence. Then rubbed my eyes. They had begun to tear up. I was not going to cry, no, not now. I'm fine.

"It's OK. I'm here now, I'm all right," said Cal. She reached out and touched my hand patting it reassuringly. "You know you could have just called."

"I didn't have your number. I thought I could contact you, if I meditated. Then a part of me wanted to break free from everything. I had this urge to run. During the meditation, I found myself running in a field. I'd entered my fox form, mentally. Once I arrived Nayla, poof-ed, out of nowhere telling me it wasn't safe."

"Nayla was right to warn you," admitted Eva.

Cal fidgeted in her seat.

"How are we supposed to block spirits? Especially, if we're searching for one we've never met?"

I shrugged. "Your guess is as good as mine. Messing with Nayla is not a grand idea. When I saw her, at the emergency meeting, she was acting out of character. She's sassy, but she took it to the extreme. Something's bothering her. Nevertheless, I trust her wisdom. She's able to sense when something's wrong."

"But, how do we know if it's them or not?"

"Who?"

"Bad spirits," replied Cal.

"We don't. Until Nayla teaches us," I answered.

"Maybe we should pay her a visit. You mentioned wanting to go-"

"Not today," said my mom, standing up from her seat. Eva handed her the empty coffee cup she'd been holding. I pushed mine aside near my mom without a word.

"Cal, you have to finish up that homework from the other day. Minder's preparing a few more assignments also. If you want to be able to meet your goal for your studies, we should get," she pressed. Then pushed herself away from the table.

"Mom, we do need to meet with Nayla. If not today, when do you suggest we go?" I asked.

"Cal, Eva, when will you be free? I'm in no hurry to visit. I promised Dan I'd come to a meeting soon regarding your training Starla."

"You did! Mom, that's amazing, fantastic, great," I sputtered.

"Hold on a Sec," she said, rinsing out the cups in the sink. "This is only going to be temporary. Eva and I, are contemplating on assisting in your training." Mom opened the cupboard putting away the mugs.

"Why? What do you know about being a guardian?" asked Cal.

Eva laughed, "Well, honey, you're looking at her."

My mom smirked at this, almost half blushed!

"Shut-up! You, were a guardian? Then why is Starla one, and not me?"

"It's how the cards fell. No, need to be jealous of Starla. The two of you are like yin and yang. After training you'll be inseparable," noted Eva.

"Yeah, similar to us until the bandits threatened our daughters. You're braver than me," said Tri, pointing a finger at Eva. "If Starla, had been captured by the bandits, I don't know if I'd be letting her train. I imagine I'd be running for the hills."

"See, that's why I was the guardian, and she was the link," whispered Eva.

"Then how come I'm the guardian?" I inquired.

"You fit the bill. Your mom knew it, Dan knew it. I had to keep my mouth shut. You and Cal needed protection at the time."

My mother nodded in agreement.

"So, When," I pressed.

"Monday after Myth class. Your dad's talking to Rascal today. Owl's there too, plus he needs to contact Jenson," replied my mom.

Cal and Eva began to get ready to leave.

"So, I'll see you, Monday? You know you should tag along."

"Yeah. Mom, is it OK?"

"If you finish your lessons. Nayla would wonder what happened if you didn't show up inquiring sooner or later."

"You got that right," added my mother. She walked to the kitchen door, peering outside.

"Are you looking for anything strange?"

"No, Fern next door has just been pretty inquisitive of our comings and goings. I've got to keep an eye on that lady."

I laughed. "Mom, come on, they are old people, pretty harmless if you ask me," I said standing up from my chair.

"Not if they find out we're foxes," Tri replied.

"Probably not," Eva added. "Come on Cal, let's go. You two take care. I'll be expecting a call soon, eh?"

"Of course. Soon," answered my mother.

Chapter 18

(Dan)

Rascal slapped me on the back. "Glad to see you finally made it over here. I hadn't heard a word since Cavin told me you had the bandits in custody. The Crusaders from over yonder, I see em now and then. That Amer, he's something else. Have you met him?"

"I chuckled, he's a character all right. We have to keep him in check now and then. Nayla is in an uproar. She's been acting strange and wants not only Starla and Cal's training moved forward, but also the trial."

He nodded, leading me into the living room. We sat down on an overstuffed green couch. Sunlight wavered in through worn curtains covering a window behind us.

"That sounds like her. She never could sit still on a case. Too bad you weren't able to get any answers out of the entity. That must have been a sight to see. Of course, no one knows anything but Cal. Starla was there at its capture. Owl mentioned they might not attend the trial. Why?"

I adjusted myself on the sofa, "Right now, it seems they're trying to help Cal-adapt to living amongst the clan. I met with Nuria the other day. Then this morning with Tri. I've almost got everyone back on track. Cal is the exception. She's reuniting with us. It's going to take time to get her to open up about situations that occurred. Things, she may not want to remember. She might be apprehensive, but it seems she trusts Starla."

Rascal placed a pillow behind his back. "It's a start. Still, they might have to testify depending on the circumstances. Even Nayla will need to realize this. They'll have to confirm what happened during Cal's rescue. For me, no news is good news. At least in the media. I'm glad they've pretty much left us alone. They're saying, bear attack. That should make the bandits happy. No one knows of our existence, well except...."

"I wouldn't worry about Jones. He's got our back. Cavin said you'd been by to see Nuria. How are the two of you?"

"Changing the subject on me, eh. We've taken a few strolls in the forest. I'm trying to understand who she is all over again. She tends to let her emotions get the best of her. We're reconnecting. What about you and Tri? Are you going to move back, anytime soon?"

"Now we're straying off the subject," I replied.

"No, no, if you can ask about Nuria and me."

"If it continues, I'll move home in a week or two. I know she wants me there. She's afraid of the clan overrunning her life again. I assumed she was ready to merge back into the tribe. I've already reassured her she will not have to give up her current life. How many times do I have to do that? I guess I should be patient. I'd be a jerk if I forced my way back into our home. Megan thinks we're silly. That we are in love, and..." I coughed, "I am in-- love with my wife."

"They'd be safer with you at home."

"I can't act like the macho man. Tri and Starla would never allow it. Megan on the other hand..."

"She's different?"

"Megan is a daddy's girl. Starla loves me but is rough around the edges. I'm not sure why it's that way. Women, who can figure them out? Still, we love them in spite of it."

"I'm sure they feel the same way about us. Night and day we are, huh?"

I shook my head a bit, looking down at the gray carpet, then looked up. "Most likely. Um, there was a bit of a disagreement during our meeting about the bandits."

"What was it?"

"Nayla wants us to allow immunity from death and banishment if they give up the person or thing that killed your son. Shellena was fuming after everything that happened at River Rogue."

"I bet she was! I'm surprised at Cavin. He goes for the Jugular."

"Everyone is speculating how much they know concerning the whereabouts of the scientist. Cavin suggested they might help us. They've already been pressuring me to do the questioning at the trial. I told them I'm no lawyer."

"True, but you've always been reasonable. Mike, he doesn't want to be involved in this? He and my son were awfully close. The only one he let in besides Owl. Oh, they should be here any minute now."

"I can go, I need to contact Jenson."

"Then you should stay. Owl said something about him tagging along. I'll make us all some lunch.

"If it's no trouble."

"Come on. You can butter the bread rolls. I'll tackle heating up the stew. Oh, and when they get here don't scare that boy."

I got up, and we headed out to the hall, then into the kitchen.

"Which one?" I asked, standing next to the dining table.

"Jenson, I don't need you putting fear into him. I have plans for that kid."

"Raz, what are you up to?"

He just grinned, ambling over to the refrigerator. Then opened the door, retrieving a container of homemade stew.

"You're not considering making him a tribal warrior, are you? The clan pretty much has dibs on him. You know, he and Starla..."

"Dating, I know, but with my son deceased, I need someone to facilitate our rituals. Owl and I have been discussing it. We think he'd be a fine man for the job."

"You may be right," I answered.

I sat down with Jenson, Owl, and Rascal at the kitchen table. We were slurping soup and devouring homemade bread rolls. Rascal sure knew how to cook!

"This is delicious. Did you make it yourself?" Jenson asked between mouthfuls.

"Course I did boy, my pappy taught me everything I know about stew. How have you boys been? Are ya just, a hankering to get in on this next case, Jenson?"

"I really can't say. I don't know a lot about it. Starla brought me up to date on what occurred with Minder. It's a good thing, Shellena and Lance dropped by the holding pen."

I nodded. "Minder needs some training. I haven't spoken to Nayla about it yet. She's placing all her concentration on Cal and Starla. Once they have a few days of instruction in I'll mention it might be a good idea to add in Minder. I don't want to get her worked up."

"Sure thing. Minder is fairly strong-willed herself. She might take offense to someone saying she lacks skills," Owl commented, scooping up the last remnants of stew out of his bowl.

Jenson picked up his cola and took a drink of it. Then set it back down on the table. "What about the assignment for the scientists? Isn't that why you wanted me to stop by today with Owl?" asked Jenson.

"The thing is Du-Vance, my son. He was a tribal warrior. He promoted our clan to the public in positive ways. Owl, and I thought you might help us out. We put on pow-wows, set up fundraisers, and often sit in during vision quests. I know you're involved with the fox clan. It's fine. We are allies," Rascal answered.

"It's a lot for me to handle on my own. It would only be twice a month," Owl stated.

Jenson swiped his bread roll in the last of his stew, brought it to his mouth, and chewed. He grabbed his paper napkin, wiped his mouth and dropped it onto the table. Afterward, leaning back in his seat, he let a sigh escape.

"Well?" asked Owl.

"I'm not sure I can commit to everything. Dan, you said I'd be on this assignment to locate the scientists. When am I going to have time to run public pow-wows? What do I know about vision quests?" he demanded.

"Right now there are no leads on the scientists. If we get any, you'll be informed. In the meantime, you'd be helping Rascal and Owl out with the tribe."

"I'd be grateful. You're not signing an agreement in stone," Rascal clarified.

Jenson stood up and began picking up the empty bowls of stew. He didn't speak. He walked over to the sink and turned on the water. Then used the old rag hanging over the spigot to begin cleaning them.

"You, don't have to do that," said Rascal, standing up.

"It's fine. You and Dan made lunch. Do you have any pow-wows, or events coming up?" he asked, looking up from the dish he was drying.

"I'll look into it," Owl responded.

"So, you're in?" I asked.

"Until you get a lead on the scientists. Then that will be my priority. My first loyalty lies with Starla's clan."

"I understand," answered Rascal.

Chapter 19

(Monday, March 29th)

(Starla)

After working a short morning shift at Denny's, I stood in the entrance of the campus cafe. It was pretty quiet. A few students mingled loitering in the hall. I'd waited for Jenson to pick me up this morning, but he hadn't shown up. I opened my mouth and out came a long yawn. Maybe he'd slept in. I stayed up late working on Math problems. I'd finally started showing up to class. One more absence and I'd be kicked out.

"So, you're still sleepy from all the excitement at the dance?"

I turned around. "Oh, hey Owl, Nah. It's more like from yesterday morning, and my late night rendezvous with math. What's up? Have you seen Jenson?"

"No, but I'm sure he won't miss class. He's interested in Native Myths."

"What tribe do you suppose Jones will focus on?"

Owl smirked, "You know Jones he'll have a smorgasbord of topics," he replied.

"I agree, he's always finding a way to mix things up. His classes are never boring," I added.

We slowly made our way up to the counter. I grabbed a cup and filled it with Mocha flavored coffee. Then started looking around for the creamer. They usually kept it in a container. I loved the cute small plastic packages of Hazelnut, vanilla, and caramel. Just then, I felt someone bump my arm.

"Are you looking for the cream?"

It sounded like Maine. I looked up, she and Molly were arm and arm.

Owl had already made his way up to the cashier to pay for his drink. Maine was wearing a long flowing blue hippie skirt and a white peasant top. Molly wore a pair of bell bottoms with a white turtleneck. She had layered over it a blue knitted sweater.

Apparently, she'd been giving Molly a few style tips. Even if, it was from the 60's.

"Yeah, how are you two? I thought you'd call me yesterday, Moll."

"We slept in late. We stayed up discussing college, our dreams, goals, and movies, you know."

"I do," I answered.

Maine raised an eyebrow at me, then grinned. "So did you and Jenson?"

"Oh, no. We shared nacho's under the stars from my favorite convenient store."

"Is she joking?" asked Maine.

"No, she's not," replied Jenson. He placed his hand on the small of my back, leaning over he gave me a soft kiss on the cheek. "We like to keep our dates PG for now until we're both ready. How about you and Maine, this was your first date, right?"

Molly blushed, nudging Maine.

"I thought with the longevity of your friendship you might. Yeah know," Maine said, shrugging her shoulders.

"It's OK. I don't take any offense. Now, Where's the creamer?" Maine picked up a container on the counter furthest from me."Thanks," I said, taking it from her. "I guess they chose the environmentally friendly creamer. No more plastic."

Maine lifted an eyebrow, "It probably just got too costly. Your welcome."

Do you have any classes today?" I asked her.

"I take this oils class. I'm into painting abstract art, but Mrs. Klutner has been forcing me to paint fruit bowls. It's getting rather mind-numbing. I can't wait til this semester is over. Once, I'm in Art II I'll have more freedom in the projects I create."

"Cool, we have an artist in the group," Jenson remarked before I could answer her.

"It was good seeing you guys again, but I have to get to class," Maine said swinging her book bag behind her. I noticed she had her art tools in a catty at her side.

"Wait," said Molly. She handed her a cup of coffee. Maine pointed to it, then the cashier.

"I got it if you want," she told Maine.

"It's cool. Anyone else craving coffee?" I asked.

"Sure, pay for everyone's after I get mine," groaned Owl.

"Hey, I'll get ya next time bro," responded Jenson.

Maine gave Molly a warm hug goodbye and a quick kiss. Then waved to us as she left, like dorks, we waved back.

I turned to the group giving Owl a playful slap on the shoulder. "I'm meeting, Cal today after class at Hunter's Park. Do you want to tag along?"

"Sounds like a plan. Jenson, are you in?"

"Definitely," he said, squeezing my hand. "Dan said there is no news on the scientists. So much for an assignment, until they get the bandits to talk."

"Yeah, Um, I'm going to go pay. I'll meet you guys in class?"

Owl nodded to me, then turned to leave.

"One minute, bro," uttered Jenson.

I leaned into him, and he kissed my forehead. "OK, see you in class, then," he whispered. I let go of his hand. Then continued to the counter. Molly trailed after me.

"He's such a gentleman. I wish I could be more confident. Usually, I let Maine handle our PDA," Molly observed.

"Jenson's sweet," I said, taking my wallet out of my purse. Then pulled out the exact amount.

"How many coffees" interrupted the cashier.

"Four, of them," I answered, and counted the money out to her.

"Thanks," she replied.

"So, can I come to this meeting? Do you suppose I'll be needed?"

"Dad did say you're an official member now. What about Maine though?" I asked. We headed out of the cafe, dodging a small group of people attempting to enter.

"Just because I have a girlfriend doesn't mean I'm going to stop hanging with the gang."

"True. Who decided on your outfit today? I've never seen you wear this era before?"

"Mom had these in the attic. Maine said she was captivated by the sixties era. I thought they might be fun to wear."

"So you dressed her up?"

"I guess you could say that. We're planning on going out again. Maybe this weekend."

"That's good," I said as we made our way down the hall to class. " Um, so what did you guys do, after the dance? Can I ask?"

Molly giggled, "We went and got a bite to eat at the all-night diner. Then went to the hotel and soaked in the hot tub. I kind of wish you and Jenson would have come. It's cool, though. We stayed up talking all night about films and art. Maine suggested we go to a local museum on our next date. She loves abstract art. Films, though, we have a lot in common there. Both of us think Michell Pfeiffer, is adorable!" she gushed.

"I'm pretty fond of her myself. Great actress. So what's up with your dad? Was he OK, when you came home Sunday morning?"

"I guess, he sort of, avoided me. Mom wanted details." Molly gave me a crooked smile, while she opened the door. Once inside we walked towards the front desks. I took a seat by Jenson. She situated herself behind us at a table next to Owl.

"Jones isn't here yet. He's never late," I observed.

"Never late," said Jones, peering into the classroom. He scanned the room to see who had arrived shutting the door behind him. "It's nice to see everyone on time today. Owl, you'll appreciate this section of my class. If you've looked at your syllabus, you know we're going to be studying Native Myths and legends. We'll focus on wolves and different views on them in myths of various tribes. I usually do not hand out material, but since this will be a broad subject we will not be using a textbook. I suggest you go to the library and check out books on the particular myths in this handout. There will be no test. Instead, you'll write a paper on your favorite Native Myth. If you discover a tribe we are not focusing on, ask me. I may share the information with the class. Now, go over your packets."

Mr. Jones made his way to his desk and picked up the handouts. He handed them to Jenson. "Please pass them out. I've got some papers to grade.

I looked up from my syllabus at Jenson after highlighting a few suggestions. "Do you think Cavin would allow me to ask the Trinity, about this? Could they be a Myth?"

Owl snickered. "I don't suppose they'd be pleased about you calling them that. Rascal may be open to discussing with us what our mixed tribe believes."

"Okay, maybe," I responded, gathering up my books, and notes. I put them into my backpack. Jones had left. I guess he had some important meeting with the dean. Hopefully, it wasn't anything bad. I'd heard him mumbling about it as he walked out of class. I finished packing up, zipped up my bag, then put on my coat and gloves. I grabbed my knapsack throwing it over my shoulder. "You guys ready to go to the park?"

"Of course, what's the plan of action?" asked Owl.

"Cal and I are meeting with Nayla regarding training. Molly, I'm not sure where you'll come in. I'd like you there, though, just in case. Cal and I have to prepare together. We're um... tethered."

"What do you mean by that?" asked Molly.

"Fixed, Cal is supposed to protect me in combat, somehow. It's a bit blurry. I found out about it Sunday at brunch."

Molly nodded. "I can just head back home. It's no big deal."

"No, it's all good. Besides your part of the clan. I'm sure Nayla will need help with something."

Owl gave Molly a comforting pat on the back. She put on her coat, hat, and gloves, and grabbed her backpack.

"Let's go. We'll take my car. I'm a bit jealous of your link to Cal," said Jenson.

I grabbed his hand, and we walked out of the classroom into the hall. Molly and Owl rushed to catch up. "You have no need. Cal and I have been friends for a long time. I'm not sure what we have in common now. She seemed a bit perturbed that I'm the guardian, and she's only the link. I would be too. Her mom was the guardian before me. My mother was only the link."

"She'll get over it. If you weren't connected, you never would have saved her. Don't ya think?" asked Molly.

93

I pulled Jenson a bit closer while we passed the cafe. "You're right, Moll. I almost certainly wouldn't have," I answered.

Stepping out of the car I tried not to slip on the ice. Afterward reaching for the door, I'd just shut. Molly got out and grabbed my arm helping me to steady myself.

"I'll be glad when this ice and snow finally melts," I grumbled.

"Me too," Molly responded.

She helped me into the park area away from the slippery cement lot. Out of the corner of my eye, I could see Owl and Jenson trying not to laugh at me.

"Come on, let's head up to the Ranger's station. Molly, nice save. We don't need Starla hurting herself. I'm sure Nayla would go haywire," said Owl. He and Jenson hiked beside us on the pathway. It had gotten dark, and I could see a faint light up ahead. Mike must have put out the lantern.

"Mike should be able to contact Nayla for me. The last time I tried via meditation, she was all over me."

"The spirit stuff, them getting-in if you can't keep them out," Owl piped in.

"Yes, and I don't know about that yet; she said she would teach me."

"She will. We dealt with that in my tribe on vision quests. They can be dangerous if not handled correctly. Nayla's a good guide, though. Jenson has some news. It in a way relates to Myth class," he added.

"What's up?" I asked as we stepped up to the Ranger Station.

"I'm going to be a 'Tribal Warrior.' That means I'll help Owl's tribe with pow-wows and events," Jenson responded.

"You're going to be so booked! It's a good thing you're not working right now," I replied. Then lifted my hand to knock on the door of the station. I rapped on it a few times peering into the window on the left.

"Yes, but I should get a job. Maybe I will, after the craziness in our lives subside."

I nodded to him, then turned to leave. "I don't think he's here. I didn't see anyone inside. Maybe we should just go to the huts. I hope Cal is there. If they are all the way out at Nuria's cabin..."

"Hey, what are you doing here?" Star asked.

"Oh, we're looking for Nayla. Once Cal finished her studies, she was supposed to be here."

"They're over at the huts. Ranger Mike's, gone for the day. He left to speak with the Crusader's tribe over yonder. It was Cavin's idea. You brought the whole gang. Good your dad's there too," she chirped.

"You sound excited about this," Molly noted.

"I haven't seen Starla, Araina since, well for a while. Now, let's be off shall we?" She sprinted ahead of us, showing off her magnificent fox form. We ran to keep up. I tried not to get too far ahead of my friends. I'd been working on gaining the ability to run well and control my breathing. Midway I stopped bending over placing my hands on my hips out of breath. "Give me a minute!"

Star raced over to me, "is everything, all right?"

"Yeah," I said, panting to catch my breath.

She chuckled, side bumping me with her body. "It's up there a ways. Cavin and the others are in the dining hall. Nayla's meeting us there. Later we'll train in the meditation room."

"What? Why would we start there first? I thought she wanted to teach us how to protect one another. Isn't that going to be a physical thing? Won't we be jetting about the forest? I'll have Cal, my tether at my side with her Kung-Fu action?" I joked.

"Nalya would like you to learn the basics."

"Yes, no meditation till we learn how to keep out evil spirits."

"Well then, you know, where Nayla wants to start. Come, we'll walk the rest of the way."

I nodded. Jenson, Molly, and Owl caught up to us. We followed her to the dining hut.

Chapter 20

(Dan)

Standing in the doorway of the kitchen, I watched Kaya preparing the snack for the meeting. My mouth began to water. Strolling over to her side, I took a piece of ham and a slice of bread. "I hope you don't mind. Something to tide me over till the others arrive." She smiled at me.

"Is Tri joining us today?" she asked.

"No, but if she does show up it would floor Cavin."

"I agree," interrupted Nuria, who was stirring a pitcher of lemon-aid.

"I hope you have coffee. My girl can't live without it. She runs on caffeine," I joked.

Nuria pointed to the pot on the counter behind her. "I'm always prepared. Cal should be arriving with Minder in a few. Star went to check on your daughter and her friends. We figured she'd go to Ranger Mikes first."

"You're right, mind if I help myself to a cup of coffee?" I asked.

"Go ahead. Kaya, I'll put those plates of sandwiches out on the big table. I'm sure Cavin will want everyone to sit together." She nodded and went to work chopping veggies for the salad bowl.

I dodged them grabbing a mug from a hanging rack below the counter, filled my cup, and headed out to the dining area. Rascal had already taken a seat. I saw he'd brought a massive mug of joe.

"No Tri?"

I sat down, tilting backward in my chair, stretched out my arms, then sat up straight.

"I told you, earlier today I didn't sense she was ready to come back."

"Well, we'll wait it out as you said. If you push a woman, all they do is run, or push back."

I made a gun motion with my hand and said, "Chu-chink."

Nayla came trotting up to the table.

"How's it going," she said, jumping up on a seat next to Rascal.

"Not bad. Who's leading this meeting?"

"Ah, well Cavin, and I thought I'd let Danny-O take the lead. We're trying to get him to man up, be our lawyer at the trial. Me? I'd like Cal and Starla to be able to protect themselves. Of course, they'll guard the perimeter when the Crusaders are unavailable. That's after all this trial stuff is over. It will be good to get the Crusaders help. They offered to be here for the court hearing. Jinx, from the small Trinity group, has been acting up again."

"What will they be doing exactly?" I asked, addressing Nayla.

"We need a jury. Following that, there's the testimony of what allegedly occurred. It's all speculation until someone comes forward."

"That's right, I'm hoping it will be sooner than later," spoke Cavin.

I got up, and pulled out a chair for him, next to Nayla. Then went to sit back down as Kaya and Nuria exited the kitchen. I stood by my chair for a moment observing the hallway leading to the mud room. A few minutes later, I heard a bustling about, then chatter.

"Are you sure everyone is here?" asked Starla.

"They're all seated waiting for us," spoke up Star.

"I'm sure, it's not going to be an extensive meeting," suggested Owl.

I caught a glimpse of Starla grabbing Jenson's hand. They marched to the table. Molly followed them, dragging behind.

"Hey Dad, mind if we sit here? Owl and Star can sit right beside us. Where's Cal?"

"They'll be here soon. I'm not sure what's keeping them," Nuria commented.

"Can we call them? Do they have a cell phone? If not, we need to get Cal a prepaid one. That way I'm not getting in trouble for inappropriate meditation," Starla admitted.

Nayla turned towards her, "You're right dear one. We should do that. I'll need to be able to get in touch with everyone. Did someone remember to bring a notepad? We'll need up to date information on everyone."

I took out my small notebook, and pen from the pocket of my coat. Then wrote down my cell with my current address. I passed it to Starla. It made its rounds ending with Molly.

"Here," she said, handing it to Nayla.

"Cal's not here, but I'm eager to tell you, what she shared with me!" Starla exclaimed.

"Enthusiasm, I like it!" I slapped my daughter on the back.

A grin spread across Nayla's face, "What's up?"

"Rumor has it, the bandits planned on attacking the scientists. Cal overheard them while being held captive. She had no other details, then, that on the subject. If we can get them to reveal a location, we could join forces."

"I did hear them," said Cal, stepping out of the hallway. She sat on the bench and took off her boots. "I was several feet from them. Sika had gotten pretty wild that night. He had, Gavin, cowering in a corner." She squinted her eyes and placed her hands on her knees. "He said, Hmmm," she bit her lower lip, trying to recall a memory.

"Tearing them apart, like a wolf, he would find someone to do it. That there were five of them, two women, and three men."

She paused. "It's getting blurry. The others were bystanders," she explained, laying her boots on the floor.

"OK, Cal. Why don't you come over here? Sit down, have a sandwich and something to drink. You, look parched," I added.

She stood up from the bench, then walked over. Kaya began to fix her a plate.

"Maybe I'll remember more, later. There was something about orders."

"Eat," said Nayla. "We'll be doing some exercises after this."

Cal picked up her sandwich and began to demolish it.

"Slow, down, there's more where that came from," chuckled Nayla.

"We need to pinpoint the murderer first. Cal, I'll have Eva get you a notebook to write down any information you may recall. If we prove it wasn't the bandits, we'll call Trinity in to be questioned. Let's not rule that out," I replied.

"Wouldn't they already have come forward," asked Eva, setting her coat behind Cal's chair. She patted her daughter on the back as she sat down beside her.

"Maybe not, if someone threatened them, they might hold back information," countered Minder pulling up a seat next to Eva.

I nodded, "Eva, is Tri, coming to this meeting? Will she be attending any of the drills with Starla?"

"Yes, later on. She called this afternoon. She's at the library in a conference."

"Thank you, Eva. Everyone's here now. Nayla is anxious to work with Starla and Cal. We need to proceed with the trial. After the incident with Minder, it's vital we resolve this issue."

"Cavin, I considered granting them immunity, if they confessed to who killed Du-Vance. After that we'll have to decide what to do with them," Nayla confirmed.

"We cannot trust those who've killed our family," blurted Shellena.

"Unless they give us a reason too," she retorted.

Lance was right behind her. He cast aside his jacket on an empty chair, pulled it out, then sat slouching low. "Cavin, I volunteer to grill the bandits. I want to be present during the trial."

Cavin nodded, "You'll be asked to keep it civil. I don't want this dining hall smashed to bits. Kaya and Star, you'll set up the tables for us. Then the chairs for the jury. Dan, you'll need to meet with Lance and Shellena regarding questions for the examination. If needed I'll get Jones, to cross-examine them. We can't have them claiming we didn't give them a fair trial."

"When will this take place?" asked Starla.

"This week, Friday. Dan, it should allow you plenty of time to prepare."

"What! Is it that urgent?" I asked.

"Yes, this adjourns this meeting."

I sat there stunned. I couldn't believe this was moving forward so fast. Cavin though called the shots. I knew that.

"Nayla, why don't you take Starla Araina, and Cal to the meditation chamber."

"Should I take Molly home?" asked Jenson.

"Oh, it's alright, I can walk," she replied.

"No, let me take you. It's freezing outside," offered Jenson.

Nayla jumped down from her seat over to Molly. She nuzzled her hand to get her attention. "As of now Cal, and Starla will need to train one on one. Today they'll be meditating and learning how to work together being in sync. Later, we'll need you to join in on our planning. For now, though, let Jenson take you home."

Molly nodded to her.

"Starla, I'll see you in class tonight. If you miss one more your tanked!"

My daughter frowned, "You know it!"

Jenson shook his head, and I observed Cal and Starla preparing to leave with Nayla.

"See ya in class Molly. Later, dad," she called.

Chapter 21

(Starla)

Nayla led us down the hall. Familiar pictures lined the corridor. I pointed to the one with the half-fox half-girl I'd noticed the first time I had been here. Cal's eyes lit up, and her mouth hung open.

"Yeah, it floored me the first time too," I responded.

Nayla pushed Cal forward with her nose. We kept moving. The door to the reflection room was ajar. Cal pushed it open. The pillows from our last meeting sat where we'd left them. I shut the door behind us. Without a word, I grabbed three of them heading to the middle of the room. Then set them down in a circle. Why was everyone so quiet? Was Cal afraid? I stood there until Nayla trotted up to me.

"Starla, Do you see the firewood over there?" she asked nodding towards it.

"Yes," I answered.

"You and Cal will start a fire in the hearth. There are twigs, dry grass, and some tinder to help it catch. This exercise will determine how well you work together. Once, the fires lit we'll sit down and begin our meditation."

"Easy peasy! When I was with the bandits, we built fires out in the open almost every night!" Cal stopped, putting her hand over her mouth realizing what she'd said. Then moved her hand away from her face to her side. "Sorry, I... spent so much time with them."

"It's okay, get started. I'm going to sit back and observe," Nayla said. A smirk formed on her lips.

I went over to the box of twigs, old newspaper, and dry leaves. "I'll make the base for the fire first. Then you place the logs on top. Is it best we put it in a Teepee position?"

"You were in Daisy Girl Scouts for a bit. We were like five, maybe? Do you remember?"

"Barely," I admitted. "They only let us watch the leaders make the campfire."

I took the box and advanced to the fireplace, placing the twigs inside I set the leaves on top of them. Afterward, I ripped the newspaper into long strips, then crumpled them.

"There, now you set up the logs," I said, standing back to give her room.

Cal took three of them, placing them in the position I'd indicated.

"Where are the matches?"

"Matches? Cal, you and Starla Araina are going start this fire using your minds. You must merge your thoughts together. Then stir up enough emotions to ignite the tinder. If you can keep it going long enough, the logs will catch."

"What?"

"I've done this before, in a large group with the clan," I told Cal, taking her hands in mine. She pushed them away.

"What are you doing?"

"It's so we're connected. We have to learn to unit mentally. It will help for now. Later, we won't need physical contact."

"Good job," Nayla responded.

Cal let me take her hands. We stood five feet away from the base of the hearth.

"We have to take our raw emotions, anger, envy, or we could use, love?" Which one works for you?"

Cal dropped my hands, rubbing her sweaty palms on her jeans. Then pushed back her tangled mess of hair. "My emotions are everywhere. I can't even stay in fox form. I keep fading back and forth. It's almost as if something else is attempting to emerge out of me."

"Okay, take the hope, faith, and what you held on to, that kept you sane. Use that," I suggested.

She nodded, taking my hands in hers.

"We'll concentrate on our own and try to combine our thoughts. You did contact me while you were held captive. Try to do that now, but let our minds collide."

"Okay," she said. Then took a deep breath gradually exhaling it out. I squeezed her hand. From my toes to my chest I let the warm intensity rise, pushing it from my arms to my hands into Cal. She could feel the heat of my hope. I heard her passion. It passed to me in a raw untethered heat. I took control of it, aiming our outstretched hands towards the fire. It began sparking, then smolder out. I stayed silent. She almost broke her hands from mine, but I held on. I felt her mind, let go releasing rage. It burned. "Push, it out, light the fire," I mind spoke to her. She took the tension within releasing it onto the hearth. A burst of flames erupted, then ignited the kindling.

"Relax, it's lit. Let go of one another."

I released Cal's hands. She let them fall by her side.

"Are you alright?" I asked.

"Yeah, a bit burnt, toasted, singed... I never started a fire like that before!"

I helped her over to sit on one of the pillows.

"Can I get some water?" asked Cal.

"Nayla?" I asked.

"Go ahead, the washroom is behind us," she said, pointing to it with her nose.

I made my way to the tiny door. Then turned the handle, but it seemed to be stuck. I pushed up against it aggressively wiggling it back and forth.

Then took a stance and pulled the knob back. I fell. Suddenly the door swung open, almost hitting me in the face where I sat.

"You okay?"

"Yeah, give me a minute."

I reached for the door frame using it to pull myself up and stood. Then inched to the sink in the small room. Turning on the water, I let it run cold, took a cup off the shelf in front of me filling it. I'd try not to spill it on the way, I thought, leaving the door opened. I didn't want to fight with it again, in case someone needed to get in.

I leisurely walked over to Cal carefully handing her the water. "Here you go."

She took the plastic cup of water and chugged it down. Then wiped the sweat off of her forehead. "Will meditation be as consuming as this?"

Nayla turned to Cal. "It requires your focus. You'll have to learn to balance your spiritual center. Starla has done well, thus far. Keeping others from entering your sacred space is tricky. You can block them by setting up a barrier surrounding your astral self. Imagine a bullet proof square box around you. You choose, who you let in. When you block out an enemy, they bounce off the box."

"Are there exceptions?"

"Always. Rare, though," she answered.

"Why does Cal, fade in and out as a fox?" I inquired.

"Technically, it's not fading. Cal's body won't stay shifted. It's extremely painful," commented Nayla.

Cal cringed, " My whiskers come out, then my fur, and for a few minutes I'm able to sustain it. Afterward, I begin to change back into my human form. It's an argument between my emotional and physical self. It has to do with a disassociation of my fox being."

"Yes. We're going to work on that."

"Um, can we get this ball rolling," I said, fidgeting in my spot on the floor."

"Do you have somewhere to be," asked Nayla.

Cal gave me a inquisitive look.

"Math class. I can't miss it, or I'm out. It's not my best subject. Molly's been tutoring me."

Nayla began to pace. "I see. OK, I didn't realize I was under time constraints today." She stopped and sat beside me looking me in the eyes. "I wouldn't want to upset Tri. Not after she has agreed to meet with us, finally."

I attempted to smile. It would be comforting to have my mother near. The pressure though for her to be here. I hoped it wouldn't force a wedge between us. So far what had happened to me brought us closer together. Would she accept her identity as I had? Or would she push it away due to fear? She seemed to be coming around.

"I'm going to lead you together in a short meditation. We'll take five minutes to relax, go into deep breathing, and attempt to meet in the field. Cal, you will try to find Starla Araina's astral form. You'll follow her in yours. This exercise should last no more than twenty minutes. If you get lost, back out, come back here. Wait for Starla and me to return."

"What about blocking baddies?" I asked.

Nayla shook her head in disgust. "You'll imagine the bulletproof box, put it up in your mind as your entering the meditation. Both of you," she said firmly.

I moved into the cross-legged position, bent my head forward closing my eyes. My hands rested on my legs. Breathing commenced. I heard nothing around me, Cal and Nayla must have also begun. The first few moments I worked on controlling my breathing, making it steady and staying calm.

Then slowly brought up an image of a box around myself. Nayla hadn't said to change into fox form, so I stayed in my human body.

A rush of air surrounded me. Was I being levitated off the floor? A whirring sound blasted in my ears, before landing roughly on the ground. Where was I? Was this the field? I opened my eyes and stood up.

"Starla, come to the meadow. Cal should be here, find her!"

I heard Nayla speaking, but could not see her. Don't panic! I took a deep breath in and let it out. I looked around me at the gold wheat.

Afterward, I gazed further on searching for Cal. Then took off sprinting in circles to find her. Had she been able to enter? If not, why?

Moving forward through the tall golden wheat, I saw nothing. Amare? Are you here? I waited for a moment. No, not even my spirit guide. I halted ready to sit down. Then considered heading back as Nayla had instructed us if we became separated.

"Starla, Where's Nayla?"

"Cal, Where are you? Nayla has to be here somewhere." I sniffed the air to see if I could locate her using her scent. I'd never done it before, but hey, it might work. Then bent down and put my hands into the earth. I brought up the soil and took a good whiff. Well, it smelled like earth. The dirt fell from my hands onto the ground. I turned to my right. There, facing me was a big black wolf! I stood up, backing up into something and stumbled.

"Cal, put up your shield! Run, don't let anything in!" A whooshing sound erupted around me. A wind storm, perhaps? I crashed onto a rock, so much for my astral form. I'd traveled pushing my solid matter into this hemisphere. From there I stumbled onto the ground. "Help me up!"

"OK, alright. You told me to run."

Cal stood, brushing off her jeans. She grabbed my hand helping me up. "How was I supposed to know you were behind this rock. I've never run so fast in my life! Did you see that wolf? Where did it come from?"

"Beats me, we're not in the middle of a thriller video. Let's hope it didn't attack Nayla."

"Thriller?"

"Never mind. Mom and her VH1 obsession," I chuckled. "We've got to find Nayla or go back without her. The last thing we need is to get stuck here. If I do, my mother will never forgive me, for failing out of college because of math..."

I backed up...

"Starla?"

"I see it again, the black wolf. Don't you see it? It's right behind you!"

"There's nothing there."

Out of the field, Nayla came trotting up to us. "Why didn't you two come further out? I've tried several times mentally connecting with you."

"There was a black wolf. I don't know where it came from, who it was, or if it wanted to attack me," I sputtered.

"Well, I never..."

"Nayla, come on. I saw it too, once. Then the second time I... I... think you were in shock," Cal said, giving me a strange look.

"You said, enemies can get in. Have you ever seen one?"

"A black wolf? Not here," Nayla answered. She turned and trotted forward. Cal and I followed. We stopped in the middle of the field.

"Sit as you are presently back in the Reflection room."

Cal and I took our positions.

"Now, as before, continue, let yourself go. Visualize yourselves back in the room. You're relaxed. Nothing can harm you. Guide your spirit back an open your eyes."

I felt a rush, then a whoosh, in between hemispheres. My body hit the floor in an abrupt manner. I hoped Nayla hadn't noticed. I shuddered, opening my eyes. During the transfer, I'd wrapped my arms around my chest. I'd been hugging myself. I released my arms, letting them rest on my thighs. Then waited for Nayla and Cal to return. Cal was the first. I saw her aura enter her body. Gradually she began to move. Then blinked her eyes. She jumped up from her seated position.

"Where am I?"

I stood up, and walked to Cal. "You're fine. We're back in the meditation room. Stay calm. We can't disrupt Nayla's return."

She nodded. We both sat down. In silence, we waited and watched.

Nayla shook, her eyes fluttered, then opened. She stood up on all fours stretching her torso forward, then back before sitting. "Starla, you were supposed to travel in astral form. Please, next time make sure you do so."

"Of course. I'm not sure, how it happened," I stammered.

"Alright and Cal, your ability to touch Starla using astral projection is impressive.

"While you have shown your ability to adapt, this mission was unsuccessful. I'm happy no harm came to anyone, and we made it back. It's the first time something has severed or stopped my arrival. Thank goodness I found you both. Generally, we'd arrive at the same place."

"What should I do about the wolf?"

Nayla held up her paw. "Be leary, watch your back. Cal, you and Starla should spend more time together. The bandits trial is Friday. We can only presume it's under control. Cal, Nuria is coming to get you."

"I should find my dad. I need to stop by my house to pick up school work," I said, standing up.

"We'll must meet again, before Friday. Your dad will prepare Jenson. He'll want Owl there too. Have you discussed anything with Molly yet?"

"You want us there for the trial?"

"Only in case, we need you to verify, what happened."

"I have to go," I said, moving towards the door.

"OK, I'll contact you then. Don't let Denny's get in the way of this," Nayla warned.

"It's a job. I'll most likely be switching to weekends only," I responded, pushing the door open.

Chapter 22

(Dan)

Rushing out of the Reflection room my daughter bumped into me! She stepped back.

"Dad, can we get out of here?"

"Is everything alright? What happened?" I asked.

"I'm a bit shaken up. Can we talk about it on the way to the apartment? I need to get my knapsack."

"OK, do you mind waiting out here? I need to speak with Nayla before we go."

Starla shrugged.

"Are you mad at her?" I asked.

"I'm not sure she believes what I saw."

"Catch me up to speed as you kids say."

"Dad, just go talk to her I'll wait." Starla leaned up against the wall.

"Are you going to tell me what happened?"

"If Nayla doesn't tell you first," she said, glaring at me.

I pushed open the door to the meditation room. Cal and Nayla sat in the middle of it.

"Come on in. Where's Starla?"

"Waiting in the hall. Did everything go alright?" I asked.

"It was a mess. We all ended up at different edges of the wheat field. It's not often we get separated. Not to that extent. Cal, you and Starla handled it well."

"She seemed upset by something," I commented.

"A black wolf, she only saw it for a moment. I know because she screamed for me to run. I saw it the first time. The second, nothing," Cal answered.

"I've no clue how it got in. We've never had one in the field before," Nayla responded.

I tapped my foot on the floor, then brought my hand to my chin. "Hmmm, well it could be anything."

"I told her to be cautious. I want to meet with her again. She and Cal need training. The trial is Friday."

"Well, I've got to get Starla home, then to class. She's insisting we pick up Molly."

"OK, make sure she's not working too much. We need her here Dan."

"Yes, but be careful," I said, raising an eyebrow.

"Tri," said Nayla.

"Yeah, you don't want her to believe you're monopolizing Starla's time."

"That, and I don't want to push her away. I'd like her back."

"Me too," I answered, turning towards the door.

"Dan, you'll get through this."

I nodded, then twisted the door handle to open it.

Cal sat watching us both."We have to," she chimed in.

"We will," I answered, shutting the door behind me.

"Dad, I'm not prepared for this," said Starla.

"Why? Nayla has faith in you. You rescued Cal from Thunder Head Bay."

"That wolf, not being able to find Cal. I guess it freaked me out," she answered, waving her hands in the air.

I kept my eyes on the road ahead. "You know you could take on fewer hours at the diner. I'd help your mom out with your schooling," I advised.

Starla slouched back in her seat, keeping her eyes on the scenery outside. I reached over to turn on the radio.

"No, it won't solve my insecurities with the clan," she answered.

Hungry like the wolf drifted out of the radio speakers.

"Great," Starla said, pointing to the radio. "Even Duran Duran has it out for me."

"You know who they are?"

"Dad. Mom plays the oldies station all the time," she sassed, folding her arms a crossed her chest.

"Why don't you, and Jenson, do some recon on the wolf you saw. Find out if it holds any meaning?"

"Not sure what it would indicate. It didn't exactly try to attack us, yet."

I turned onto the street of the apartment complex. Starla unfolded her arms and adjusted herself in the seat. I was unsure of what to say to help her believe things would be alright. Nayla would make sure she was safe.

There was no way in hell Tri would let anything happen to her. If it did, the whole Starla and clan-emersion would be over. She'd run. I knew my wife.

"Dad, you OK?"

"Yeah, I'm just thinking."

"Are you worried too?"

"I'm a dad. That's my job," I admitted, glancing at her. Then turned my attention back to the road while I pulled into the parking lot.

Starla smiled. I circled the lot trying to find a place to park. The complex was pretty full.

"Is someone, having a party?" I asked.

Starla shrugged, "Who knows. Anyway, dad recon is a good idea. Owl will be able to help us. Jones has us studying wolf legends. That man is always one step ahead of us. Psychic or something."

"He's just doing his job," I said, opening the car door. "Come on, go get your things. I should talk to your mom before we head out again."

Standing in the middle of the kitchen, I eyed the coffee maker. Tri had apparently just made a pot. It smelled pretty amazing. "Hey there, mind if I grab a cup of coffee to go?" I asked.

"Sure," said Tri, standing in the middle of the kitchen. "Where's Starla?"

"Oh, she went to get her things. Math class. Molly mentioned she'd tank if she didn't show up. Whatever that means."

"Fail Dan," she said setting her coffee cup down on the counter. "So how did the meeting with the clan go? Is she alright?"

I sighed. Then went over to get some coffee.

"Here, let me get it for you." Tri grabbed a cup off of the counter and poured some brown liquid into it, then handed it to me.

"Thanks," I said, taking a drink. I tried to steady my shaking hands. I hadn't realized they were until now.

"Starla's a bit spooked. During the meditation, they were separated. A large black wolf appeared to her. Nayla had been attempting to coach them to block out spirits. She's never had this happen before. We're not certain if it was in fact there or what. Starla assumes Jones holds the key to some of this. Says he's having them study wolf legends." I shrugged.

Tri's eyes grew wide, "That's a possibility. It didn't attack them. Did it?"

"No, she only observed it. Nayla's concerned, it will return. I advised Starla to look into it."

"Good idea, I'd like to help. I can research at the library. You said it was black."

"Yeah. The trials Friday."

Tri raised her eyebrows at me, "That's pushing it."

"Everyone wants me to question them. I don't see a way out. Jones will cross-examine them."

"You'll do fine," she said, taking my empty cup from me, and setting it on the counter.

"Come here."

I stood inches away from her. Tri placed her hands on my shoulders, leaning into me. Her warm lips brushed mine. She pulled away. I stood staring into her eyes. She brought her hand up and stroked my face with her fingertips. We parted.

Megan peered into the room from the hallway. "Dad, are you and mom done now?"

"Yes, come here and give your dad a hug."

She rushed over to me, almost knocking me over. It's difficult to admit she's in eighth grade. She's almost, as tall as me, I reflected. I felt her wrap her arms around me. Then gave her a soft bear hug.

"It's good to know you're not too old to cuddle your dad."

"Never, just not in front of my friends," she sassed.

116

I tousled her hair. "Okay," I said as she backed out of my arms.

"Dad, are we ready?" asked Starla glowering at me from the hallway.

I let go of Megan. Tri leaned against the counter, then brushed her strawberry blonde hair behind her ears. A small smile spread on her lips.

"Dan, I've been contemplating things. Although, we don't have everything figured out yet. I'd like you to come home."

My heart raced, she wanted me home. I wanted to be home. I probably looked like a deer blinded by headlights. Yes, she loved me, but there were unsettled issues. I'd have to be patient.

She put her arm around my middle and pulled me close. "I'm serious. It would be good for me, and the girls. I don't want to wait any longer."

I pulled her into me and held her. "OK, I'll have to get my things together. Let the landlord know. How soon?" I asked, dumbfounded.

"As soon as possible!" Megan chimed in standing off to the side.

"As happy as I am for you both. If we don't go I'll be late for class," Starla grumbled.

"Alright," I said, pulling away from Tri.

"So I'll see you tonight. For dinner?"

"Um, I'll have to check in. I do need time to pack," I admitted.

She nodded and turned to the dishes in the sink.

"I'll have to remember we both have priorities."

"You are one of them," I replied, opening the back door for Starla.

"Bye mom, see ya after class?"

"Okay, bye." Tri turned to me, "Are you bringing her home?"

"Starla?" I asked.

"Um, I'll catch a ride with Mrs. Fretner."

"Fair enough. Call if you need anything, both of you," said Tri.

I grabbed her hand, squeezed it, and smiled at Megan before closing the door behind us.

Chapter 23

(Starla)

Standing outside of the classroom, I stared in. Mrs. Price was at her desk. Fingering my assignments, I decided it was time to face the music. I'd had to turn in a few of them via her mailbox. I had attended classes and then skipped out again. Big mistake. Molly stood up from her seat and turned. She noticed me standing in the doorway.

"Don't be chicken," she mouthed.

Still, I was. I pushed open the door. It made a loud creaking noise. At any rate, no one else had arrived, yet. Mrs. Price looked up from her desk a frown scrawled a crossed her face. She set aside a several papers. "Well, come in," she instructed.

Molly sat back down and opened her syllabus. I watched her take out her notebook. She began to write down a few of the new math problems. I looked away, shuffling over to the instructor's desk.

"Here's the last assignment," I gulped.

"You will not be able to miss any more classes. One more, absent will result in your expulsion from this class.

"I understand."

"Good. Molly said, she'll continue to help you. We have two more assignments plus one more test. You'll need to get a B average to pass this class. Then, as I understand, you'll be moving on. I don't want to see you back here."

"Yes, here," I said, holding out my homework to her. Reaching out, she took it from me.

"Thank you, you can go sit down now."

I took off my coat and hung it behind the chair, then sat down.

"Drill instructor," Molly whispered under her breath.

I tried not to giggle. "Don't make me laugh Mol. She'll frown at me more. How's it going?"

"I sort of feel left out of the clan stuff. Are you going to give Cal back her moped?"

"If she asks for it."

"You're such a brat! Open your math book. We'll go over the steps for the next set of problems."

"Now you sound like Mrs. Price," I countered.

"Maybe I will be someday. I don't plan on being the math militia."

I laughed, "Okay, let's get this over with."

"Are you ready to get out of here?" I asked. Molly crinkled her nose. Then twitched it several times.

"What are you doing? Your not Samantha on Bewitched," I joked.

She slouched in her seat and gave a long sigh. Mrs. Price had dismissed class. Then left.

"Anything irritating you?"

"I'm ready for this semester to be over, aren't you?" she asked. Then threw her pencils in her pouch and started to put away her books.

"If I could, I'd quit school like Buffy did. Although if I'm correct she did it so she could take care of Dawn."

Molly rolled her eyes at me while she stuck out her tongue. I snickered at her absurdity.

"Come on. My mom will be here soon to pick us up."

I stood to push the seat under the desk. Feeling chilly, I grabbed my coat off the back of the chair. "Do we have time to get coffee?"

"We could have it at my house. Why not invite Jenson," she pressed.

"It sounds tempting. I don't have anything planned tonight. Maybe you could help me with the last two math assignments?"

I finished putting on my winter gear. Then walked to the exit. Molly followed beside me.

"Sure, if that's what you want to do. Wouldn't you rather see Jenson? I could ask Maine to join us."

Molly gripped the door handle, twisting her body back to look at me, then opened it. We strolled out into the hallway.

"Well, it's better to get it completed, before I get in over my head with the demands I'll need to meet for training with Nayla. I'm sorry they're not including you currently."

"It's Maine, isn't it?"

"Yeah, vulnerability, rules, excuses. My new hidden life!" I threw up my arms. A deep sense of hurt built up in my chest. I pushed back my girly emotions. Then took a breath of air, and exhaled. "Sorry, I'm getting worked up again."

We stopped to stand in the alcove to wait for Molly's mom. "So what has been going on? How'd the training go with Cal?"

"She's a bit shaky regarding her abilities. In spite of that, she's able to unite with me. We started a fire in the hearth using our minds. That part went well."

"And... What part didn't?" she asked.

"Once we went into, a deep astral travel meditation. I should have pulled back the second I realized we were separated. Cal had never attempted it before. I wasn't going to leave without her. Stumbling around the field, I called out to Nayla. Afterward Cal. Out of nowhere, this black wolf appeared!"

"I don't know what it means. Cal saw it too! Nayla can't figure out how it entered our realm. Once I found Cal, Nayla came accusing us of not venturing further into the field. Soon after we went back to the Reflection room."

"What did your dad say?"

"At first, I wasn't keen on discussing it with him. After I did, he suggested recon."

"More research. Well, your mom does work at the library, do you think he's discussed it with her?"

"Most likely, they seem to be understanding each other lately. Before class today my mother asked him to move back in. She also agreed to attend my next training session."

"Those are big steps! Last I knew she didn't want anything to do with the clan or Hunters Park for that matter."

"Exactly. Do you suppose your mom will ever let you borrow the car?"

"Probably, she had a meeting tonight at church," Molly replied.

"Ah, Okay," I answered.

A black blazer pulled into the parking lot. The headlights reflected off of the door where we stood.

"Ah, mom. We'd better get," she said, pulling open the door.

"I should call mine on the way. See, if she doesn't have any plans for us this evening." Molly held the door for me. We left letting the door shut behind us.

"And you think that my parents are super strict," Molly replied.

"Within reason," I answered.

We shuffled our feet so we wouldn't slip on the icy sidewalks. Then got into the mega car. Ha, mega car. Well, it's how I viewed the blazer.

"What have you done to your room? It's girly," I commented, sitting on the pink bean bag. My math book spread out on my lap.

"I like pretty, things like Maine." Molly gave a long sigh.

Shaking my head in defeat, I picked up a pillow sitting next to me. I tossed it over at her.

"Starla!" she exclaimed, catching it in mid-air. She threw it back at me.

"Molly!" I echoed her. The pillow hit me, then landed on the floor. "Thanks for helping me with this last assignment."

"Are you getting it?"

"Yeah," I said, picking up my pencil to start another problem. I crinkled my forehead. Then worked through the order of operation to come to a conclusion. I continued until I got to the last problem on the page.

"Can you help me with this?' I asked.

"Sure," Molly answered.

"I hate imaginary numbers! I'm so glad this is the last math class I'll be taking," I answered.

"How's that?"

"I'm considering a degree in the arts. If not, maybe I could get paid to train the kits from my clan."

"Oh, your mom would love that. Let's finish this problem."

"We should get Jenson and Owl over here for recon."

She nodded, taking my pen, then showed me how to break down the equation to solve it more simply.

"I always forget I can't combine real parts with imaginary parts when solving for a complex number. It's like me. To the world, I would be part imaginary! Heck, I'm half fox," I noted.

Molly smirked. "How's lit class going? I know it's one of your stronger suits."

"I'm just finishing some reading. It's a comprehension test so it should be fine."

"That's good. One class that isn't turning your brain into mush. I'm glad Megan and I are good at math."

"If not I'll be working at Denny's for life, or some other dive," I said, then shrugged.

Molly got up to get her cell. She took it off the dresser and pulled up another pink beanie chair to join me.

"I have my phone. I'll call Jenson."

"Sure, and I'll contact Maine. Set up our mid-date for Wednesday."

"No church?" I asked.

"No church. Dad hasn't been happy about my truancy. Oh, well," she commented starting to dial.

Maine was making Molly brave. I pulled my phone out of my jean pocket, dialed, and waited for him to pick up.

Chapter 24

(Dan)

Rascal grabbed the books off the top shelf of the bookcase. He placed them in boxes on the floor.

"Thanks for your help. I know it was short notice. Tri out of the blue asked me to move back! I'm in awe of it!"

"Man, enjoy it. You have been waiting for this for a while."

"I have, and it feels good to be getting out of this cramped one-bedroom apartment."

Rascal finished packing up the box of books. I took my suitcase out of the closet. Then walked over to the dresser to pack up my clothing.

"You have any plans for dinner tonight?" he asked.

I paused, then pulled open the dresser drawers. I took out my socks, T-shirts, and other items, stuffing them into the suitcase.

"Tri wanted me to come over. I told her it would take me a while to get things in order here. I can pack, but I have to give notice to the landlord. If he doesn't let me out of my lease, I'll need to sublet the place. Otherwise, I'll have to pay a fee."

"That makes sense. Are you hungry? I thought we'd order a pizza or something," Rascal suggested.

"Sounds good," I answered, closing the suitcase. "Say, do you know anything about black wolves? Starla had a meeting with Nayla. She went on a vision quest or meditation? She said a black wolf appeared to her. It upset her. Tri and I were going to do a recon. Then this," I said, spreading out my arms to indicate the fast track move.

"How much more do you have to pack?" asked Rascal.

"Not much. I plan on giving most of my dinnerware to Goodwill. It's where I got it from."

"OK, what about the living room."

"I have a flat screen T.V. Do you want it?"

"No joke?"

"Heck, why not? Goodwill won't take it," I laughed.

"Thanks, man."

"No problem. Now let's get this finished, order pizza. Afterward, maybe research the black wolf," I answered.

He picked up the boxes of books, placing them over near the door against the wall. I began to pile things up there. All that was left was my bed and empty dressers.

The smell of cheesy pizza with meat toppings filled my nose. Rascal insisted he'd pay after offering him my fifty- inch T.V. Who needs two televisions? Neither Starla nor Megan needed one in their rooms. I wasn't going to have an argument with Tri about the bedroom either.

Rascal opened up the pizza box. He took one piece out and started to eat.

"Let me get us some plates. What do you want to drink? Is soda OK?"

"Sure, any kind, but diet. That stuff will kill ya!"

I chuckled. "You've got that right." I took two cans of Orange Crush out of the fridge. Then grabbed the plates off of the counter.

"So is this furniture yours?"

"Nah, it was here when I rented the place. I kept it in pretty good condition. I'll get my deposit back, minus the carpet cleaners."

I set down the soda's and paper plates on the table. Then grabbed a slice of pizza from the box. Rascal opened his soda, taking a long drink. He set it down, wiping his hand on the napkin beside him.

"Black wolves, are not always a bad omen. It could mean many things. Do you know anything about it besides the color of the wolf?"

"No, I just thought you might know something since you're from a tribe."

"It could be a warning or a sign she's on the right track with her training. Either way, I'd recommend being cautious for now."

"Can you at least give me a general overview?" I asked grabbing another slice.

"No problem. The wolf is a pathfinder. He helps guide you when you've gone astray. Pushing you to discover what is making you unbalanced. He or she encourages you to trust your instincts and intuition. If the wolf came to her, it has to be for a reason. They usually don't leave their pact even spirit wolves. It could be carrying a message."

"So, what do we do?"

"Wait, it out. Let me talk to Owl about it. He and my boy were close if he knows anything, I'll let you know. OK?"

"Thanks. There's one more piece left. Do you want it?"

"Nah, Can I get another soda?"

"Sure, help yourself."

"OK, then I'll help you load your car," he replied getting up.

"We can move the boxes and your suitcase into the living room for the time being. I'll call Tri later. I hope to be home by Wednesday. Megan is extremely excited. It also might be best if Tri and I show up together for Starla's next training session."

"Nalya won't allow you to take part, though," he replied, shutting the refrigerator door. He leaned up against it sipping the drink.

"True. We'll figure it out." I pushed my seat back and stood stretching.

"What do you suppose your kids are up to?"

"Hopefully, Starla is doing her math homework. Megan is playing sudoku unless she's found a new hobby."

Rascal downed the rest of his soda. Then put his empty can on the counter. We began to tidy up a smidgen. Once we were done here, I'd plan on getting some shut eye. I wouldn't be getting up til work called in the morning.

Chapter 25

(Starla)

"Owl and Jenson are on their way. How's Maine?"

"Ah, working on art stuff. She's an only child. When she asked what I was doing tonight, it left me feeling guilty. I told her you and I were hanging out. We needed best-friend time. It sounded crazy lame. What else could I say?"

"Not much," I answered.

Molly took her laptop off of her desk, positioning it between us on an old coffee table.

"Do you want to get started?" she asked.

"Yeah, I told the guys we'd hack the info before they got here. Jenson was like I'm the computer king!" I rolled my eyes.

Molly pulled up the Google Search engine on the computer. At first, it was difficult locating useful websites. A lot of them were stories. None related to a visitation by a black wolf. We'd done research on spirit animals. The wolf, however, was not mine.

"I guess we should have paid better attention in Myth class. It was on that test we took a few weeks ago," I blurted.

Molly shrugged, "Here, let me try. I'll look up spirit-animal for a wolf. Let's see what description comes up."

Molly typed it in and up popped a link. She clicked on it and read. "Strong connections, loyalty, following your instincts, a need for freedom."

"It doesn't explain why it would show up out of nowhere."

"Nope, let's keep looking."

The door to the room swung open. Jenson and Owl walked in.

"So you girls got started without us," Owl commented.

"Yeah, we're trying to figure why Starla, is encountering this black wolf," answered Molly. She pushed the keyboard aside for a moment.

"Wait, was it in a vision, meditation, or astral travel?" asked Owl.

"Meditation mixed with astral travel. Nayla is teaching Cal and me, how to block out unwanted entities."

"Uh huh," said Owl, stepping over to where we sat. Jenson came over to me. I moved to make room for him on the bean bag.

"Miss me?"

I wrapped my arms around him giving him a brief hug.

"Did dad tell you the trials Friday? They've moved everything forward. I'm pretty sure Wednesday will be my next day to train. If this wolf comes back, most likely it will be then."

"Don't worry. Usually, these spirits are only meant to warn you. Did it say anything? Make any noises?" asked Owl.

"None," I answered.

"OK, mind if I take over," Jenson offered.

"Be my guest," said Molly, moving the computer closer to him.

Typing a mile a minute he made side notes in the word document. Molly left to get us coffee. By the time she came back, Jenson had papers printed out sitting on the table with the laptop pushed off to the side.

"Jenson, let me explain some of this to Starla. It's not going to make much sense until she can communicate with this spirit or being."

"Alright, go ahead, Owl."

"The black wolf you're seeing, either means you're on the right path or lacking trust in your life. It could be a person you are close to, mentor, or a friend. If this isn't the case, It could be calling attention to the strength, courage, and loyalty you hold within yourself. My last and most crazy thought, it has to do with Du-Vance."

"That is wild! What would it have to do with him?"

"I'm not sure. If there is a next time, or you get any funky visions, dreams, make sure you have a pad and paper. "

"Are you going to be present during the trial?" I asked.

Owl struggled trying to get his coat off. Finally, placing it on the back of a nearby chair. Then sat on the floor.

"Of course, I'll be there. I don't see why not. Rascal will either criticize, observe or remain seated quietly. Cavin will make sure the bandits are in restraints. Not sure who is going to do it. We're not supposed to use magic on them to contain them if not in combat. I don't see how they'll come willingly."

"It has to be the entity that killed Du-Vance. They hired him to capture Nuria and Cal. That way they could get me to go after her, potentially assuming he or it could gain my powers and abilities," I spoke up.

"How did the entity know you?" asked Owl.

"Cal might have talked about me. She knew I was half fox. She wouldn't have done it intentionally. They told her they rescued her. She believed them until Minder told her the truth. It's that simple."

"Back to square one," Jenson admitted.

"Agreed," stated Owl.

Molly stood up and pulled Skip-PO off a shelf. "Let's play a few rounds. Take the edge off."

"Sounds like fun," said Jenson, placing his arm around me. I leaned into him.

"Hey, does Maine have a super power?" I asked.

Molly played with the heart necklace Maine had given her biting her lower lip. It looked like she was pouting. Was she hiding something from me? Us?

"I wasn't going to reveal this. I figured you'd freak out."

"What?!" I demanded.

"You love Willow, right?" she asked, letting the necklace fall back into place.

"No way! She's not Willow in disguise!"

Molly began to giggle. "No, she's not Alyson Hannigan. She's studying Wicca. It's hush-hush, so shut up about it, OK?"

"A Native American, a half fox, a soon to be Wiccan. And..."

"I"m just Jenson."

"And I'm just Molly."

"Somehow we all balance each other out. Now let's play Skip-PO," added Owl.

Chapter 26

(Tuesday, March 30th)

(Dan)

I turned my watch over, checking the time, 10:15 a.m. Megan had already left for school, Tri was at the library working, and Starla had dish duty at the diner. If I had a key to Tri's, I'd go drop off my stuff. No one would be home til six. What should I do with myself? I'd let Rascal take the television last night.

Pulling out my cell, I searched for Ranger Mike's, number. Then dialed.

"Hey, um, hi. I was wondering if you could use some help today. I'm in the middle of moving back home. Everyone is out, and my landlord won't be home til Wednesday. I'll give him my key back then."

"He let you off the hook on the lease?" asked Mike.

"Ah, maybe you could help me with that. Do you know anyone looking for a one bedroom apartment? It's near the college."

"No, but I'll help you make flyers. Why don't you stop by, I have the materials to make them here. Later we can visit Cavin and Kaya. I'll be there during the trial. Jones too. We have to keep our guard up. Anything new with you? How's Starla?"

"She's well, a bit spooked. Nayla has her training with Cal. She's doing OK, college wise. It's this black wolf that appeared to her. It happened on Monday. I'm sure the kids have done recon by now. I spoke with Rascal about it."

"Well, get over here. Can you stop by and get doughnuts? I have coffee."

"Yeah. Sure, give me ten minutes. I'll be on my way."

I stood at the ranger's door, juggling the doughnut box in my hands, and knocked. Then took a step back.

"Hey, thanks," said Mike, opening the door. "You didn't have to buy the large box."

"Yeah, well that was all they had left. A glazed and chocolate dozen," I answered.

He nodded, shutting the door behind me. I walked in and set them on the counter next to the monitor station. Mike pulled out a chair for me. I sat down unbuttoning my winter jacket.

"I can hang that up for you. If you want," Mike offered.

"No, it's fine. I'll let it hang on the back of the chair," I replied.

"Other then Minder's injury, it's been pretty quiet around here. We could go over the interrogation," he said, sitting down near the monitors. "I think Lance will be helping you."

"What about the Trinity, and Crusaders. We should hold a meeting with them before the trial. Has anyone spoken with Jones?"

"He's been monitoring the area on his morning runs. He hasn't mentioned seeing anything."

"We need to bring them in on this, even though there was never any suspicion they were involved, it's not good to just dismiss them, they're still suspects. We just don't treat them as such," I confirmed.

"They were questioned after Du-Vance's death," Mike replied.

"Who questioned them?" I asked, picking up a glazed donut. I glanced around to see where the coffee pot was.

"Cavin spoke with them. They don't leave the park often. Usually, if they're going to hunt, Kaya or Cavin are the members who give them permission. We don't have any proof of them being in our territory on the day of the occurrence."

Mike got up from his chair, grabbing two cups to the left of him on the counter. He moved a few items revealing the coffee pot. Then poured the coffee. He set the mugs down in front of us at the monitors. I reached for mine and let it warm up my hands. Then brought it to my mouth, taking a few sips, then set it down. Mike took his seat beside the monitors.

"Meeting with the Crusaders before the trial would be a good idea. I've seen a few of them lingering on the outskirts. They nod their head to me or bark in a friendly manner. I have yet to see any them in human form. They don't care to mix with us," Mike admitted.

"How many of them are there? It could be a problem fitting them into the dining hut."

"It may. The best bet would be to have the main leaders there. I suspect not all of them are wolves. If we need to call any of them in we can," suggested Mike.

We finished up our doughnuts and coffee. I stood up from my chair and grabbed the mugs. "Where do you want these?"

"Leave them, I'll put them in the sink in the other room."

"Okay," I said setting them back down.

"Do you want to visit Cavin? I'd say let's look in on the prisoners, but we have no questions lined up."

"Yeah, that and it was suggested we leave it alone until the trial," I answered.

"Anything unusual going on?" asked Mike. He stood, grabbing his coat off the hanging rack.

"Why?" I asked.

Mike put on his coat and finished buttoning it. "Well, you brought up Jones. He may not have seen anything. However, we had a group from the college out here Snowshoeing. A recreational week long class, adult education."

"What happened? Was someone attacked?"

"Nothing like that. A student claimed to have seen a black wolf roaming in the woods. Could it be the same one Starla saw?"

"It's possible. She encountered it during training. I suggested she and her friends do some research on it. Tri and I also planned to."

"You'd better get your coat on. We'll go to the dining hall and see if anyone is there. I'm not sure what everybody is up to today. Better that than having to drive out to Nuria's. It's quite a ways," said Mike.

I fumbled for my coat behind me, put it on, buttoned it up, and threw the hood over my head, tying it so it wouldn't fall off.

"You ready?"

"Yes," I answered. All thoughts, on the flyers for the apartment, had been forgotten. I had too much on my mind regarding my daughter.

Mike shut the door behind us and turned, locking it.

"We haven't had any problems with unknown predators. It may be a spirit. The Crusaders and Trinity group confirm when they have visitors. So I don't suppose it's a cousin or a relative. I'd know."

"Okay," I agreed.

We hiked towards the path leading into the pines. The snow was packed on the ground, which made it easier to travel.

"Have you spoken with Owl about the wolf Starla saw?" Mike asked, picking up his pace.

"No, but by now, I'm sure he knows."

Mike opened the door to the dining hall, switching on the lights. We sauntered in and looked around. It seemed deserted. A faint light shone under the door leading to the kitchen. It sounded as if someone was in the middle of washing dishes.

"Maybe Kaya's in there working on preparing meals for a few of the elders. I'm not sure why you haven't met them, you having been here since Tri left us. I never felt the need to concern you with it. We have three in our clan, and a few others from the Crusaders. Kaya and Star take them, meals, now and again."

"Do they live like the other foxes and wolves? Ah, sorry stupid question," I answered.

"No. No, it isn't. Mango lives in a hut. So do the others. Nuria and Eva helped to build them. Weird, right?"

"That name sounds familiar, maybe I met her once," I replied, opening the door to the kitchen. Kaya was scrubbing dishes while Cavin rinsed and dried them.

"Hi, I thought about contacting you today," she said. Then handed Cavin another dish to dry. "Star isn't going to be able to set up the trial room. She had to assist an elder. Mango can't seem to keep her hut up, by herself anymore. She's a sweet old fox."

"Yes," Cavin commented. Then placed a dish in a cupboard. "One who always thinks of others. You may find it odd, but around the solstice, Kaya would go out and buy her yarn. She'd crochet blankets for the newborns," he said.

"The reason he brings this up is, she mentioned one was given to Tri when Starla was born. Mango has an amazing memory! Ah, well, I could go on and on. Mango helped train Nayla."

"Ah, I think I recall her now! She came by once to congratulate us," I answered.

"So, do you want some help setting up today?" interrupted Mike.

"That would be great!" said Cavin. He finished drying a few dishes and put them into an opened cupboard. "Do you mind if we go, start set up," he said turning to Kaya.

"No, I've got this, you guys go get things ready. I'll check on Mango and Star after," she offered.

Cavin set aside the dish towel leaning over to Kaya. He kissed her cheek sweetly. "See ya later, Hun."

"Yes, I'll see you tonight," she answered.

We stepped out of the kitchen back into the dining hall.

"Now, I want to move all these tables over to the left first. Then we'll take two of them and set them up front. One will be for the judge," said Cavin.

"So you'll sit there?"

"Yes, this is only the second trial I've coordinated."

I nodded and didn't ask about the details. "So, why don't you set up the judge's table. I'll put a table next to it for the defendant. We're only bringing up one of the bandits at a time. It would be a disaster otherwise."

"I don't trust any of them," Mike scoffed.

"Let's get started, once everything is finished, we might as well discuss what's to come. Are you in?" asked Cavin.

"Yes, with only two days left, we can't wait around," I admitted.

"No, we don't want to go into this blind. I'll call the others in for a meeting tomorrow. Nayla needs to get a hold of Starla before she makes plans. Although I'm sure training will continue after this is over."

"How much longer will Nayla be here? You said she only visits once a year. It's been almost two months since she arrived," Mike commented.

Cavin motioned them to start moving the tables. "She may stay on until Starla Ariana's training is finished. Now, let's get this done. Afterward, I'll pull out my log book. We need to start making notes, come up with questions. It shouldn't be too difficult."

Chapter 27

(Starla)

I placed my apron on the notch in the break room. Then headed over to the sink in the corner to wash my hands. What a shift! I'd had to work on the line, making burgers, which was rare. One of the cooks called in. So I covered while Gina and Marla waited tables. After washing up, I grabbed my coat off one of the hooks on the wall. I'd been thinking about taking a ride over to Cal's. I probably should give that moped back. I hadn't used it as often, as I thought I would.

"Hey, chica. Thanks for flipping burgers for us," said Marla, entering the break room.

"Sure, now I have to get home and shower," I said, putting on my gloves and hat. "I was contemplating visiting a friend. Jenson and I, have had so little time together. Maybe he'll want to come over to study."

"Is that what you'll be doing?" she chided while bumping me with her hip.

I had had thoughts about a full make out session. It's not like I'm a total saint.

"I suppose we might snuggle a bit. If I'm real crazy, watch some television," I admitted.

"You got a ride home?" she asked.

"I've got the moped."

"Alright then," she answered, patting me on the shoulder.

"I'll see you later."

"Later," I replied.

Outside the diner, I put on my helmet, climbed on the moped and started it up. Home, or Cal's? I pushed up my coat sleeve to look at my watch. It was six. I felt like I'd been neglecting Jenson a bit. At the same time, though I'd have to give this bike back. Why put it off? I adjusted my messenger purse and pulled my cell out of my pocket. If I didn't call mom, she'd flip out.

It rang a few times until someone answered.

"Hey, Mom?"

"Starla, did you just get out of the diner?"

"Yeah, do you care if I head over to see Cal? I thought I'd return the moped to her. Molly had mentioned it yesterday in class. Would that be cool?"

Mom gave a loud sigh. "I don't want you walking home in the dark."

"What if I ran home in fox form," I whispered into the phone.

"Call me if you need a ride. Fern and that, old man scope out the house every morning since they saw me one day. It's why I've been avoiding the whole change a Roo. I'm sure if Eva is around, she could drive you back."

"OK."

"Be home by nine, and call Jenson. He called asking for you."

"Will do, after I get home. Then I'll take my shower. I had to work the line today. Gotta, go, mom, love you!"

"Love you too, and be safe," she replied.

I hit the end button, shoving the phone into my purse not wanting to chance it slipping out of my pocket. Afterward, I started up the bike. OK, traffic isn't too bad. I waited til it slowed, and pulled out into it. The wind whipped at my hair. It felt amazing to be riding again. I'd taken a few trips with it since Thunder Head Bay. I'd even taken Molly out once, just to get Slurpee's from the convenient store. It had been a while since I'd gone to the Sunshine Cafe. Tomorrow's Wednesday. Hmmm, lunch with the crew? Didn't Molly have a date with Maine? If I scheduled it right, maybe I could ask her to join us. I'd like to get to know her more plus her learning Wicca might come in handy one of these days. I would love for her to teach me! I should be careful, though. I didn't want it to seem like I only liked her due to her belief.

I pulled up to a red light waiting for it to change. Half-way there I told myself. After it turned green, I revved my bike moving onward. The cold wind blew my hair behind me.

I stopped the bike in front of the cabin near the porch railing. There I secured the moped to it. Then skipped up the front steps. Cal popped open the door.

"I see you brought the bike back."

"Yes. It was the right thing to do. Besides, you probably can use it."

"Thanks. Minder and Nuria are overprotective," she stated, rolling her eyes. "Yesterday, I convinced them to let me, explore the woods a bit. When I didn't come back right, away they came out looking for me. I get it! They don't want to lose me again. The problem is I need my space."

"Sure, doesn't everybody?"

Cal laughed, "Yeah, we do."

"Can I come in for a minute?"

"Sure, sorry." She opened the door wider.

I slipped inside taking off my coat.

"Here, let me get that for you," Cal offered.

I handed it to her, and she placed it on a nearby coat rack.

"Thanks, should we just hang out here?" I asked, gesturing to the couch.

"Sure, take off your shoes, if you're going to put your feet up. Minder hates it when I put my shoes on the furniture."

"So, Where is everybody?" I asked sitting down.

"Minder was contacted to help with the kits. Nuria has plans to eat dinner with Rascal. I heard your dad was there today. I'm not sure if he still is, though."

I leaned down, took my shoes off, and placed my feet up on the couch. "Ah! He better, fill me in if anything went down."

"I'm sure if it did, we'll hear about it. Have you seen our black wolf lately?" Cal inquired raising an eyebrow.

"No, nothing. Molly, Jenson and I did some research. We suspect the wolf may be trying to warn us about something. What, we're not sure. Owl suggested it could be related to Du-Vance. I found it inconclusive."

"So we don't have anything to go on, great," she sighed. Then leaned further back into the sofa.

"When researching we discovered this wolf's visit could mean, I'm on the right path with training. The wolf may represent my strength, courage, and loyalty to the clan. The bad news, it could also symbolize a lack of trust in someone I'm close to or an individual I shouldn't trust," I admitted.

"That's mind boggling! I don't know of anyone you can't trust currently."

I scoffed, "Yeah, not sure who that could be right now."

"Are you edgy? " Cal asked.

"Nah, I'm good."

"My life is mind-numbing. I've been in study mode."

"How's that going, what grade are you in now?" I asked mischievously.

Cal laughed, "Fourth or fifth, I believe. I finished a math lesson, read *Little Women* and started a book report on it. I don't even want to talk about the science project I need to tackle." Cal pushed her books off to the side of the table. "You want some coffee? Nuria or Minder will be here soon."

I nodded, standing up from the couch. Then stretched out a bit.

"I'll get it started. Come sit with me when you're ready."

"Oh, I'll sit down. Um, have you mastered full fox form yet?" I asked, meandering to the table.

"Yes! That is one thing that happened. But I have to confess something to you."

I raised my eyebrows at her before pulling out the chair. Then sat down with my elbows on the table.

"OK, spill!"

Cal grabbed cups out of a cupboard nearby. Then started to make the coffee, leaving me to anticipate her revelation.

"Are you going to transform for me? Why are you, being so quiet?"

"The reason I was having a hard time changing is-- Mom's half wolf. I have some of her genetic material. It tries to flip-flop me from a fox into a wolf. At first, I wasn't able at all. When I was younger, my body was still evolving. I could only transform into a fox. Now..."

"Yes," I asked with eagerness.

"My genetics choose for me which one I'll become. I can't fix on, the fox form. When I switch over from my human body to an animal body, my genes choose which one. There are times I'm both. I don't get to choose what parts though. It's wack!"

"Wow, how do you deal? Will it affect our training? Have you and Nayla talked about this? When did you find out?" I babbled.

Cal poured our coffee into mugs handing me mine. She sat down next to me.

"Nayla isn't worried. It shouldn't affect my ability to protect myself. Each has its own, desirable traits."

"Your mom is half fox, half wolf, though. She's not one or the other when her body form chooses," I speculated.

"You're right. The clan isn't sure how it happened." She rolled her eyes while sipping her coffee.

A sputtering sound came from the front of the cabin. We heard a loud bang, and then a thud. I jumped up from my chair.

"Everything's fine. It's just Minder," Cal reassured me. "She's out there working on her motorcycle. That's the first thing she does when she gets home. Mike found one used. Cavin had Kaya pick it up for her."

"We all need transportation. Mom talked about getting me a car. I guess it's time."

The door to the cabin opened. In popped Minder a bit dirty from tinkering with her bike.

"Hey, Cal, Nuria will be back soon. I see you have coffee. What about dinner? Have you eaten yet?" She glanced in my direction, then back at Cal.

"No, Starla's here. I wanted to catch her up on what's going on."

"I see, do you have a way home tonight?" she asked me.

"I can call my mom. She'll pick me up if you want," I offered.

Minder put the wrench on the living room table, then brushed her hands off on her jeans. I watched her pull off the bandanna wiping the sweat from her face. She grinned.

"Cal, you and Starla can make some sandwiches. After we eat, I'll take her back on my bike. She can wear the helmet you lent her. I'll bring it back for you."

"Sure, that's fine. Will mom? Eva, joining us tonight?"

"She has a meeting to attend with Cavin. She'll be by tomorrow," replied Minder stomping off to the bathroom.

"Is she mad?" I asked.

"No. She always, stomps. It's because of her wolf feet," said Cal.

Chapter 28

(Dan)

A cold chill crept up my back. I shuddered. Cavin, Mike and I sat waiting for the others to arrive. Kaya had begun preparing a meal for us. It had taken longer to set up than we'd predicted.

"I'm not sure where to start. There's a lot we need to get out of this trial. Not only do we want to find out if they killed Du-Vance, but also what do they know about the scientists? Starla would be adamant about that," I suggested.

"I'm sure she would. First, we are going to begin questioning them about Du-Vance's death. Where were they February 19th? Do they have any witnesses to their whereabouts? Cal and Nuria will play a significant part in this since, as far as we know, they were still with them at the time. We'll need to figure out when, exactly, Minder took Cal away from the group," said Cavin.

I heard a door shut and turned to see Shellena and Lance. They meandered up to the table.

"Have a seat. We're discussing the trial, what's going to happen during questioning. Kaya's making us some food. I'd help, but..."

"You're the head guru on this," commented Shellena. She and Lance took their seats.

"Star and Eva should be here soon. I'd call Minder and Nuria, but Cal's been busy with studies. I believe we should wait til Wednesday. Nayla will have to set up a time for training them and discussing the trial," admitted Cavin.

"Where's Starla Araina, tonight?" asked Shellena.

147

"She worked. Then most likely went to Jenson's I assume. If not maybe she and Molly went out, for a bite to eat," I said.

Lance lifted an eyebrow. Shellena elbowed him.

"Ouch! What did you do that for?" he asked.

"You, acting as if you know what goes on in that girl's mind, bro," she replied.

He rolled his eyes at her. "Has anyone talked to old Sika lately. How's he getting along?" inquired Lance.

"I've been taking them their meals. There has been no communication. They just growl, Gavin tries to escape, but cannot. As I said, they can no longer harm themselves due to the spells we placed on their confined quarters," Cavin answered.

The door to the dining hall swung open. Star made her way to the table with a basket in her hands. She placed it on the slab. "Mango and I made some homemade rolls. She insisted on it. Is Rascal, coming?"

Cavin shook his head. "No, he had plans with Nuria later tonight. Right now he's in a meeting with his tribe. Owl and Jenson are there with him. Dan, you'll fill them in on this?"

"I will, besides what are we going to have Jenson do? I don't have any recon for him right now on the scientist issue unless we get the bandits to crack," I acknowledged.

Kaya stepped up to the table setting down a basin of soup. "True enough." She glanced at the rolls. "Those will be perfect. You and Mango made them?" she asked Star.

"Yes, she was pleased to do so."

Kaya smiled, then turned making her way back into the kitchen. Star pushed her chair aside and got up to help her.

After they had left Cavin cleared his throat. He was about to speak as Eva moseyed up to the table taking a seat. She'd arrived in human form. Her reddish brown hair done up in braids pinned to the back of her head.

"Thank you for joining us this evening," he said to her. Then turned to face the rest of us. "Nayla is going to be at the trial. I don't want to stop anyone from attending if they wish to be there. The kits will need someone to look after them. Thank goodness we only have three of them.It will be mandatory for those of you who were involved in the Thunder Head Bay mission to attend."

"That is a given," Lance spoke up.

"Right. What is you would like me to do during the trial. Should I go about my Ranger duties as usual? Who's going to take over the park?" Mike asked.

"We, don't know. Let's get through the trial first," suggested Star. She and Kaya set down empty bowls in front of us. Star took an open seat, and Kaya pulled out a chair by Cavin.

"Let's give thanks, and then eat," said Kaya.

We bowed our heads in silence and then lifted them. Cavin took his soup first. Then the rest of us served ourselves. The rolls were warm, buttery and sweet. I passed the basket along to Shellena next to me. We ate for a time in peace.

I looked up from my meal thinking I should tell them. I rolled back my shoulders, then stretched out my body. I needed to ease my tension. Why was I nervous? They would be happy Tri was willing to help out. I was pleased to announce this, wasn't I? It was good news.

"Dan, is there something you want to say?" asked Mike giving me a strange look.

"I'm moving home." My lower lip trembled. "It was unexpected. I didn't plan on it being this soon. It will be good to be home," I stuttered.

Cavins eyes widened in surprise. "It's a start. Eva, you told me she's planning to attend Starla's next training session."

A smile played upon Eva's lips. "Yes, that's right."

"Dan, make sure Tri knows it's this Wednesday. If we have to, we can work around her schedule. Do you know what time she gets off work?"

"It varies, I can give her a quick call if you want," I added.

"No, it's fine. Um, let me know. Things are tight. Nayla needs to contact Starla Araina."

"Eva, you'll make sure Cal is in attendance. It's imperative we have everyone here tomorrow. Especially Tri," said Cavin, eyeing me.

I gave him a silent nod.

"Shellena and I could pay Starla a visit later this evening. Is that OK? It's been a while since we've seen the kid."

I chuckled, "If you want to attempt it. Make sure you're in proper form. Tri said the neighbors have been suspicious. The Crusaders would be incredibly upset if news got out of the clan." "No problem," said Lance.

I finished the rest of my soup. Afterward, wiping my face with a napkin. I picked up the last roll letting each morsel melt in my mouth. Oh, I hope no one minds, I thought.

"I'll have to tell Mango her rolls were a hit!" said Star. She clapped her hands together, got up from her seat, and started taking care of the dishes.

"Let me do that," offered Cavin. "I want everyone else here to stay seated. Make a list of questions you'd like answered at the trial. I'll go over them tonight. Dan, and Mike, would you mind helping me with dish duty?"

"Sure, why not," I answered standing up. We grabbed some of the bowls off the table. Cavin took the large basin with the ladle.

"I'll call Rascal tonight, update him on all this as you asked. Then Jenson, and Owl. That is, unless I can meet with them all at once," I commented.

"I'm grateful, you and Mike showed up today. There is an awful lot to arrange for this. Nayla has been focusing all her energy on Cal and Starla. I suppose, she's also trying to figure out why Starla encountered that black wolf."

"She told you?" I asked.

"Yes. It has to be, related to a Native American tribe. A legend, another Myth, or a spirit animal. Thus, when the trial is going on if it isn't linked it could bring more chaos," Cavin admitted.

Mike and I got up from our seats to help Cavin gather the plates.

"Let's hope we're wrong," I said, grabbing the last dish.

Cavin held the kitchen door open. We stepped inside to begin dish-duty.

Chapter 29

(Starla)

I held on tight to Minder as we headed back to the apartment. Music blared out of the small speakers. Hip hop? Was it Missy Elliot? No, couldn't be. I ignored the music and concentrated. I wasn't supposed to meditate, but I wasn't going anywhere. I might as well space out til I got home. There was no way I could talk to Minder over the noise her cycle was making. I closed my eyes clearing my mind and thought of nothing. It almost lulled me to sleep when we came to a screeching halt. My eyes popped open. Whoa, I tightened my grip on the bike so I wouldn't fall. Lance and Shellena pulled up beside us on their motorcycles.

"Is there someplace we can talk?" asked Shellena.

Minder scanned the intersection for restaurants and coffee joints. I gave a little wave and said nothing.

"Um, yeah, there's a diner across the street. Sunshine Cafe, I think? We'll meet ya there. I have to get Starla home. Make it quick," she added. They nodded and off we went speeding towards the diner. Again, I held on to Minder so, I wouldn't fall off the bike. A nagging feeling came over me. An ache in the pit of my stomach. We'd just eaten recently. I couldn't be hungry. I glanced behind us, nothing. Then looked to my side, just a bunch of old buildings. I turned to my right. A black wolf ran beside us. I felt the color drain from my face. It smiled at me. His tongue hung out of his mouth as if he had been laughing. He stopped and held up a paw. Okay, what was he trying to tell me? Before I could say anything to Minder, a car passed through him. He faded into mist.

"Starla, we're here. Take off your helmet," said Minder. I hadn't even noticed we'd stopped. I paused for a second.

"Sorry, I thought... I saw something." I took off my helmet handing it to Minder.

"We already ate. Do you want to go in?" She addressed them.

"I bet Starla would love coffee," Shellena suggested.

"I suppose just a cup. Do you mind?" I asked.

Minder gave a sigh. "I guess one cup won't hurt. Don't you have class or something tomorrow?"

I shrugged.

"Kiddo, you, have a meeting with Nayla. The trial is in the works!" shouted Shellena gesturing with her arms. She kicked down the stand of her bike. Then proceeded to the diner door. "Come on, I'll buy everyone coffee," she added. Lance winked at us.

Minder and I followed them inside. I hoped no one would freak out over their appearance. The jeans and T-shirt didn't hide their wolf selves. If it were me, I'd be freezing. I didn't have fur, though. Then again, they had the ability to manipulate people. Which meant they could just charm them? Make them believe they were human? I speculated as we shuffled into a nearby booth. I played with the napkin beside me. I was supposed to call Jenson. Had I been neglecting him?

"Starla, is something bothering you?" asked Shellena.

"Um, can they see you as wolf-vamps," I whispered, pointing to the staff and customers.

"No, we reflect ourselves as humans. Do you want to see?" Shellena asked.

"Um, No. Is that why Megan wasn't afraid of Minder the other day?"

"Guilty, but not all of us have this ability. Sika, Gavin, and Gladiator. They can't mix," Minder informed me.

"Something else seems to be bothering you, though? Not just us, what is it?" asked Shellena.

"Oh, thinking about Jenson. That's all. And..."

"And," said Lance.

"The last time I was with Nayla I saw a black wolf. Then again earlier," I admitted.

"When?" asked Minder.

"At the last training session. I don't want to rehash the story. Anyway, it followed us tonight after you'd suggested we meet. It held up its paw. Maybe it was trying to signal me for some reason. I've done some recon on it," I said.

"Recon?" asked Minder.

"Yeah, research the internet. Obviously," I answered.

"No need to get huffy about it," Lance remarked.

A tall brown haired young woman walked up to our table, holding a pen with a notepad in her hand.

"I'm Susan. I'll be your waitress. Can I get you guys anything tonight? I can tell you our specials."

"No, just a round of coffee for everyone, cream, and sugar. Put it on one bill. I've got it," said Shellena.

I checked my watch. Still pretty early. Mom wouldn't start to worry til nine. The waitress came back to our table. She sat down a handful of creamer, along with an assortment of sweeteners. Then placed four mugs in front of us filling them with coffee.

"That was fast," I noted.

"Ain't nothing to pouring coffee kid," she commented, walking away.

I grabbed a handful of creamers, opened them, and stirred them into my coffee. Shellena nudged me insistently with her arm. Then pushed the sugar over to me.

"So is that the only reason you dragged me in here, caffeine and Nayla?" I asked.

"This trial is going to be wicked. I'm sure you can handle it, though. I know Nayla will question you about what occurred, at Thunderhead Bay. Of course, Cal will be asked to describe her time there. She's given us fragments. We only know what you've both shared with us so far," Lance answered.

My eyes lit up with rage."Are you trying to intimidate me, scare me? I'm going to do my best to handle myself and not bash in those evil creatures. They took my best friend. Now she's trying to play catch up with everything and everyone. She's doing better, but it isn't how it should have been. Not for myself either. If they didn't exist, I would have never been..." I ran my hands through my greasy hair.

"We want you, to be prepared. It's why you and Cal will continue training with Nayla. Afterward, we'll all meet up with Cavin. Your dad and Mike met with him today. We set up the dining hall for the trial. It's Friday," Shellena stated.

"Yeah, Nayla told me. She wasn't specific about when she wanted to meet. Should Molly come? Will Owl be there? Jenson?"

"Everyone involved in Cal's rescue will be there, this affects us all," she scolded.

I put my hands around my coffee cup and took sips. Minder slouched against the back of the booth.

"What about the wolf? Do you know what it means?" asked Lance.

"Not yet, I'm hoping it will give us answers. So far we've figured out it has something to do with strength, loyalty, and trust. It could be clan related. I may lack trust with someone or myself in my life. No one comes to mind at the moment. Can we change the subject?" I asked, turning my head to see Rascal pushing open the diner door. He glanced our way. I waved him over.

"Hey, fancy meeting ya all here. What are you doing?"

Lance moved over making room for him in the booth. He sat down, took off his hat, and placed it on the table.

"Lance and Shellena, pulled us over," I joked.

"What was your offense?"

"Failure to meet with the clan," Lance smirked.

Rascal chuckled. "Owl and Jenson helped me set up some displays today for the next pow-wow. Are you interested in going?" he asked me.

"Depends on when it is. The trials Friday. That's the real reason they stopped us," I said, pointing to Lance and Shellena. "Minder was taking me home on her bike. Cavin wants us all there. Are you going?"

"Am I going? Of course, no doubt about it. I'm hoping to grill the dang blasted things!"

"You don't have to worry, Lance here has it all under control. Cavin told him, he can't smash the dining hall, though," blurted Shellena.

Susan trotted back over to where we sat.

"More coffee? Do you want some sir?" she asked Rascal.

"Yes, coffee's good. I assume we'll all take another round?" He nodded to the lot of us.

"Yes. Caffeine good," I joked, then grinned.

Lance, fist bumped me continuing down the line with the others.

"So tomorrow we need to be there, what time?" asked Minder.

Lance hit his head with his opened palm. "Geez, Cavin never mentioned when. Now I feel like one of Sika's dumb sidekicks."

"You're not, but we should get going," said Shellena. "I don't want to upset Tri. Things are finally coming together for you, Starla. Dan will be back home soon, and Tri's coming to your training session. Lance, let's get out of here. I'll see you guys later."

I stood up from my seat, putting my coat on. "Call me, let me know what time I should arrive. Dad will probably drive me. I returned the moped to Cal. There isn't time to shop for a vehicle now, evidently."

"See ya. I'll call," answered Lance.

Minder and I headed out into the dark. I climbed back on the bike behind her. Then I put the helmet I'd borrowed on. She nodded her head to me, and I gave her the okay. Leaning in I held on tight as we sped away. Then attempted to clear my mind breathing in the night air.

Minutes later, Minder stopped the bike in front of the apartment.

"Here you are," she said.

"Thanks," I answered, getting off the motorcycle. "Do you want to come in?" I handed her the helmet back I'd borrowed. Then straightened out my mess of tangled hair.

"Nah, but make sure you talk to your mom before you head upstairs for your shower."

"How did you know?" I asked, fumbling for my keys in my pocket.

"When I was human. I worked at a diner. The grease was something awful. I'll see ya tomorrow. Okay? Now, contact your friends, shower and get some rest."

"Yes, Mom." I joked, turning my key in the lock. At that moment the door swung open. I almost fell on my sister but caught myself before we collided. I heard Minder chuckle as she started her bike. It roared to life. I glanced back at her taking off.

"Sis, Jenson called twice. Mom told him you were with Cal. That something probably came up."

"Okay, would ya let me in already?" I asked, trying to push past her. She opened the door wider for me, and I slid in.

"Here, I'll hang up your jacket for you."

I handed it to her, turning my body towards the staircase.

"You smell," she complained crinkling her nose.

"No, duh. I worked the line today. I'm going to take a shower. Tell mom we have a meeting with the clan tomorrow, ah and training. Lance is going to call."

"Whatever, I'll tell her," she hollered heading to the kitchen.

Sisters, I thought as I climbed the stairs. After my shower, I'd call Jenson and tell him all about my day. Then maybe I'd catch up with Molly later. What about her date with Maine? Gah, hopefully, this meeting wouldn't ruin it.

I guess her not getting involved made sense. She wasn't at Thunder Head Bay and knew zilch about my clan. Once, I was at the top of the stairs I stopped. Then turned to my room. I leaned my head against the door. It creaked open. Reaching in I switched on the light. My bed looked extremely inviting.

Chapter 30

(Dan)

I pushed open the door to my apartment. Maybe I still had a cold soda in the fridge, I thought, locking the door behind me. I leaned against it scanning the bare room, then shuffled out of my shoes. Boy, did that ever feel good! I placed them against the wall laying my coat beside them. I wondered what Tri was doing? I got my phone out of my pocket, checking the time. Eight O'clock. She should still be awake if I wanted to talk. I turned towards the kitchen and froze. A faint glow appeared in the doorway. I couldn't quite make out the shape, but it looked like a dark creature of some sort.

"Wh... what are you doing here?" I stammered.

A chill crawled up my back. Whatever it was, crept out of the shadows into view. I stumbled back a few feet! A large black wolf stood between the table and refrigerator. It let out a low growl from deep in its throat. *Was this Starla's wolf?*

"I asked you, what you're doing here," I demanded.

It looked up at me sitting on its hindquarters. "Keep the clan safe. The scientists are not far. Du-Vance was interested in something far more relevant than a peace treaty. In time you'll uncover the reason for his elimination. I'll be keeping an eye on Starla. Do not, I warn you. Do not try to find them. Not now," he said.

"What about the trial?"

The black wolf shook his head in frustration. "Go ahead with it. Do not attempt to establish contact with the scientists.

"Never, then how will we bring justice to our people?"

159

He smirked, then licked his lips. "They will pay for what they have done. Jones will see to that." The wolf turned his long, lanky body around. Then trotted away from me heading to the wall. Where was he going? Little by little he faded out of view.

What the heck? Where did the damn wolf go! I flicked on the light in the kitchen. What the hell was he talking about, not to go after the scientists? What was it Du-Vance had planned? None of us were aware of any secret mission. He had wanted to be a Ranger. He was going to take over Mike's position. What could he have possibly wanted to do that would have put our clan in danger? None of this made any sense. Should I call Tri? Nah, she'd only flip out. I'd wait.

I looked down at once. My cell phone was still in my hand. I dialed Rascal's number. It continuously rang. Ah, no machine I'd forgotten about that. He didn't have a mobile phone either. I terminated the call deciding to try Jenson. He picked up after the third ring.

"I'm not sure where to start," I stuttered.

"Okay, Dan. Ah, can I call you Dan?" asked Jenson.

"It's better than Starla's dad, sure. Something has happened. We're going to have to lay low. We cannot attempt to locate the scientists. Where are you at?"

"Home, working on homework. I was positive Starla would call me tonight. I haven't heard from her or Owl," he explained.

"I need to meet with everyone. Starla is training with Cal and Nayla tomorrow. We could get together before the session in the dining hall."

"What happened?"

I pulled out the chair from the dining room table sitting down. Then got situated, I rubbed my forehead with one hand. "I can't talk about it over the phone. Tomorrow?" I asked.

"The gang was going to meet Molly for lunch," Jenson answered.

"Then plan on driving to Hunters Park afterward. I'll be home in the morning. It should give me time to talk with Starla first."

"OK, sir, - Dan. Are you going to be alright?"

"Yeah, I've just been shaken up. Can you do me a favor?"

"What kind?"

"Keep an eye out for Starla. Don't go snooping online looking for answers about how the scientists created the bandits," I suggested.

"I hadn't thought of that. Now, Dan, don't go giving me any idea's. I might not be able to handle myself."

"Jenson, I'm serious. There's something about Du-Vance we don't know. Hopefully, we'll uncover it during the trial."

"I'll do my best to restrain myself. Afterward, I cannot make any promises. If we can't pin Du-Vance's death on the bandits, or the entity who else would have killed him?"

"I don't know," I admitted.

"Alright, then tomorrow. What time should I be there?"

"No later than three-thirty. Will you drive everyone?"

"Of course! We're all meeting for Brunch. Talk to you later," he answered.

I hung up the phone. I didn't feel like calling Rascal again. If I contacted Tri and told her what happened, she would lose sleep. The wolf had not given me any reason to believe he was dangerous. Most likely he was Du-Vance's spirit animal. I couldn't prove it. However, there was no other explanation, unless he was, or is an actual wolf who saw the murder take place.

Chapter 31

(Starla)

I stepped out of the shower feeling refreshed. Then grabbed a towel and dried off. Warm fuzzy jammies! Yes, now I could finally relax. I put them on, enjoying the soft feel of the fabric against my skin. Before I could hit the dream land button, I had to make a phone call. Turning off the bathroom light, I slipped into my bedroom, grabbing my phone off the dresser. Hmm, it would be great to hear Jenson's voice after today. I sat on my bed trying to get comfortable, then flipped my phone open to call him. It was late! Ten thirty to be exact. I hoped he was awake. I shrugged dialing anyway.

"Hey, Starla. I was hoping you'd call. Did you miss me?"

I yawned, "Sorry, it's been a long day. I had to work on the line at Denny's. After that, I returned the moped to Cal," I answered.

"How's she doing?"

"Good, she's in fourth, fifth grade now? Online that is. Nuria and Minder have been on her about her studies. I'm not sure about Eva. Math is driving her nuts, but not for the same reason it makes me."

Jenson laughed.

"I heard you had a meeting with Rascals tribe. I'd like to come to the pow-wow once you guys have it together."

"Yeah, that's not til late April. It should be well after the court hearing."

"My meeting for training is tomorrow. I'm not sure what time. We'll have an early lunch with Molly. Maine may or may not be there. Molly said something about a date with her the other day."

"I know, your dad called me. He said I shouldn't try to locate the scientist. I haven't, but found it rather odd. He wants to meet at Hunter's Park tomorrow. He wanted me to take you, do you want to go?"

I smiled and blushed. My heart started to beat fast.

"You, OK, Starla?"

"Yeah, I'm here. It would be sweet. We haven't had tons of time together since the dance," I admitted.

"I know. We did hang out at Molly's but does recon count?"

"Nah," we both said in unison.

I bit my lip and thought about the black wolf that had followed me. It didn't seem as vicious as I had thought it was when I'd encountered it in my meditation.

"Your thinking again?"

"Lance and Shellena hunted Minder down tonight. She was taking me home. Once, they had pulled us over we decided to meet for coffee. I saw it again! The black wolf. It ran behind the motorcycle. It wasn't ferocious. In fact, it seemed to smile at me. Then it stopped in the middle of traffic, put up its paw, and faded in and out. What's up with that? Cars just whipped right through it, as if it didn't exist at all," I explained. Then yawned pushing the covers down with my feet sliding underneath the sheets. I positioned a few pillows behind my head. "It's definitely, a warning, not a threat. Maybe it's protecting me, us? If so, why?"

"Good question. Recon sure didn't do any good. If Nayla allowed you to attempt to contact it, then perhaps we could get some answers. However, she seems pretty uptight about stuff like that. Unless I'm wrong," he replied.

"She can be. I'm not, freaked out anymore. Not in a, oh, it's going to get me, way. I would like to know why and what it's trying to do, or tell me." I admitted.

"Me too, No one likes to be left in the dark."

"Jenson, that's so cliche'. I need to get some shut eye."

I heard him yawn into the phone. Followed by, drawers opening and closing.

"Are you searching for something?" I asked.

"Information Rascal gave me on tribe pow-wows. Also, my black fleece sleep pants. It's cold."

"I'm wearing blue jersey pajamas. They're soft and comfortable," I teased him.

"I'd love to see that, I bet they're perfect. If I was there, I'd wrap you in my arms and snuggle you."

"Hmm, I wish, and cover me with kisses," I added.

"If only," he answered.

I snuggled deeper under the covers as I held the phone to my ear. My eyelids heavy with the need for sleep.

"Hmmm, so tomorrow at 11 a.m. We'll kidnap Molly. Then see if she wants to double date with us for an early brunch. Later we'll let the girls have their own alone time," I suggested.

"It's a plan, sweet dreams," Jenson said.

"You, too. Hugs."

"Hugs and kisses, night," he replied.

I hung up, placing the phone on my nightstand. Afterward, I pulled my pillow close to me thinking about Jenson.

Chapter 32

(Wednesday, March 31st.)

(Dan)

How had I made it into bed last night? The last thing I remembered was contemplating calling Tri. I leaned down scratching at an itch on my leg. How late was it? I threw off the covers, swinging my legs over the edge of the bed. I had to take all of my things home to unpack, then there was the clan, and talking to Tri. I wasn't looking forward to either of them. I'd shower later. My phone buzzed on the floor, leaning down I picked it up.

"Hello?"

"Hi there, I didn't hear from you last night and was worried. What happened?" asked Tri.

I took a deep breath and exhaled. "I had to pack. Rascal was here Monday helping me. I considered dropping my stuff off Tuesday morning. Then decided to wait til the evening. By then I had gotten involved in setting up the courtroom for the trial. I found myself back at the apartment last night. I'm sorry I didn't call. I should have," I stuttered.

"It's Okay, Are you coming by today?" she asked.

"Give me half an hour. I should be home by at least ten thirty. We're meeting at three-thirty in the reflection room with Nayla. You'll want to be there. Starla and Cal's training starts at four. I can't discuss what's happening til we meet."

"I don't like the sound of that," she answered.

"Yeah, well, I don't know what else to tell you. My hands are tied, at this point. Nayla is happy you're willing to be there, for support if nothing else."

"I will be for you, and Starla. I'm just getting Megan's lunch ready for school. She's been taking the bus."

"How's she doing?"

"Great, she's happy you're coming home. I have to go. I'll talk to you...?"

"I'll be there within fifteen minutes. The car is already pretty much loaded."

"Sounds good. I love you," replied Tri.

"You too," I answered, hanging up. I was still in my clothes from last night. Did I even have any clean ones left? Rascal and I had practically cleared the place out the other night. I stood up making my way over to the chest of drawers. Nothing. Now, what was I going to wear?

It had taken me ten minutes to unpack a clean shirt and a pair of jeans. The car was a disaster. I looked back at the mess one more time before pulling up to the apartment complex. Once parked I checked my watch. Ten-forty-five, oh well. Close enough. Before I could open my door, I heard a knock on the hood. Startled, I looked up to see an older gentleman hitting it with his cane. What was going on? I pushed my car door open, stepping outside.

"Can I help you with something?" I asked.

"Ah, are you Dan? I've heard about you. Your daughter lives in Apt B211. You must be moving back in. Do you want some help carrying those boxes? I can get Fern if you want. She's my wife. She can be a real nag if ya know what I mean."

I forced a smile. "No, it's fine. I'm sure my kids will be happy to get me moved in. So you know my name. What's yours?"

"The name is Earl. Well, if you ever need anything I am a handyman. In spite of what my wife thinks," he winked.

"I'll keep that in mind," I said, shutting the car door. He nodded to me then went about his way.

I pulled my coat around me strolling up to the building. Then found the door to Tri's, apartment. I knocked a few times and waited. When no one came, I turned the knob. It opened.

"Tri? Are you here?" I called, walking in. Then shut the door behind me.

She popped her head out of the alcove from the kitchen.

"I was putting on a pot of coffee. I can help you bring in your things if you want."

"It can wait."

"Are you sure? Especially if you left that car of yours unlocked."

"Ok, but not everything at once. It's mostly just clothing. I have a few board games, books, and a lamp. The lamp was mine," I said.

She nodded and shuffled into the hallway. "Can you grab my coat off of the hook please?" she asked, pointing to the puffy blue jacket. I took it, then helped her put it on.

"Thanks, I bet it's pretty cold out there."

"It is, hopefully, it warms up. Cavin is planning, for the crops to be planted soon," I answered. I turned back and opened the front door. "You know you have some noisy neighbors. Earl, he offered to help me bring in my stuff."

Tri shook her head. "Yes, that is Fern's husband. I told you we have to watch out for them. They are nice but noisy."

We walked toward my vehicle. "Is Starla still home? Jenson said something about them having brunch today. I was curious if she'd left yet?"

"You know the kids, they are always running late," she answered.

"Hmm, that's true. I wanted to see her before she left. I asked Jenson to make sure she gets to her training sessions afterward."

"It will be interesting. It's been a long time since I..." Tri leaned against the car. I pulled open the door on the driver's side. Then started taking out a few boxes, setting them on top of the car roof.

"It'll work out. You'll be there for Starla. I'm sure Cal and Eva will be glad to have you too. Don't feel obligated to stay long. Unless you want to," I offered.

"We'll see what happens, hand me a box," she said, holding out her arms. I picked one up and gave it to her.

"Come on now, I can handle another," she pushed.

Tri had three boxes. I didn't think she could hold anymore. I took two out of the back seat. Then locked and shut the doors.

"Ready?" I asked.

"Of course," she grinned.

"This is exciting. I'm a bundle of nerves our whole family is reunited," I stated.

"Yes, it will be good to have you home." She turned away from me for a moment. I could see her blushing a deep red. I almost wandered back to the apartment when she caught me off guard. She leaned in and kissed me.

I smiled, touching her cheek. Then pulled away. We turned back to our dwelling. I would have taken her hand in mine. If her hands, were not full. These boxes, my life fit in them. Now, maybe, I would have a better sense of permanence. I was officially home.

Chapter 33

(Starla)

Wham! Bang, thud. Startled I sat up in bed. What the heck was going on downstairs? I turned to my nightstand and reached for my cell phone. Ten-fifty-six a.m. Damn! Jenson would be here in fifteen minutes. I sprang out of bed, sliding a crossed the room. No time to bother with the racket below. Whatever it was, mom had it handled or, she'd have been knocking my door down. I pulled open my dresser drawer. OK, green sweater, white T to go underneath it, and a pair of faded blues. I threw off my PJ's leaving them in a pile. Then scrambled to get my clothes on. There, now if only I could find where I'd tossed my shoes, scanning the room, my ears perked up. No, no time to go all foxy! I had on my favorite sweater. There, my shoes! I pulled them out from under the bed and put them on my feet. OK, feet let's go. Stuffing my cell phone in my pocket, I headed downstairs. Almost falling as I went.

"Mom, Do you know if Jenson is here yet?" I hollered from the hallway.

My mom stuck her head out of the kitchen alcove. "You're right there. See for yourself. I'm making pancakes if you want some. Um, that is if you're not planning on eating out with your friends."

My eyes darted between the doorway to the kitchen and the one leading outside. If I ate pancakes and then had brunch. Ugh! I'd better not. "No thanks, mom. I won't be back until tonight. I have that meeting with Nayla."

"I know, I'll be there," she said, holding up the dish towel in her hand.

"Mom, were you doing dishes again?"

169

"Guilty, if you girls wouldn't just pop in and out. Your sister's becoming quite popular! She always off somewhere with Carol. There's this new girl too. I haven't got a name yet."

"Mom, it's Megan. The mega math genius. I wouldn't worry," I answered.

"Mom's worry," she replied, winking at me. Then disappeared into the kitchen.

I pulled out my cell phone, Ten fifty-nine. "So what was all the noise this morning?" I said, turning towards her.

"Your dad brought his stuff today. He sure didn't have much. Can you come into the kitchen if we're going to talk?"

I took a few steps and peered in. Dad was sitting at the table eating some cereal. I went over and leaned against the counter, observing the scene. Mom was drying dishes and dad mowing down on cornflakes. Is this what it would be like having him home?

"Hey, so I'll see you, later at the meeting?" he asked.

"Of course, do you think I want to upset Nayla? Besides, I'd like to figure out what's going on with this black wolf," I pressed.

My dad pushed away his cereal bowl and got up to stretch. He rubbed his eyes. Then rolled his shoulders back a bit.

"You OK? Dad?"

"We'll discuss the situation tonight. Give me a chance to move in?" he joked.

"Trying to make light of things I see. Sure, dad." I sighed forcing myself to grin.

"We'll figure it out. Nayla will be ecstatic to see me," admitted my mom. She placed the dish rag on the rack off to the side of the sink. "You know, it was nice seeing Eva the other day. It's going to be weird for a bit, but I'll adjust."

"Mom, are you asking me to give you time?"

"Yes, time to get used to you being independent. It's a new phase of your life. I'm going to be here for it. Also, it's going to be new for me."

"Um, Mom. Would you consider going for a fox run with me? After all, this. You, and me. Mother and daughter, racing into the wilderness," I smirked.

"Are you joking, Starla?"

"No, mom, it would be fun. A bonding experience, we've never had. Who knows, maybe Nayla will ask you to join our meditation," I offered.

"Let's not go, that far yet! However, I wouldn't put it past her," she replied, lying the dish rag in the sink.

A sharp rap on the front door surprised me. "I bet that's Jenson."

"Go ahead, your mother and I will see you at the park."

"Yeah, see ya," I said.

Back in the hallway of our apartment, Molly peered into the small window, at our door. She was making funny faces attempting to get me to laugh. I pulled it open, letting her enter.

"Is everything OK? Jenson was supposed to pick me up," I said, irritated.

"What, you're not happy to see me?" she asked, leaning against the door frame.

"I didn't say that," I answered, grabbing my coat off the hook. "So where is my silly boy? Is he OK?"

"He's with Owl. They'll meet us at the Sunshine Cafe. I guess they had some things to do for Rascal."

"He called me this morning asking me to pick you up. Maine's waiting in the car. She's driving us."

"Cool, let's jet."

I zipped up my coat. Then reached into my pocket, taking out my hat and gloves. I tugged them on ready for the chilly weather. Molly closed the door behinds us as we left. The sunshine outside energized and awakened me.

"It's beautiful. A great day, for a drive. Well a short one anyhow," I said.

Molly nodded to me pointing to Maine's car. It was pink. Pink!

"Wow, your lady has class." I jogged up to it, placing my hand on the window, backed up, and waved to Maine. She smiled at us. Then mouthed, Come On! Molly grinned back at her.

"I'm head over heels," she said, opening the back door for me to get in. I pushed my hair behind my ears and sat. Molly shut the door behind me. Then got into the passenger's seat next to Maine.

"So how are you doing? Anything new?" she asked, glancing back at me.

Wow, wish I could tell her. Hey! I'm a fox. Your girlfriend and I are going to be at a trial. I'm preparing to be a guardian in my clan. You're soon to be Wicca skills would be wicked cool! Instead, I answered with "I'm doing OK. My dad's moving back in. That's good news. It was a weird situation."

"I bet, how long was he away? Molly's been hush-hush, about you."

"She has?"

"Yes, on particular questions. She's respectful like that," answered Maine, looking over at Molly. She turned the ignition starting the car and pulled out of the driveway.

"Has she told you I'm obsessed with Buffy?"

172

Maine stifled a giggle. "Yes, that was one of the first things she said when I told her I had taken out a few books on Wicca from the library. The dance was fun, but we barely got to know one another."

"Right, you sure can boogie. It was great, though. I don't get out often unless it's to work or class."

Maine nodded in agreement. I glanced at Molly, who laid a hand on her thigh. I melted back into my seat. Gah, I missed Jenson. Oh, stop acting like a fifth grader. I scolded myself.

"You, OK, back there? You sort of, have this gushy look on your face," said Molly, looking back at me.

"Yeah, I'm just thinking about Jenson. We haven't gotten any us time, since the dance. He's been off with Owl. Then the other night when we hung out. You know with all the family crap I've got going on, it kind of sucks."

"I understand. It'll get better," Molly reassured me.

Maine lifted an eyebrow and shifted the topic. "I don't know if anyone around here teaches the craft of Wicca. I haven't felt this place out yet. No one seems too stiff or uptight. Life is crazy."

Didn't I know it! Hadn't Star said she'd trained with a Shamen when I'd first met her? Perhaps she could teach Maine. If not her, someone in our tribe must practice. My dad had said not to involve her. Maybe he was right. If after the hearing things went back to whatever my tribe felt was normal, then I could introduce her to the real me.

Molly fidgeted in her seat. "Look, Owl and Jenson are already here."

I saw Rascal's pickup parked near the entryway. Owl must have borrowed it. Didn't he have a car of his own? I let the thought slide out of my head. My stomach let out a loud growl.

"I can't wait to get a stack of chocolate chip pancakes!" I announced. Then pushed open the car door while Molly unbuckled her seat belt. Maine hopped out of the car slamming the door behind her. She raced up to the entrance holding the door open for Molly and me. Once inside, we dashed over to Jenson and Owl sitting at our regular booth.

"Hey, guys! We already ordered. We were starving," Owl emphasized.

"Hi, Owl," I said, scooting in next to Jenson. Molly and Maine took seats a crossed from us.

"Rascal had us set up a display this morning for the Spring art market. It's going to be off the hook. Most of it was setting up tables for the craft booths," Jenson explained.

My hand found his underneath the table. I felt him squeeze it reassuringly. I leaned over and kissed him. Then slowly pulled away.

"What was that for, it isn't like you."

"I missed you," I admitted. Everyone at the table was blushing except me.

"How about those pancakes?" asked Maine. She picked up the menu off the table. The rest of us began to look over it. Then ordered when the waitress hustled over.

We'd been busy stuffing ourselves with pancakes when a thought occurred to me. "Has anyone done anything for Jones class yet? I haven't even started trying to decide on a project. Jenson you should already have everything set. You and Owl, have been hanging, out a lot. I'm sure he's given you some idea's."

"We've been focusing on the pow-wow coming up. This Spring art market was dropped on us earlier today. I wasn't planning on it," he answered.

I pushed aside my half eaten stack of pancakes.

"You're full already? Can I have the rest?" asked Jenson.

I pushed them over to him. "Sure, knock yourself out or your stomach. If you wish," I scoffed.

"Are you mad? You seemed happy a few minutes ago."

"I'm not mad. I'm just wondering what I'm going to do for Jone's class. Then the meeting at Hunter's Park today. Mom and dad seem psyched about it," I said, forgetting Maine was there.

"Is someone trying to cause trouble again?" she asked.

"Sort of, it's all supposed to be on the down low," I acknowledged and rolled my eyes. Jenson placed his arm around my shoulder.

Molly looked up from her potatoes she'd been pushing around on her plate. "After class on Thursday, we could go to the library. Do you have to work?"

"Only before class, after would be great. I've been contemplating how to work on a project related to what's happening."

"You mean with Hunter's Park," commented Owl.

"Yep," I answered.

Maine picked up her glass of water and took a long drink. She set it down. Molly grabbed her hand moving a bit closer to her. I pulled my hair up into a ponytail using the band on my wrist. Owl looked questionably at us.

"Is something going on?" asked Maine.

I shook my head and sighed. Then stretched my arms above my head, attempting to get the knots out of my back. Afterward, I pulled them back towards me propping them on the table.

"I can't say. I've been sworn to secrecy," I muttered.

"It's about your family, isn't it?" asked Maine.

I played with the dirt under my fingernails. "It's complicated. I've only known you since Moll had a crush on you. It's not like I don't want to trust you."

175

"I see. I'm just curious if maybe I could help in some way."

"Come on, Starla. You're an adult. When did you, start letting people tell you, what to do?" asked Jenson.

"Peer pressure, but you're right. What I don't need, though, is anyone freaking out on me. I don't want to create conflict." I sighed, then laid my chin on my hand. I stared out the window at the parking lot in silence and drummed my knuckles on the table in aggravation. My mom wanted a normal life for me. Maybe I should have accepted that. No! I'd done the right thing by rescuing Cal. I had to become a fox. I needed the clan. I turned to my friends. Then looked directly at Maine. "I'm going to tell you a secret. Please don't flip out."

Chapter 34

(Dan)

Tri slammed the door shut behind us. I set my boxes down against the wall in the entryway. Tri placed her's, on top of them.

"Want me to help you unpack. After that, we could take a walk. What do you suggest we do?"

"I can unpack later. It's just clothing. Is there a place you want me to put the lamp? Or we could..."

"Dan," Tri said, sauntering over to where I stood.

"What?" I asked, staring at her strawberry blonde hair. It fell onto her shoulders out of the hair tie. It was a mess. A beautiful one at that.

She touched my shoulder, placing her arms around me. I stared at her with my silly grin.

"That smile is what got me into trouble in the first place, you know," she admitted, letting her finger trail down my face.

"You sure about that?" I demanded.

"There is nothing else I have been surer of in my life. Now you're here. Leading us right back where we were. I hope I've made the right choice."

"You give up on being a sort of widower then?" I asked, admiring her hazel eyes. "Foxes do mate for life," I reminded her.

"Even though I don't agree with that rule, yes," Tri replied.

I embraced her. "Starla's safe now," I whispered in her ear.

"No one will ever be safe. Not 100%. No one can guarantee anyone's safety. It's time I've admitted that to myself."

"I love you, Tri," I answered.

She pulled me closer. I put my arms tightly around her. Then placed my hand under her bum lifting her up. She laughed at this.

"You think I'm this easily played?" she asked, staring into my eyes.

"It's been a long time. We haven't since Megan."

She playfully slapped me on the chest. Eventually, leaning her face in close to mine. She admired my eyes mischievously inching her lips closer and closer until I felt them on mine. Little by little she pulled away from me.

"I love you, but it's not going to happen today." She patted my chest gently eyeing the ground. "Let's unpack your clothes. Afterward, we'll go for a walk. You are a gentleman still, correct?"

I smiled at my wife putting aside my hormones. Then gently set her down on the ground.

"OK, it's alright. I'll unpack myself. Did you empty some drawers for me?" I asked, turning towards the hallway.

"So now you won't let me help you unpack?"

I could feel the tension in the room. Hadn't we just had an incredible moment? Wasn't I getting my wife back? I took a deep breath before replying to her question.

"I'm not mad at you. I thought you might have work to do, for the library. I was trying to be considerate," I answered.

"So later, we'll go on a walk?" she asked.

"Of course, I'm not going to fight over intimacy. When the time is right, we'll come together again. I know this is happening a lot faster than we'd planned."

"The whole Starla, being a guardian, finding Cal, and me possibly being a part of the tribe again. Yeah, that happened way too fast. Us, though, I'd always hoped we'd find our way back to each other. I know you've felt the same."

"Sure as peaches and cream," I chirped.

"I understand you want to unpack yourself, but I do need to show you where the bedroom is. It's the one room you haven't seen yet. You'll love it! Even Megan has her own bathroom."

"I guess that's why they call it Springville's Luxury apartments," I added.

"Yes, and watch out for the sprinkler system. It' easy to turn it on accidentally."

"Who turned it on?"

"Starla, one night she came home from work. She said it went off. It was a mess to clean up. The room is just to the," I paused as he started to walk in the direction of my room. "Yeah, how did you know?" Tri asked.

"Um, the one night you had me stay to watch films with you. I kind of, snooped around. You let me use the guest bathroom. It's a crossed from it."

"So you'll grab the boxes from the hall. I'll be in the living room going over several new books. I have various choices. We only have funds for twenty novels. There are a lot of new writers presently."

"Go ahead. I'll be finished in, say twenty minutes or less," I answered, glancing at my watch. "I'd like to shower after. I didn't want to bother at my last residence."

"I'll be in the living room if you need me," she offered.

I watched her swing her hips as she left the room. I wasn't a teenage boy anymore. Still, inside I ached. It would happen, I told myself and turned back to get the boxes waiting for me in the hall.

About half an hour later....

"Are you done already?" Tri asked, poking her head into the bedroom.

"Yeah. Let me, grab my coat. Where are we going?"

"Have you been to the library? I imagine you've visited the college version. Not mine, though. We could see about digging up more information on that black wolf," she offered.

"About that, I have news. I shouldn't discuss it, til tonight."

"OK. We could get a slushy. I swear Megan and Starla live at that convenience store. I've kept reminding them. I still pay for their dental bills."

"Come on. The girls are pretty good. We're lucky that Starla hasn't moved out yet. She still wants to be at home. You know that time will come. Has Megan started dating yet?" I asked.

"Nah," answered Tri. We strolled into the hallway, then onto the landing near the front entryway. She pulled our coats off of the hooks on the wall.

"Starla and Jenson haven't started..." I stopped and cleared my throat not wanting to have to process it.

"Dan, you know, you can say it," she said, turning towards me.

"Having sex?" I gulped.

"No," she stated, opening the door. I closed it behind us.

"Then we're doing pretty good. You have had the talk right?"

"With Starla, yes. Megan is just becoming interested. I've frequently thought about leaving that one to our other daughter."

"You're kidding!"

"No, Starla's pretty smart. Plus I told her how I ended up pregnant. That's usually the best warning, there is."

I put my arm around my wife as we sauntered along.

"So how about that slushy? Can I buy you one, love? It'll ruin our teeth, though," I joked.

A grin formed on her lips, slowly the cute dimple on her face I loved appeared. "That sounds good, but only if you buy me a chocolate chip cookie."

"You got it, babe," I replied.

"Kind of like old times," commented Tri. She was too choked up to continue. I could see the tears starting to form in her eyes. I stopped where we were.

"I realize, you, don't want to be rescued. But, we are going to be OK."

A tear slid down the side of her cheek.

"I'm happy, but in-between knowing how to feel."

I cautiously placed my arm around her shoulders."We've got each other and our girls. It's not about me protecting you. We protect each other," I said.

She nodded at me somberly. After that, we continued on our way, to buy slushies.

Chapter 35

(Starla)

Maine remained silent and played with her bracelets on her arm. "It's a lot to take in. No wonder you freaked out at the dance."

"I have to ask you to keep it under wraps. I don't want my dad finding out you know. He'd flip. Besides that, this group the Crusaders. They aren't keen on the human public having knowledge of our existence. We're this myth only a few people are aware of. It keeps us safe."

Molly took Maine's hand. She looked back at the rest of us. Then again, at Maine. "We trust you. Starla and I have been friends for as long as I can remember. She doesn't like keeping things from people."

"It's a weakness," I acknowledged.

"I'd call being open a strength," said Jenson.

"It can be, but it can hurt those around you. We can't let anyone else in our circle. It's closed for now. Maine, will this be a problem?" Owl asked. He shot me a stern look.

"No, I'm not popular. I was a long time ago. It changed real fast. I woke up one day to how fake they were. I caught them gossiping about me behind my back. I'd thought they accepted me. I was wrong," she replied.

I turned towards Maine, "When you choose to be yourself it happens. I've dabbled in things others don't always understand. I'm interested in Wicca. I've, used spells a few times. They held, but I thought they'd tank."

"You already have the gift. It takes practice. That's what the book I'm reading says. It's trickier to practice without a coven.

182

Um, but we shouldn't discuss it here. We'll make plans to meet up."

"I'm not sure when I can. My training with Nayla is going to pick up real rapidly. She hasn't given me a timeline for how long it will last. Then there's the trial. I have to be present for that."

"Let me know. Other than classes my schedule is open," Maine offered.

"Sure, if it doesn't interfere with whatever you and Molly have planned," I replied.

"Same for you and your man," she winked, pointing to Jenson who blushed.

The waitress dropped off the bill. Before I could pick it up, Jenson grabbed it. Molly pulled Maine towards her. She whispered something in her ear.

"Maybe you could heal me," Maine giggled.

Molly laid her head on her shoulder. "That would depend on the type of healing. I'm all for helping with physical ailments. I haven't learned how to ease emotional ones. If I could do that I'd get my dad to understand us," Molly said, shrugging her shoulders. "He's tolerating the situation, seeing as he doesn't want mom to leave him."

Maine put her arm around Molly. "I'm sorry he's being, a jerk. I haven't had to go through that with my folks." She looked down at her watch, "It's two O'clock. I don't think I can eat another bite," she announced patting her stomach.

I smiled at my friends while Jenson pulled me into a hug. I sunk into him. I loved being surrounded by people I cared for. Owl wore a smirk on his face.

"You guys are disgustingly adorable! Why don't we take a walk? There's a park not too far from here," he suggested.

Jenson let go of me. He stood up and shimmied out of the booth. "I'm going to pay our bill," he said grabbing his coat. He put it on. Then strolled to the front counter.

I pushed my hands into my jean pocket, taking out five bucks. "That should do it unless anyone else wants to chip in."

"Sure," said Maine. She laid down three dollars. "The food rocks here," she smiled. "I mean it. Thanks guys for inviting me."

"Come on girls," said Owl, putting on his coat. I peered out the window to see tiny snowflakes flying around. It had gotten warmer. The snow kept trying to take over what would soon be spring. I shook my head in annoyance.

"Everything alright?" asked Owl.

"Yeah, I'm waiting, for the sun to arrive. I miss L.A. The palm trees, the sun," I grumbled. Then stood up, placing my hand on one side of the booth. Molly and Maine were now leaning against it. They grasped each other's hands, waiting for us to make our exit.

"Ready?" asked Jenson, making his way back to us.

"Yeah, let's go," I announced, letting my hand linger on the booth for a second. Leisurely we headed to the exit. The waitress behind the counter waved to us. I waved back and managed a smile. "Thanks, the food was amazing." Turning back to my friends, I asked. "Does this park, have a swing set?"

"My kid at heart," acknowledged Jenson, holding the door open for us.

"A whole playground, and it's not the school you're thinking of," answered Owl. The cafe door banged shut behind us.

"Um, so is there room for me in the truck?" I asked Owl glancing at the parking lot.

"If you want sure! Molly and Maine can follow us. It's not far from here." I nodded, trying to keep up with Owl and Jenson.

Maine and Molly zig-zagged towards her car. "Sounds good, so we'll be there in what, ten minutes?" she asked.

"Yeah, we have an hour to fool around. Cavin and your dad won't be happy if we arrive late. Then tomorrow we have classes."

"We'll meet in the cafe for coffee?"

"Sure, but I have to work before class." I rolled my eyes.

"You know you love Denny's," chided Jenson.

"Well, Marla and Gina make it bearable. Who wants to hit the books with me after Myth class? Toss them around a bit," I joked.

Molly side bumped me pointing to Maine's vehicle. " See ya when we get there?"

"Yeah, oh wait-a Sec." I grabbed the sleeve of her coat. "We're going to work on Jone's assignment together right?"

"We'll need to do some major digging for this," she acknowledged.

"I'm considering something regarding wolves," I admitted letting go of her sleeve.

"OK, well, Maine is waiting, so are the boys." Molly pointed to Jenson resting against the truck waiting for me.

"OK, see ya." I skipped to the truck catching myself when my foot slipped on the ice. I grasped the handle on the door and pulled it open. Then looked up to see Owl in the driver's seat. Owl turned the ignition. The engine of the truck roared to life.

"Go ahead, crawl over me. That way you won't slip again. They should put some salt on this asphalt."

Awkwardly, I did as he'd asked, positioning myself between Owl and Jenson.

"Herc, let me help you with your seat belt," Jenson offered, pulling it out of the cushion it was stuck in. He helped me adjust it. Once buckled up, I laid my head on his shoulder.

"Are we ready to go?" Owl asked.

"Yep," I answered.

Jenson slightly nodded at Owl. He pulled out of the parking lot. I noticed him, keeping an eye out for Maine and Molly in his rear-view mirror. Then felt myself drift off for a bit.

Jenson and I skipped along the track surrounding the playground stopping near the jungle gym. I picked up the first snowball-flinging it at him. After a few more he grabbed me around the middle tackling me to the ground.

"Prepare to be tickled," he roared.

"It's not going to work with this jacket on buddy," I warned him lightheartedly pushing him aside. I got up, dusting the snow off of my jeans. Boy, it was cold!

"So, should we try the ice rink? Maine and Molly seem to be fairing well," he said.

"Yeah, Maine's fallen how many times?" I quipped.

"A few, but it is fun."

"I suppose, I could use a little of that."

"Where's Owl?" I asked, looking around.

"He'll be back. He ran into a friend from his tribe. Come on," he said, taking my hand, leading me over to a small building.

"Skates, two of them please?" he asked.

"Sizes, please," asked Taylor.

"Ten, and..?"

"Eight," I answered.

Taylor handed Jenson the skates. "The first hour is free, after that, it's about two bucks an hour. It's pretty cheap. It helps us keep the park up," he explained.

"It's nice, thank you," I told him.

"Yeah, thanks," said Jenson.

We walked over to some benches and sat down. Man, I was going to freeze. I put my skates, on. Too bad, Jenson wasn't aware I had a handful of lessons. Nothing major, just skating at the Y back in L.A.

"Are you all set?" he asked after he'd laced up his skates.

"I'm good."

We left our shoes sitting on the bench. I hoped Springville was an honest city. Jenson took my hand, and we skated onto the rink.

Chapter 36

(Dan)

The cold cherry-drink slid down my throat. I took a bite of the chocolate cookie. "This is too good! Now, I know why our daughters are obsessed with this place," I commented.

"Don't go getting used to it. I'll be paying your dentist bills soon too." Tri slapped my back lightly.

We sat at a small table in the store. This place had everything. I'd never stopped here. I always hit up this pizza joint on, fifth street. Tri pushed her strawberry blonde hair behind her ears. Then let her hands lay flat on the red table. I watched her take a drink of her frozen concoction.

"Ugh! Brain freeze," she said, pushing the drink aside.

I chuckled. "Will it function for the meeting tonight?"

"It's going to be," she paused. "Odd, strange, awkward."

She threw the words out at me. "Maybe it won't. It could end up similar to an old friendship. You may pick back up, where you left off. I don't see anyone upset or trying to punish you for leaving. They understand."

"Star's one person I haven't thought of in ages. Starla, is she still interested in Wicca? If so, she'd be the go-to-girl."

"She told me you banned her from those books. In place of them, she viewed documentaries. How was she able to watch them? You never allowed the girls cable-television."

"The library, I couldn't deny her anything with educational value. She got wrapped up in the Salem witch trial era for a bit. It relieved me when she started watching Buffy instead," laughed Tri.

I touched her hand gently. She squeezed mine back.

188

"Sorry about today. I'm, I do want to be with you. Tonight, OK. Privately," she said, raising an eyebrow. A smile gradually spread a crossed her lips.

"We'll both probably.."

"Don't say need it," she interrupted me. Then gave me an evil stare. "It's about Love."

I picked up my cherry drink and crumpled up my napkin. "It's almost time to head out. We can go to the cabin first if you want. Nuria and Cal should be there. It's only two-thirty."

"I ought to talk to Nayla. I haven't seen her in ages. Since she is training our daughter, it's important for me to recognize what's happening. Earlier, you said, you can't discuss anything til the meeting tonight. My guess is that wolf came to visit you," she whispered standing up.

I pushed my chair back, almost falling over. Did Tri have ESP?

"It's not back, not yet," she admitted. "I've had a few, Deja Vu' moments." She pushed the chair underneath the table. "Let's get out of here. I can't drink any more of this. It's too cold for frozen drinks. See what nostalgia does to us?"

"Yeah, but you've got to admit it was a great, idea."

Tri trudged through the snow up to Nuria's porch. Then peered into the window on the left. She waved at whoever was inside.

"Eva's here! I don't see Nuria or Cal, though," she commented, standing back from the window.

I made my way up the stairs and stood beside my wife. The door swung open. "Hey you two, I wasn't expecting to see you til this evening. Come in," she offered.

"Thanks, how are you, Cal?" I asked.

Eva shut the door behind us. She took our coats and hung them up. Then led us over to the dining room table. "I made a pot of coffee if you want some," she offered.

"I'll take a cup. Tri?"

"It would warm me up after that slushie. I'm pretty full, though," Tri answered.

"It was your idea, a bit nostalgic I suppose," I added.

"Maybe later then. Did you have a reason for stopping by?"

"Has Cal seen, the black wolf?" I asked.

Eva poured herself a cup of coffee and sat down. "No, she told me Starla saw one during their first session. Nayla is trying to find out if it's related to the case."

"Have you pulled out the cards yet, consulted them?" Tri asked.

"Cavin, he's not that cool about it," she admitted

I nodded, "playing with the future. It worries him."

"Yeah, but it's necessary. Had we known Martin Du-Vance was in danger all this could have been avoided," Eva added.

"Do you feel the same way about River Rogue?" I asked.

Eva's hands trembled. "Dan, the cards don't always hold the correct answers."

"It helps right. We can plan based on the prediction. We have to be cautious of course," Tri responded.

"Hmm," Eva took a sip of her drink. "Yes, I usually don't go against Cavin's advice unless Kaya supports it," she stated.

"What happened to my girl. The one who defied authority," my wife joked.

"Steve left. I haven't told Cal. She assumes he disappeared. It happened before, she vanished."

"When we went to his office, he was gone. Maybe that's why I... I've let the men push me a bit. Let them handle conflicts and problems. Steve always had to solve things, to be right. He didn't like it when I had the upper hand in our relationship. We're supposed to mate for life. So much for that," she stressed.

"You don't have to stick to it. It's such an old-fashioned rule. Dan here has been teasing me about it." Tri rolled her eyes at me.

"I'm glad he's gotten you this far," admitted Eva. She winked at him.

I blushed, "She has me ensnared." I quickly changed the subject, "Please don't pull out the Tarot cards. Not unless we have to. That black wolf. If I'm right, it's a spirit. The other night it came to me with a warning. We cannot attempt to locate the scientists. It demanded that we don't," I stammered.

"Now I want to pull out the cards! Where did it come from, and why did it wait to reveal itself?" questioned Tri.

Could it have been searching for Martin's soul? I thought. Maybe it needed to find him before we could get the information we needed. I shrugged it off. "I'm sure we'll uncover it soon enough. Jumping to conclusions isn't going to help. It may make matter's worse. Better to heed the warning, go on with the trial, and then go from there," I suggested. My eyes shifted to the clock on the wall. "We need to get going. Eva, do you want a ride?"

"OK, let me turn off the coffee pot. Then I'll get our coats," she answered.

I turned away, allowing them a brief moment of privacy. I watched them embrace. Tri held Eva close to her. Most likely, comforting her for her loss. Steve, had left her? Where had I been? Looking into cases, for Cavin probably. It had been years. Eva? Strong, beautiful, loving. I shook my head. What a mess. He didn't know what he'd lost.

191

Chapter 37

(Starla)

(The Reflection room)

"Where did you drop Jenson off to," prodded Nayla.

I stood at the door. I'd just walked in and wasn't ready for an interrogation. Cal must be on her way. I glanced down the hallway, then back at Nayla.

"He's with my dad in the dining hall. They're discussing the trial Blah, blah blah. Sorry, I'd like to get it over with its dragging," I admitted. Then, stepped into the room.

"Anymore black wolf sightings?"

"Once, on the way home. It seemed to be protecting me. It smiled, and put its paw up to its mouth."

"An omen. Be careful who you trust. Also, what you say to whom," said Nayla.

"I've wanted to try to contact it. Figured I'd discuss it with you first." I lowered myself to the floor sitting down.

"Thank you, once Cal gets here, it's an option. You'll turn today. Cal's seen you in fox form. You haven't seen..."

"I've never seen her change."

"No. You'll need to, she's doing better. We worked yesterday at the cabin. She's coming along well."

A shiver crawled up my spine, then ceased. Nayla placed a paw on my leg, then laid down next to me, resting her head on the floor. Afterward, she closed her eyes.

Wait, this was no time for a nap! What was she doing? Instead of calling her out I stroked her fur. Footsteps! Maybe it was Cal? I turned my head to the door. It creaked open.

My mom glanced at Nayla sitting at my feet. Casually she walked over to us. Kneeling down, she pulled out a deck of cards from her back pocket. "These are for you."

I took the cards pushing them into the pocket of my jeans, not giving it a second thought as to what the cards were.

"Is Nayla in a trance?"

"I'm not sure. She didn't say anything. I figured maybe she was meditating. Do you know where Cal is? Have you spoken with Eva?"

"Your father and I came from there. Cal's with Minder. Nayla, wake up! What are you doing, sleeping on the job!"

She jumped up on all fours. Then glared at us. I was consulting the goddess. I assumed you'd be here much later." She shook her body and pranced around the room in a circle twice. Then turned her head up towards the ceiling.

"Shh. Shh..."Tri whispered.

I closed my eyes. The shiver, I'd experienced earlier came again. It would pass. Nayla would finish, and we'd start the session. Ugh, I hoped I didn't black out! All of a sudden the floor shifted beneath me. Was I being transported? If so, who the hell had initiated the spell? Small dots, black ones, then red, appeared as if I shut my eyes and held them creating images. I felt along the floor. Grass, wheat, brush maybe? My eyes opened. The black wolf trotted up to me.

"Listen, be on your guard. Follow Nayla's instructions I've been tethered. They're doing their best to keep me from reaching you. My soul was trapped."

"Who? Why are you following me? Am I like your new person? Do you know what happened to Cal's dad? The scientists? Can't you just tell us?" I complained.

"If I had all the answers I would. You're the guardian. I trust you. Now, only speak of me, if you must. Do not mention my name," it stated.

193

"I don't even know it, so how could I?"

It scoffed, then coughed, "Trigger."

"What kind of name is that?"

"A spirit-guide, once, you and Cal are completely tethered I"m yours."

"What? How do I use you, are you meant to be used?"

"You're evolving Starla. Soon, you'll have two tails, not only one."

What else, did I need to freak me out!

"I'm not here for that. Du-Vance was planning to infiltrate the scientists. Right now, they have an army. They're forming an infantry. You're going to think I'm crazy. Their leader Sika is a fool, but if you can get them on your side. I suggest it."

The ground began to shake-- fading was I fading!

"Go they're waiting."

"What do I do!"

"Put your hands on the trigger, but don't shoot yet," he cautioned me.

My eyes fluttered open. Ah, Cal had shown up. Eva was holding her daughter's hand. I looked down, Nayla's paw rested on my chest. Why was she holding me down?

"Here," said my mom as she held out a bottle of water to me.

"I'm OK. Let me up."

Nayla withdrew her paw from my chest, stepping aside. I pushed myself off the floor. Then, stood, stretching out my arms, arched my back, and pulled my legs behind me as if I was preparing to run. I wasn't really. I had to get reacclimated to myself. I reached out my hand, taking the water from my mom.

"Thanks," I said, taking a long drink. Afterward, I put the cap on the bottle and handed it back."

"You gave us a scare. Where did you go? I tried to follow you after you collapsed. Whatever it was, it only wanted you," Nayla commented.

I repositioned myself back on the floor. "The field of gold wheat. It's usually where I always end up. This wolf claimed Du-Vance was going to infiltrate the scientists. He said he'd been trying to contact me, but they had his soul trapped. I'm not sure if they are the scientists or someone else." I paused.

"Go on," urged Nayla.

"The scientists are building an army. He said it would be best if we could get Sika on our side as crazy as he is."

"Sika!" exclaimed Eva.

"Yeah, exactly what I thought. Then to top it off, this is the kicker. Once Cal and I, are tethered. This wolf claimed. He belonged to me. Not only that, he's a spirit guide. He was specific I continue to follow your instructions," I said, looking at Nayla.

My mom moved closer to me taking my hand. Nayla, Cal, and Eva sat down, forming a circle. Should I tell them about evolving? It wasn't as if it was going to happen now. Trigger hadn't made it seem earth shattering.

"Starla, are you with us?"

"Yes," I said, looking up at her.

"Our session must go on. We cannot let it effect this," stated Nayla.

"Of course not, am I going to get to see Cal turn? Are we going back to the field of wheat?" I asked, raising an eyebrow.

"It wouldn't be a good idea. It's best if you and Cal turn today. I'll have you complete some mental exercises that will specifically connect your souls to each other," suggested Nayla.

"Are these similar to spells?"

"No, you'll be spiritually joining Cal's spirit," Nayla answered.

I froze. What? I thought that was something you only did, physically like... Sex? In a way, I was horrified. *What about Jenson?*

My mom put her hand on my back. I turned to face her.

"It's OK. It's not like that. This way, you'll be able to maintain a protective circle, around each other. Once completed the only way an enemy can harm you, is if you disconnect. It's why the entity wanted you."

I should have been excited, ecstatic even, at learning this data. "Mom, there's something else. The wolf said," I gulped. "I'll evolve. I..I.. I'll have two tails," I stammered.

"Never mind that now. We need to focus on you and Cal. Let's get started. Then we'll discuss what you've told me," answered Nayla.

"Okay, so do I just change into a fox?"

"First, we'll let Cal change. Next, you'll transform. Afterward, you'll both begin the meditation, but you're not going anywhere. You'll be connecting to each other mentally."

"How can Eva and I help?" asked Tri.

"We need to observe them, make sure nothing goes wrong. Cal is the most vulnerable. Starla has had, experience connecting before." Nayla turned to me, "It was when you learned to use memories, against others."

I nodded to her. Cal got up off of the floor and began stretching her arms and legs. She positioned herself on the carpet like a child ready to crawl for the first time. This was going to be strange. What fox and wolf qualities would she have?

"Quiet your thoughts. Cal needs to concentrate. I don't want her to pick up on you mentally yet," mind spoke Nayla to me.

Cal let out a yelp, and a whine as her legs began to take shape. They were strong muscular wolf legs.

Her body lean and gray. Out jutted whiskers and a fox-like face, her tail emerged from her backside. Again she stretched out and pranced around the room a few times before stopping to sit next to Nayla.

"As you can see, Cal has the body and the legs of a wolf. She has the head, and tail of a fox. It is extraordinarily unique. You two will be fitted well together. Soul sisters."

"Now that I've seen her turn do I?"

"Go ahead dear, and I'll instruct you," Nayla answered.

I took my stance to do so my body trembled in anticipation. Concentrating I recalled what Nayla had told me. I needed to learn to switch without pain. My hands became paws, my legs thicker yet lean. I felt my whiskers materialize and face re-shape, while my tail emerged. Then shook my body, stretched and trotted around. I stopped plopping down next to my mom.

"Now, that you're both in the proper form you'll sit in the circle," instructed Nayla.

Cal and I both stood up, trotting into the circle the three of them had created. Cautiously we sniffed each other. Then backed off a bit, I let my tongue hang out and playfully swatted her with my paw. She jumped on my back, pushing me down. We began to wrestle.

"Girls, this is no time for play! Now, sit down, and we'll begin," Nayla ordered.

Cal and I broke out in hiccups of laughter.

"Come on. I"m serious," Nayla stressed.

"Okay, Okay," I replied.

"Memories play, an important role in your ability to attach to one another. Starla was able to save you due to her gift to hold this bond. Now, you must not only pick a memory but find a way to link to her soul. Once done, it should not be too difficult for her to do the same."

"Is there a way you want me to attempt it? Can I handle doing it alone?" asked Cal.

"We'll try your way first. If you are unable to, then we'll do things my way," Nayla smirked.

Cal inched towards me to touch my paws.

"No, touching, when you're out guarding the perimeter, or one another you will not be able to stay linked that way. You need to be able to connect mentally," Nayla said.

I pulled back, staring up at Cal. "You called out to me before I heard you," I mind spoke to her, repeating it several times.

Moments later she responded, "How are we supposed to combine, link, whatever. I hear you. I see you in front of me."

"What connects us, what makes you and me different from others who surround us. Parents, friends, people, the bandits, what?" I asked her silently.

Nayla watched us, her eyes darting back and forth. We had to do something to impress her quick or else she would intervene.

I pulled out the memory of us defeating the entity. The necklace that we used to contain it. Where had it gone? What had been, done with it? I supposed Cavin had found a safe place for it. I shrugged it off trying to concentrate on our connection again. A strong tugging sensation pulled at my chest. It gravitated me towards Cal.

"What are you doing? What?"

"Relax, I'm pulling you in. Accept it," prodded Cal to me in my head.

I assimilated to her soul's presence. A warmth spread, little by little overtaking my being. It wasn't a memory that was binding us. It was something else. I wanted to pull back, to run. But I stayed. Maybe this was a part of evolving.

"Cal, can you make me a little more comfortable. It's like your trying to take over my body," I admitted mind speaking back to her.

Memories, what kind did Cal have of us? Were they different? Out of the blue, my mind was flooded with an image of us on a fall day, playing in the park. Fall leaves fluttered to the ground. Cal and I ran along a path. My mom and Eva were behind us. Was this in Springville or L.A.?

A rush of adrenaline filled my body, then heat, we linked. Cal was with me. I couldn't see her soul. It wasn't a physical form, but I could feel it. How were we supposed to use this? Would it protect us from outsiders? Tri and Eva, stood up, moving briskly towards the circle. An electric buzz sounded. Pulsating vibrations surged out of us. Electronic waves radiated to the invaders. Wham! They fell a foot away from us. We were keeping them out. How had it been that easy?

A loud clap hit the ground. Startled, I shook dropping to the floor, placing my paws over my head. Cal backed away our connection broken. After a few moments of silence. When nothing else occurred, I stood up, surveying the damage.

"Mom? Eva? Where is everyone?" I asked. Then looked down at my body. I'd reverted to human form while Cal remained a fox-wolf. I did my best to cover myself using my hands.

"Is everyone OK? It's just lightning. Rare, but it does happen. Nothing to get worried about," said Eva. She stepped back into the room, shutting the door behind her. "Nayla and Nuria left to get your father. We're impressed you connected so well. There was a strange glow, though. It has Nayla a bit concerned. We fear another spirit, may be guiding you," Eva said.

The black wolf no doubt. However, I wasn't ready to say it out loud. You'd think they would have figured it out. How else had we been able to connect so quickly? Unless it was the bond we formed when I'd saved, Cal's life.

"Um, can I get some clothes? Mom, you packed them right?" Gah, I'd forgotten I wore my favorite sweater. I'd have to be more careful about what I wore on training days.

The door to the reflection room swung open. My Mom pushed my dad back practically shutting it in his face.

"Mom!"

"Well, you are naked, let me get you those clothes I stashed. Nayla tossed the ones you discarded while transforming. After that, I'll let your father in."

I blushed. Mom walked close to the fireplace. She'd tucked a paper bag behind the chair near it.

"Here," she thrust it at me.

I pulled on a pair of yoga pants, a clean sweatshirt, socks, and noticed I hadn't any shoes. When I turned back to Cal, she'd already taken human form again. She was putting on clothes. Eva must have brought her. The door burst open. My dad leaned half way into the room.

"Is it safe to enter?" he asked.

"Yes, is Nayla with you?" questioned Eva.

My dad opened the door wider. Nayla trotted inside in front of him. He left the reflection room door ajar.

"You girls have performed exceptionally today. It's key you don't let distractions bring you back from your link. We'll work on that," said Nayla trotting over to where I stood near Cal.

"Will there be any more lessons today?" asked Tri.

"No, why don't we meet in the dining hall. The Crusaders are there. We're discussing the trial. It won't be long. Dan, will you lead the way?"

"Of course," he answered.

"What happened, before Cal and I connected?"

"Generally, it's a combination of emotions, bonding, and friendship. Oh, and fear. It happens," acknowledge Eva. She turned to Nayla. "Are you ready to head to the dining hall?"

"Okay, Starla and Cal. When you're ready, we'll see you there."

They ambled out of the reflection room, leaving the door slightly opened. I caught a glimpse of my mom and dad standing in the doorway.

Cal took my hand pulling me aside. Then glanced at my parents. "Give us a minute," she demanded.

"Sure, you girls can meet us there," my dad replied.

"Thanks," answered Cal. The door closed quietly behind them.

"When we joined what else happened?"

I paced back and forth. I felt like Nayla when she was anxious. Then let my hands fall to my sides, staring at Cal.

"What?" she asked.

"It could have been the wolf in-between us. It claimed you and me, had to unite first, though. It can't be anything else. We are not anything else!" I screamed.

"Starla, hey, it's OK. We're friends, kindred spirits. We have this bond. It's scary. I'd give my life for you. You already practically did for me a few weeks ago," she admitted.

I nodded, leaning against the wall embarrassed. Cal gave me a sympathetic, puzzled look.

"Would it be weird if I hugged you? I mean after all that emotional stuff, and fear?"

I shook it off embracing her. Then let go. She pushed my hair back behind my ears. The bit that always wanted to cover my face. "We've always been best friends. We have a tougher job now than ever before. All these people, are depending on us. I overheard Nuria talking about it on the phone to Rascal. I guess, I'm just good at ease dropping."

I laughed, "Yeah, those were the good ole' days."

"When?"

"L.A., ease dropping on mom. Megan and I would deliberate on when she would date. She never did."

"Did you ever find that odd?"

"Hmm, I never thought about it. Mom and dad were on and off. It was confusing. Now things are gradually getting back on track."

"We should get going," suggested Cal. She slightly bounced away from me to the door, pulling it open. The hallway dimly lit. Would I be here again before the trial? How much of it would, I attend? This black wolf had ideas of his own. I shook it off as Cal and I walked in silence to the dining hall.

Chapter 38

(Dan)

Starla and Cal stood in the doorway of the dining hall. I got up from where I sat to greet them.

"Hey, come on in. Sit down. The food is ready, you both need to eat something. Cavin will introduce us to the Crusaders. They're helping with the trial. I've let him know we need to speak to the group concerning this black wolf."

"Sure dad, sounds like a plan. Cal, why don't you sit here next to me?"

"I would, but I should stick by my mom. I'll be going to Nuria's tonight," Cal answered.

"Oh, she's going to be here?" Starla asked.

"Everyone is here," said Star, wandering up to my daughter.

"Oh, hey," she said. We followed Star to the main table.

"There you are. Your Dad and I didn't imagine you'd be this late. Is everything alright?" asked Tri.

"Yes, mom. We just had some things to discuss. We're good. I should sit down."

My wife nodded to Star, who trotted off to talk to another fox nearby. I looked a crossed the room. Lance and Shellena waved while standing next to Owl. I nodded to them as Jenson jogged up to Starla. She immediately stood up.

"I almost forgot you were here! I've been so wrapped up in connecting with Cal and what happened," she stammered.

Jenson laid his hand on her shoulder, then turned to me. "I should have come with you Dan, but I thought I'd stay here. Owl and Cavin wanted to discuss the scientists. No leads. You said not to pursue them. I've been keeping it hush-hush."

"Jenson, if he told you, not to then don't!" she exclaimed pulling away from him. Jenson's hand slid off her shoulder. He let it fall to his side.

"Starla, he's only looking into the facts, where they have been. Not where they are. I'm trying to get an idea of what's going on. This way we have a chance to prepare for what might occur," I added.

"I'm sorry, I didn't mean to jump to conclusions. It's just I had another visit from the black wolf."

I nodded at my daughter, "Yes, and once the meeting begins you may speak. You'll need to tell Cavin precisely what happened."

"Of course," said Starla sitting back down. I got up and pulled out a chair for Jenson to join us.

After everyone had finished eating and the plates had been cleared Cavin clapped his hands to silence us. "I would like your attention. We have three guests with us today. The Crusaders are here to listen in on our idea's and plans for the trial. I'd like to introduce you first, to Jun, she is half human and wolf." Jun stood bowing to us.

"We're pleased you trust us enough to allow us to help. We're not here to interrupt your proceedings. All you need to know is we'll be assisting you, should anything go wrong. My partner Amer is a full wolf. He's capable of most human functions except for changing into one. Please, stand up Amer."

I observed Starla engulfed in this lecture. My eyes fell on Jenson, holding her hand. It was mildly amusing that Tri didn't seem nervous at all. She looked comfortable with her clan. I brought my attention back to the meeting. Amer was now pointing to a human. What?

"This is Sensi. She came to us. It isn't explainable. I'll let her introduce herself," he said, sitting back down.

"I came to the group two years ago. The Crusaders took me in. I've been training in martial arts for a while. The plan was to stay out of the human world. I've got this problem." She held her hands and began twisting them together. Then looked back up at the crowd. Amer gave her a thumbs up.

"It's alright, go on," he urged her.

"At night, I turn into an Owl. It's great, for keeping an eye on each and every one of our members. It's why I feel guilty about all that has happened."

Sensi sat down as Jun reached for her hand to comfort her. Automatically I glanced at Tri who managed a weak smile. Turning back to the front of the room, I noticed Cavin. He stood up while Kaya stayed seated.

"I want you to observe that this room is now set up for the trial. In front of us, is what will be the jury seats. A big thanks to Dan, and Ranger Mike. They helped set most of this up. With the hearing only one day away. I want to hear from clan members." Cavin paced back and forth staring at the floor. Occasionally he looked up at us.

I rose to speak. "The planning is nearly finished. I'll be questioning the bandits and Jones will cross-examine. If it's needed Cal and Starla are to testify as to what happened during the rescue from the entity. We will not be releasing it. The point is to get Sika to admit who killed Martin Du-Vance. Then, if that doesn't work Lance will further interrogate them. What I'm concerned about, are the warnings I've experienced. This black wolf has appeared to myself and Starla Ariana. It's cautioned me not to attempt to locate the scientists. It promised Jones would find a way to bring us justice."

"That's absurd!" Cavin screamed, slamming his paws onto the table.

I touched my daughter's shoulder and with the other hand motioned for her to stand while I sat back down in my seat.

"Cavin, according to the wolf, Du-Vance planned to infiltrate the scientists. He was going to go after them himself. There was no peace treaty." Starla lowered her eyes to the floor. *The next part would not be received well.* "What's confusing is this spirit told me we need to get Sika on our side. The scientists are preparing to attack us."

"Is that all Starla Ariana?" he asked in a low growl.

"No, this spirit claims it's soul is trapped. I'm not sure if it's by the scientists or someone else."

"This is more unsettling than I anticipated. I'll contact Jones this evening. If this spirit guide-wolf, was not so cryptic," Cavin pressed.

"Tell me about it," Starla answered. I pulled out her seat for her, and she sat back down. Afterward, Tri got up, taking her position on the floor.

"Why would this guide advise us not to protect ourselves? Is it in any way shielding us from danger? Does it assume we'd stir up trouble trying to stop it ourselves? How do we know those that created the bandits won't pay us a visit during our integration!"

"We don't. We trust that this wolf has been placed, as a protective barrier. It's defending us for the time being. I don't believe we are meant to know the reason yet. It sounds like it's doing everything in its power, its able," Star responded.

"How can you presume that? Trust is, built. All it has done is notify us. It hasn't shown us any truth, or reliable facts," Shellena interrupted.

Nayla hopped off her seat. "We shouldn't attack the unknown. Any premonitions or even Deja Vu' should be reported to me immediately. No one is to act without consulting me, or Cavin first. Dan, Friday will continue as planned. If this spirit visits any of you, please contact me."

"Yes," I answered, observing Kaya who laid a reassuring hand on Nayla's back. This wolf would have its say even if it didn't directly show itself.

"What if it's in the middle of the night?" Starla asked.

"Meditate, it's fine. If you experience anything odd, you'll report to me. I can't believe I said that!"

"Thank you, Will we be training again? I have work and class tomorrow. There's this project for Myth class."

"I'd hoped Minder would be able to join us for a session. Perhaps Friday, before the hearing. In the morning?" Nayla asked.

"That works for me. I'd be happy to help the girls prepare. I suppose you'd like me to brush up on some of my skills too," Minder chimed in.

"Yes, exactly. Cavin any guidelines until we next meet?"

"Be on guard. The Trinity and Crusaders are looking out for us. Jones is acting as security. Mike, keep the visitors out of the woods til the end of the trial. I don't need them stumbling upon us should we have to leave abruptly."

"Not a problem," he answered.

Jenson. The boy hadn't said a word. I looked over at him and my daughter, her head rested on his shoulder. She slightly slouched into him. He'd wrapped his arm around her waist.

"You alright," I heard him murmur to her.

She shrugged her shoulders and then pulled away, sitting up straight.

"I'm ready to find out who killed Du-Vance. I agree with Cavin on the whole cryptic wolf thing," she said a little too loudly.

I tried not to chuckle. It came out as a snort.

"Dad, why are you laughing. It isn't funny," Starla answered.

"No, it's not," I responded. Tri shot me an angry look.

Lance got up from where he sat, "I want to know if Sensi saw anything? Do you have any idea who might have been in the forest, the night Du-Vance died?"

Sensi scuttled back to her chair nearly knocking it over. Then re-arranged it upright. "I heard noises. I'd been hunting for mice. That's what I told Mike when he asked. Too scared to investigate anything I fled from the area. I saw flashes of red. As if, something was running. Quick, like lightening. Maybe it had on a cape," she stammered.

"And you're just telling us now!" Lance shouted.

"I only recalled it, at the moment. I cannot control when I remember things. Whoot-Whoot..." Sensi's eyes darted back and forth in a crazy frenzy. Amer pushed his chair aside quickly assisting her.

"Calm down before you turn," he told her.

"Sensi is not on trial here. When and if more pieces of the puzzle emerge you'll know," Amer said glaring at Lance.

"He's right. There is no need to attack each other," I stated, pushing my chair back. I turned to see Rascal, standing against the door to the mud room. How long had he been there? A scowl appeared on his face.

"Right in the middle of chaos. It's how I like to show up. How's it going Cavin?" he asked, unfolding his arms. He shimmied towards the table. "It seems things are getting stirred up. This wolf business, then the girl having seen flashes of red lights, the bandits, and now the scientists and an army! It just all keeps coming at us."

Cavin threw his paws up into the air out of frustration. They fell onto the table where he laid his head on the slab. He appeared hopeless for the moment.

"Are you here to save the day Rascal?"

"No, but at least we're on track. Friday Owl, and I will come together." He turned to Sensi, "Thank you for the information." Rascal took out his card, placing it on the table. "We'll fit these pieces together. Do you suppose The Bandits did this?" he asked.

"It's possible, however, unless one of them likes dressing up in a red cape, is red, or carries a red flashlight." Sensi shook her head in dismay.

"Well, it wasn't little red riding hood," Starla admitted.

Jenson laughed, and I glared at Starla. Tri stifled a chuckle.

"Let's all stand down," Kaya declared. "We'll meet here on Friday morning 10 a.m. Starla, please bring Molly. Cavin will call Sika to the stand first. Then we'll go down the line of importance. For now, there's to be no harassment based upon suspicion. Nayla is here if you need her."

Chapter 39

(Starla)

Pandemonium, my head was spinning from the madness. I sat on my bed. Jenson rubbed my back trying to soothe me. Dad and mom were downstairs sorting things out. She'd done well during the gathering. I reached behind myself with one arm moving Jenson's hand off of my back. Then, turned to face him.

"It felt like nothing came together at the assembly. Sensi having seen a red light only adds to the craziness of the black wolf. We're not any further than when I stood in the clearing where Du-Vance was killed," I complained.

"Don't beat yourself up. It will come to you, relax. Maybe you should pull out one of your magazines, cut out pictures for a collage."

"Why, what good would it do?" I argued. "I can't be focused on art when I need to figure out how to help the clan. I didn't see Du-Vance get killed. We don't have any leads."

"Come on, Buffy wouldn't give up," Jenson teased me.

I grinned, "You know how to make me smile."

He got up and pulled out a few magazines off of my dresser leafing through them. "Should we order a pizza."

"We just ate a few hours ago."

"My stomach must not remember," Jenson joked.

"What about everyone else? I'm sure Megan will want some," I commented.

Across the hall, a door slammed shut. I heard footsteps approaching. Abruptly the door to my room swung open. Megan slipped in and stood with her arms crossed.

"Hey, Megs is something wrong?" I demanded.

"I heard you discussing pizza. It sounds fantastic. Do you think I can get in on this?"

Jenson smiled as he walked over near the bed. He set down the magazines next to me. Then took my hand. I got up and stood beside him.

"Well?" she demanded, her hands now on her hips.

"Why don't we go downstairs. Your mom and dad are probably famished. What time is it?" Jenson asked Megan.

She pulled her phone out of her pocket. "Eight O'clock. No wonder my stomach wouldn't shut up," she said. Then stuffed the phone back into it.

I would have laughed at my sister, but my stomach had started to grumble. Jenson gripped my hand tighter. My eyes darted to the floorboards. I needed time to contemplate everything. Nayla had warned me not to contact the wolf again. Still, I wasn't sure if waiting was the right thing to do. If she was there during contact, she might consider it. What would Nayla think if I brought Molly with me? Should I involve her in this or just ask Cal?

"You OK sis?" asked Megan.

I had been staring off into space.

"That's how your sister gets when she's trying to make a decision about something," Jenson commented.

"I'm irritated. We can't figure out who this black wolf is, or who killed Du-Vance. These are the missing pieces of the puzzle. You remember the information I filled you in on after Thunder Head Bay."

"Yeah, but you didn't tell me about the black wolf! I only knew about Du-Vance. I'm sorry sis," she stated, putting a comforting hand on my shoulder.

"I'll be OK. There isn't anything you can do about it right now. Let's go downstairs. We'll see if we can talk mom and dad into ordering a pizza. I didn't realize how late it was getting," I said, glancing at Jenson.

He nodded to me. Megan pushed the door open wider.

We stood in the kitchen not sure what to make of the scene. Mom and dad had flour all over the place. It was on the counters, floor, and the table.

"What happened? Flour doesn't explode," I commented.

Jenson and my sister had their hands over their mouths trying not to laugh. Both my mother and father were covered in the stuff.

"I was trying out a spell. All of a sudden the kitchen cupboards flew open. The flour immediately burst everywhere! You know how many bags of flour I've been storing," said Tri.

"Mom, when did you become interested in learning spells? And ah, what are these?" I asked, pulling out the stack of cards from the pocket of my jeans.

"Those are Tarot cards."

"Ah," I acknowledge examining them. Yep, definitely what they were. Mom didn't need to know I'd had some before. I muffled a snicker.

"Hmmm, why are you laughing? A lot of people, won't understand. They'll tell you they're evil. It's not accurate. The readings give you guidelines, what might happen. It's a way to prepare for what may occur. Please don't start waving them around in college. I'll have to show you how to use them correctly. Not today, though," she said.

I put them in my pocket for safe keeping. Then changed the subject. "So can we order pizza? We're kind of, hungry."

My dad dusted the flour off of himself turning to my mom. "We should clean up. Have them order pizza. We can get two large's and then have left over's later. Tri, the next time you want to attempt, a finding spell we should consult the books first."

"You're right," she answered him, glancing at us. "Go ahead. You can order what you want. I"m up for anything. Oh, and we'll pay. Don't go overboard!" she warned us. My mom took my dad's hand, leading him out of the room.

"What kind of pizza do you guys want?" I asked, taking my phone out of my other pocket.

"Anything but anchovies, little fish. Sick!" Megan exclaimed.

Jenson shook his head in disbelief. He slung his arm around my shoulders. Then looked at my sister. "Dan said to order two large pizza's."

"If only we could eat that much," I replied gently removing his arm from my shoulder. I wandered over to the refrigerator. Then, removed the magnet holding up the menu. Pillar's Pizza. It features some of the best pizza in town. That's what mom claimed.

"We could try the BBQ veggie and then go with a regular supreme," I suggested, biting at my fingernail. "Mom says it's always good to try new things," I admitted, taking my hand away from my mouth. I was almost ready to dial. "What do you think?"

Megan shrugged, "Sure, I'll try it. If I don't like it, I'll just eat the supreme.

"Me too," Jenson offered.

I placed the order and told them we'd pick it up, setting my cell on the kitchen counter. "What should we do now? Mom and dad are apparently still cleaning up," I answered dusting the flour off the counter with a dishrag.

My sister bounced over to the table and sat down. Jenson automatically started to take plates out of a cupboard.

"We, usually use paper plates," I said, then stopped dusting. I opened one of the drawers below the countertop to retrieve them, then gave them to Jenson. He shut the cupboard door he had opened.

"Sorry."

"It's okay," I replied, grabbing some plastic cups. I placed them in the middle of the table.

"So are you going to tell me about the black wolf? What's going on?" Megan demanded.

Jenson and I situated ourselves at the table. I guess I might as well tell her. She'd find out sooner or later. "Cal and I have been training. This black wolf has made itself known to me. So far I've figured out, it's a guide of sorts. It's trying to warn us of what not to do and to help us solve this case. Something is trying to keep it from reaching me. It's holding it hostage. It'll work itself out somehow. You shouldn't worry."

Megan's face went from curious to pouty. She pushed her chair back from the table. She almost stood up but stopped.

"I'll watch out for your sister. It seems as if this beast is too. If he wasn't; he wouldn't be shadowing her," said Jenson.

"He's right. Now it's your turn. Who's this new girl you're hanging with, what happened to Carol?"

"Oh, Tasha's cool. Carol and I, still go skate now and again."

My dad glanced into the entry way of the kitchen. "Did you order the pizza yet?"

"Yes, two large's. One BBQ veggie and a supreme. I figured we should try something new," I replied.

"Sounds good." He ambled over to the table, pulled out a chair, and sat down.

"We have to pick it up in... five minutes," Jenson said.

"Okay, not a big deal. Ah, Starla is Molly still looking for a place?" he asked.

"Not sure, why?"

"I'm looking for someone to take over the apartment. I was going to put out flyers. In fact, Ranger Mike said he'd help. We got sidetracked therefore it never happened. I thought if Molly still wanted to move out it would be a great location for her. It's near the college."

"I'll let her know tomorrow. She's going to help me with the project for Jones. Funny, he wasn't at the meeting," I added.

"Starla, he's undercover. He'll be at the trial." My dad patted his pocket, then shoved his chair backward. "I'll go get the pizza." He stood up, grabbing his coat from behind the chair, and walked Fonzi style to the back door.

I rolled my eyes at him. Jenson slapped the table once. My sister glanced from us to my father and just shook her head. We watched him depart.

"That's dad, for ya. He's trying to be 'the bomb'," giggled Megan.

"Certainly is," I answered, twisting back to Jenson.

"Do you think Molly will still want to move out?" Jenson asked.

"Maybe. If not, perhaps I could get a place of my own."

"Yeah, like mom would let you do that. We're finally all under one roof again," scoffed Megan.

"You're probably right," I added.

Jenson left after dinner. We'd mostly just devoured our food. Normally, Megan would try to embarrass me in front of him. I sprawled out on my bed surrounded by magazines.

I'd cut out several nature scenes, animals, and foxes. I selected a picture of a pine tree, placing it on the blank paper.

"Starla, get down here. Molly's on the phone! She says it's urgent."

I must have forgotten my cell phone downstairs.

"Mom, I'm coming," I hollered pushing aside my art. I rushed out of my room trying not to trip on the stairs. My dad was heading out of the kitchen when I bumped into him.

"Be careful. Molly isn't going anywhere."

"Sorry dad, so my phone is?"

"On the counter. Don't stay up all night."

"I won't," I replied, hurrying into the kitchen.

My mom leaned against the counter reading notes. She must not have heard me come in. I stood patiently. She glanced up at me and promptly set them down. Then picked up my phone beside her on the counter. "It sounds urgent. I heard your dad. Let me know if you need anything, OK?"

"Sure, Mom," I answered, taking the phone from her. I put it to my ear. "Hey, Moll. Give me a minute. I'm heading to my room. I'm in the kitchen with Mom right now," I stated.

"OK," she stammered.

I walked into the hallway towards our front entrance. Then turned right heading up the stairs to my room. I pushed the door opened, shutting it behind me practically diving onto my bed. "What's going on?" I asked almost out of breath. She wasn't sobbing, but I could tell she was crying. She sniffled. Then blew her nose rather loudly. I pulled the phone away from my ear to put it on speaker, making sure the volume was low enough so only I could hear her.

"Today I overheard my mom and dad fighting. They've been arguing a lot since I came out. I feel partly responsible. I don't know if I can do this. I mean, I don't think I can be straight. Starla, I don't want them to get a divorce because of me," she said.

"If your parents are having problems it's probably more than that. I.. Have you seen your mom and dad hug, kiss, or be affectionate in the last few months, or has it been years?" I asked.

"It's an on and off affair with them. To top it all off Maine and I had our first fight. It's like everything is collapsing around me," she cried.

"Do you want to come over?"

"No, it's ten O'clock. My mom would never let me."

"What did you and Maine fight about," I asked, pulling at a loose string on my comforter.

Molly let out a sigh. I wondered if she had one of her hands on her forehead. She usually did when she was upset about something.

"I wasn't ready," she whispered.

"Molly, is this about sex? If it is, then you know you need to be clear about boundaries. You've only been dating, for what less than a week?"

"I know, but I really, like her. Most people our age, have already done it. I still plan on....- waiting you know?"

"You mean til you're married?" I asked.

"Maybe, if..."

"If what? No matter what you need to be true to yourself," I said, trying not to scream into the phone. I waited anxiously for her response. Molly remained silent on the other end. I sat for a minute thinking about all the years Molly had talked about waiting till she found the right person. I'd always thought I'd find someone like Jenson. That it wouldn't be a question of if I waited, but if I loved him, then it would happen. "Are you still there?"

"Yeah."

"If Maine cares for you, she'll get over it. Oh, so did you stop her or?"

"I pushed her away. She asked me why I didn't want to. Honestly, I didn't know what to say. My body wanted to, but my head told me no."

"Where were you? She didn't try to break up with you, did she?"

"No, simply that she wanted to show me how much she cares. That this would bring us closer," Molly murmured.

"Be careful Moll. I don't want you getting hurt. It's hard to say if you guys will be together for the long haul."

"I know, It's why I'm scared, giving a part of yourself away. You can never forget it happened. It's a part of you forever, even if that person isn't."

I wanted to hug Molly her words were wise and true. Most of the people I'd known in high school gave themselves away hastily. How many times had I thought about it? Once almost did. Gah, George. So glad that didn't happen.

"Are you OK?" asked Molly.

"Yeah, I was just pondering about the past. Nothing had happened. Good thing too," I answered.

"L.A. George?"

"Yeah, that was a total foul," I admitted.

"Molly, you need to get off the phone!" Mrs. Fretner yelled.

"Sorry I should go, it's getting late," Molly said.

"Ok, I'll see ya tomorrow, then. We'll meet at the college Cafe after I get out of work.

"Sounds good, Bye, and thanks."

"Bye," I answered, hanging up the phone.

Crap! I was supposed to tell Molly about the apartment. Oh well, she has a lot on her mind. I hopped off of the bed and stretched out my arms. Reaching into my pocket, I pulled out the tarot cards. Curious, I opened up the deck thumbing through them. The first cards to appear as I turned them over were: The Star,

Empress, and death. I shivered, turning around. Then pulled open the drawer of my nightstand dropping them inside.

Chapter 40

(Dan)

I shifted back and forth on the couch attempting to follow the game, but couldn't concentrate. Jones hadn't contacted me yet about the trial. I looked up at the clock on the wall. It was getting late. Starla had recently bumped into me in the hall. I'd heard her race back upstairs. She'd taken her phone from Tri. Hopefully, everything was all right with Molly.

I decided to stand up to stretch my legs. Then picked the remote up off the table and turned off the T.V. Why bother? If I couldn't focus, on the game. I'd find out if Illinois won against Ohio later.

"Hey, are you done watching television already?" asked Tri, peeking into the living room.

I sighed and ambled over to her. "I can't focus on it. My minds on the trial. I can't believe Jones hasn't contacted me. I'd call him, but I bet he's either fast asleep in bed or working on an assignment for his class."

"Well, does that mean we get our alone time?" she asked.

I took a deep breath in and exhaled, "I should call him. I won't sleep a wink tonight, if I don't," I answered.

"You're right. You won't. I'm going to do some light reading. When you're ready, I'll be waiting."

I chuckled, "Do you know where I left my phone?"

"It's beside the television controller, silly man," she replied, ruffling my hair. I watched her spin out of the room like a teenager. Afterward, I grabbed the phone off of the table. Adjusting myself back onto the couch, I dialed his number. It rang, a few times, then someone picked up.

"What? Who's calling me? What time is it?" Jones stammered.

"Hey, it's Dan. Sorry if I woke you up. I hadn't heard from you regarding the trial. Ranger Mike, said you'd been keeping an eye on the bandits. We only have one day, til you have to be in our court. Why weren't you at the meeting?"

"Cavin told me, my cross-examination would be brief. I'll be direct and to the point. Lance will step in if needed. Is Starla there? I hope she's been preparing for her assignment," he said changing the subject.

"There's no reason to worry. You'll see Starla in class tomorrow. She has it in her head you're psychic when it comes to knowing what's happening with the clan."

Jones chuckled, "I am pretty receptive. I wouldn't say I'm psychic. What's up?"

"Since Starla began her training a black wolf has been appearing to her. Mike mentioned an adult Snowshoeing class was startled by one. They observed it running in the forest."

"Ah, I guess she wants to write a report on the Windigo Myth, concerning the black beast," Jones added.

"It's a possibility. She hasn't said anything to me. Jenson's eager to find out what it wants. I advised him not to go snooping around searching for the scientists."

"Let me guess. The black wolf told you not to?" he asked.

"Right. I'm trying to believe this spirit is trustworthy. It's only protected Starla, so far. That's what it's claiming."

"Cavin, is he concerned?" asked Jones.

"He's leery, but not off the wall," I answered.

"I'm free after class, do you want to meet, then?"

"Ah, around four?"

"Sure, that's when I let them loose!" he exclaimed.

I laughed, "OK, then. I'll catch you tomorrow."

"Tomorrow," he responded and hung up.

I pushed myself up off the couch and strolled out of the living room. What was Tri planning? One minute she was warding me off and the next pulling me into her arms. It wasn't unusual. Human nature I guess. I peeked my head into our bedroom. She was lying on the bed with a coy smile. My wife in her flannel jammies. I leaned against the door frame.

"Well? Come on," she pressed.

I took off my shoes setting them inside of the doorway. Then off came the socks. My eyes lingered on my wife watching me. It shouldn't have felt so strange. Earlier I'd been ready for this. I was the guy after all. I coughed to clear my throat.

"Are you getting shy all of a sudden?" she asked, bringing her knees up to her chest. She wrapped her arms around them, then looked up at me.

Those eyes. The ones I fell for.

I joined her in bed, and we pulled the covers over us.

Chapter 41

(Thursday, April 1st)

(Starla)

Disaster! That's what Denny's had been this morning. First, I clocked in late for work. Then Marla had called off, and the new guy never showed. Thank goodness I'd remembered my change of clothes. I hated my Denny's uniform with a passion. Leaning against the building, I waited for Jenson to pick me up. He'd called at the crack of dawn to ask if I needed a ride. I suppose I should have been more appreciative. I looked around hoping he'd be here soon shielding my eyes from the shining sun. I tried to see a crossed the street.

"Hey, do you need a lift?"

"What, uh." It sounded like Maine. I turned around to the diner entrance. Maine held the door half opened.

"Jenson's picking me up? Don't you have class today?"

"Yeah," she answered shutting the diner door behind her. She drew her coat around her for warmth.

"Do you always come here to eat breakfast?"

"Molly was going to meet me. She didn't show," answered Maine.

I looked away from her at the oncoming traffic from the street. Should I bring up what Molly had discussed with me? Was it my business to defend my friend? I felt like I should say something.

"Um, ah, yeah, she called me, last night. Maine, she seemed awfully upset. I don't know how you deal with things where you're from, but Molly is a pretty conservative girl."

"She told you!"

223

"She's my best friend. I've known her for several years now. You've been dating for, what? A week, a month! Of course, she's going to talk to me," I responded, throwing up my hands. I pushed my backpack up higher on my shoulder.

Maine glared at me then turned her eyes to the ground. She kicked at the cement beneath the snow.

"What did you do?"

"You said she told you," replied Maine, shrugging.

"Yes, but how did you leave it? Did she storm out, after? Did you talk to her about it? Did she tell you how she feels emotionally?" I demanded.

"What are you my new psychologist?" she spat.

"No, I'm Molly's friend. I was hoping to be your's too." I turned away Jenson was just pulling in. I twisted back to Maine. "You need to work things out with her. Don't push her. She's been through, a lot. You were there when her dad and Mom were arguing. Has she told you what's going on with her folks?"

Maine took a deep breath, ignoring the question. Then left walking towards the diner. She pulled the door opened, but before entering glanced back. "He's waiting for you," she said, pointing to Jenson's car.

"I know. Are you going to be at the Cafe? What should I tell Molly?"

"I'll call her. I should meet with her alone. I'm not sure it's a good idea for me to see her right now."

"Better sooner than later, she could crawl back into her shell." I wasn't joking either. How long had it taken for her to admit the truth to herself? Maine nodded at me. I turned back and hurried to Jenson's car. I opened the passenger's door, then got in.

"What was that about?" he asked.

I rubbed my hands on my jeans. Then put on my seat belt. Leaning over I hugged him.

"What's that for?"

"Because, you get me," I said, then pulled away. I sat up straight.

"You're not going to tell me what's going on?"

"Maine and Molly are having troubles. It's mostly Maine's issue," I said.

"Girl on girl problems," joked Jenson.

"Don't, just drive, okay?"

"Sorry, didn't mean to hit a nerve."

"I love Molly. You know that. She's my sister."

"Not biological," he argued, pulling out of the parking lot.

"No, but we're tight, it took her a long time to come out. Now Maine's pressuring her to have sex outside of marriage. Religion is important to her, Jenson! It's the one thing she's held on to for so long. Then finally accepting herself, loving herself even though the church might shun her?" Tears formed in my eyes. "Yeah, I'm emotional. I don't want to see her go back into her shell. I want her to be happy. Maine needs to get her shiznit together."

"She sure does, or you'll go all Buffy on her won't you?"

"You can bet your bottom dollar on that!" I answered.

I stood outside the Cafe wrapping my arms around Jenson's waist. I pulled him close to me.

"I know you're concerned with Molly. What I want to know is how you're doing?" he asked, pushing a stray piece of hair behind my ear. His hand rested on my shoulder.

"Things are a bit confusing. Cal and I are developing the knack for linking. I 'm worried. It could be more than that," I said, leaning into him.

"How so? Like Molly and Maine?"

I shrugged, not wanting to answer him. I'd never thought of Cal that way. Not even during our sessions, I was just freaked. Why? That was the question I wish I knew. "I don't know. I haven't had any of those thoughts if that's what you mean," I answered.

He touched his forehead to mine. Reaching out my hand, I stroked his cheek. Then tugged him closer until there was no space between us. Gently I kissed his top lip, then the bottom one.

"Ah hem," said Molly.

Jenson and I untangled ourselves from one another.

"Eh, hey. I thought maybe you were already in the Cafe waiting for us," I said, fixing my backpack on my shoulder.

"No, I'm right here! We should get coffee before class starts."

"Yeah, you're right." I needed my caffeine fix. It was going to be a long day.

Molly looked at Jenson, "Can I borrow her for a bit? You don't mind ordering us our drinks do you?" she asked, handing him a ten dollar bill.

"I guess. I'll meet you girls wherever you sit."

"Sure. That works," said Molly grabbing my hand. She guided me over to a table near the window, pulling out two chairs.

"Thanks," I said, sitting down. "There's something I need to tell you. I forgot last night. My dad mentioned, there's an apartment for rent near here. Are you still considering moving out?"

"I'm not sure yet. Um, did you see Maine today? I was supposed to meet her at Denny's. Then mom and dad got into this screaming match. I was right there in the middle of it. I don't want to take anyone side on these issues. It worries me. One of them had to do with money. Before, it was all about me. My mom doesn't spend a lot. He insists she has a problem."

"He sounds controlling," I remarked.

"A smidgen, yes," she admitted.

I glanced over at Jenson, who was ordering our drinks and then turned back to focus on Molly. "About Maine. Since I worked today, yeah. I didn't' wait on her or see her come in. She offered to give me a ride home. Then we argued a bit. I was trying to give her advice on how to work things out with you. I don't want to see you recoil into your shell. As far as your mom and dad's troubles, you'll have to let them work out their problems. There's not a lot you can do."

"I'm aware of that," Molly answered.

Jenson shuffled over carrying the drinks in his hands. He set them down beside us on the table. Molly took hers, sipped the hot liquid and then pushed it aside.

"Thanks," I stated, grabbing my drink.

"Did I get it right?" he asked us.

"Yeah, thank you," I managed.

"Thanks, Jenson," said Molly.

"I'll leave you girls to chat. Um, see you in class?"

I nodded, he planted a kiss on my head.

"Catch ya later." He waved as he left the cafe.

Molly turned back to me. She held herself as if she were cold. "Um, so. How did she react to you?"

"She wanted to speak to you alone. She didn't think it was a good idea if she showed up here. I may have upset her. I promise I was only looking out for you."

Molly pulled her hair back. Then tied it with her elastic band. "What kind of looking out are we discussing?"

"I asked her if you'd talked about what happened. She didn't seem to approve of that. Then I tried to explain that I care about both of you."

"Thanks, so was that it?" she pressed.

"Pretty much, Jenson had just pulled up into the parking lot. She notified me of that."

Molly shivered, "It's drafty in here today. Don't you think?" She took another sip of her drink, setting it down on the table. I tried to read the expression on her face. She slouched in her chair which wasn't usual. Mrs. Fretner complained that all of us should maintain good posture or we'd be hunched over in our old age.

"Nah, I hope you're not coming down with a cold. Do you want anything to eat before class?" I asked.

"I'm all right. Why are you going to eat?"

"I thought about it. I left the diner without grabbing something." I pushed my chair back, glancing in the direction of the line. Then looked back at Molly. "Um, are you going to be OK?"

"You mean if you leave me here?" she asked.

"No, this whole Maine thing. If you need to vent, hang out, or anything. I'm right here."

"I know. If I need anything, I'll let you know. Now go, get something to eat. I can hear your stomach growling from here."

"Okay, you sure you don't want a chocolate chip cookie?"

"Sure, then we'll walk to class. I'll eat it on the way."

"Okay," I said. Then stood up, pushing my chair aside. The line wasn't too long at least.

Molly opened the door to the classroom. "Everyone decided to show up today. Good thing since we're going to the library."

"We are?"

"You didn't look at the syllabus did you?"

"No," I answered.

"Yeah. Well, I did." Molly scanned the front of the room. "We'll have to sit behind Owl and Jenson. I guess they decided it would be their turn to sit in the front row."

I followed Molly to the desk behind them. She chose a seat behind Owl. I sat behind Jenson. Why bother, taking out my work if we were going to the library. Jenson turned around to face me.

"Hey, did you girls get everything worked out?" he asked.

"We're good," Molly said.

"What's up Owl?" I asked.

He shrugged and turned back facing the dry erase board.

"He's a bit upset. Melina blew him off last night. They were supposed to go out for drinks," replied Jenson.

"Yeah. I'm pretty humiliated. Rub it in, why don't ya," said Owl turning back to us.

"At least you aren't dealing with peer pressure," I answered.

"What, Jenson? Are you?" asked Owl.

"No, not us," he replied.

"It's me, and Maine, OK? I don't want to talk about this. It's private," sputtered Molly blinking back tears. She gave Jenson an evil stare. The guys turned back to the front of the room as the door opened. Jones, strolled into the classroom.

"Why aren't you in the library? Did you not understand the syllabus?" he asked, glowering at the classroom full of students. "Well, grab your things. We're going to explore your options for the assignment. First, find out what you'll write about for your composition. Remember, it needs to focus on one Myth. I'd prefer, one you can relate to on either a personal level or imaginative. Has anyone given any thought to this?" he demanded.

I immediately raised my hand.

"Yes, Starla."

"Black-wolves," I replied.

"You'll have to find a myth about them. It needs to be more specific, than the animal itself."

"A spirit wolf from a tribe?"

"That might work. Does anyone else want to share?"

Molly put up her hand. Jones called on her.

"I'd like to do a paper on healers of the Winnebago Tribe. You know those that cared for the sick. I'd plunge into their beliefs and how they affected the process. How they endured, their viewpoint on healing medicines, and if the spirits had anything to do with reviving those injured."

"Good idea. Now, off with you. I expect you to have notes and the beginning of a paper by the next class. Remember freshman, this is college, not high school!"

"That's it!" exclaimed a girl in the back row.

"It is, I have to prepare for an important meeting. If you have any other questions, you know when my office hours are. Don't use this time to fool around. You don't want your G.P.A., taking a dive," he advised us.

Jenson and Owl marched ahead of us to the library.

"They're getting awfully chummy," Molly commented, walking beside me.

"Oh, they've been planning a tribe Bizare of some sort, as well as a pow-wow. I'm not too worried. They'll get tired of each other."

"Do you suppose Maine wanted to because she loves me?" asked Molly out of the blue.

"It's too soon for that. If it isn't, then she falls fast. Jenson and I haven't even said I love you yet," I added.

"True. You're probably right. Hormones. The ones our mothers warn us about," she scoffed.

"Yeah, most likely. I've thought about it. Ya know, with Jenson," I said, trying not to blush.

Molly pushed me playfully as we turned the corner. The library was just up ahead.

"Haven't you?" I asked, noticing my right shoelace had come untied.

Molly stared at the basketball trophy's in the case as we neared the library. "Maybe once or twice," she admitted.

I stopped at the library entrance to tie my shoe. Once finished, I stood back up. "Come on, really?"

"Seriously," she answered.

Jenson grabbed the library door and held it open for us to enter while Owl waited inside the entrance.

"Come on ladies. We've got studying to do!" Jenson blurted.

Molly laughed, "I'm excited, but not overjoyed."

"Would you rather be, at the trial? It's tomorrow. We have to be there by 10 a.m.," I added.

"That early?" asked Owl. The doors closed behind us.

"Alas, yes. I'm not working this weekend so, that isn't an issue. Didn't Rascal tell you about the meeting?"

"He's been somewhat preoccupied. I saw him the other day, but he didn't mention it, weird."

I shook my head in astonishment wandering over to our usual table. Jenson pulled out a chair for me. I sat down beside him. Molly sat a crossed from me.

"You're coming, aren't you?" asked Jenson.

"I'll be there. Now, where do we begin our research? Should we, use google or check out the books?" Owl pondered.

"Books impress Jones. He's old school. You of all people should know that," I offered.

Jenson took his laptop out of his backpack for me. Then set it on the table. "It's faster and easier. Who wants to go first?"

I pulled his computer towards me while I turned it on. Why not? I might as well try to find something that resembled a myth on black wolves. Molly and Owl got up sauntering into the stacks.

"You got this?" Jenson asked me.

"Yeah, go ahead, I'll find you. If I need to."

He nodded, then drifted off to do his research.

I typed in Wolf spirits, the Winnebago tribe. A list of several sites popped up before me. The first two were not helpful. One contained information on a wolf sanctuary. The second a short Myth. None of them even mentioned a black wolf. I sighed to myself, then looked up. Molly was heading to the table with an armful of books.

"Did you find anything yet?" she asked, placing them on the table.

"Not yet," I answered, bringing my attention back to the computer screen. I struggled to pick out pieces that would merge with my understanding of what I'd been experiencing. Well, the third one is a charm, I thought then clicked on it. Wolf and dog spirits, this had to be it! An article or Myth about four wolf brothers. One of them a black wolf who controlled the night. Maybe this was something useful. Hadn't I mainly encountered it at night? It discussed foxes and wolves being, linked.

"I need to print a copy of this. Do I need to hook the computer up to something?"

Molly turned the computer so it faced her. "I'll set it up for you. Then order the print. You have the change right?"

"Change like Nelson Mandela or the sort you buy things with?" I taunted.

She shook her head slightly. "Your humor is leaning towards nerd."

"Yum, I should get some of those."

Jenson came up behind me putting his books on the table. I glanced back. Owl was still searching through the stacks.

"You better watch out. I sense your girlfriend is becoming a cannibal," announced Molly.

Jenson placed a hand on my shoulder. Then pulled out a chair sitting down beside me. "No way. What did you say to her?"

"That I wanted to eat a nerd, especially the grape ones," I responded.

He smiled at me also cocking his head to the side. "She's talking about the candy."

"Ah, the strawberry ones are my favorite," Molly commented.

Jenson opened one of his books leafing through it. I pushed a notebook over to him.

"I'll just Xerox it. It's faster and easier than writing it down."

"Yeah, but you'll remember it better if you've written it."

"She's right. I learned that from one of my high school instructors," Molly replied.

"I'm going to get my information. What printer is it?"

"Number Four, it's just over there," Molly pointed.

"Thanks," I said, standing up. Then headed to where the printers are. I pushed my untamed hair behind my ears. You'd have thought I'd be familiar with this library by now. How many times had I been here? I shook it off. One day til the trial. Would the black wolf materialize again? Was there a way to free him from whoever held him prisoner? He must be under a spell. It seemed the only plausible explanation. I stopped at the printer and retrieved the article

"What did you find?" Owl whispered.

"This article, I'm trying to understand it," I answered, handing it to him.

"Oh, this is an Origin Myth. This one focuses on the gray wolf. The black wolf is only a part of it," he said, looking up from the paper. "Are you trying to incorporate information regarding the wolf you've been seeing?"

"Yeah, maybe it's crazy," I replied, taking back the papers. We started walking back to the table in a zig zag pattern avoiding other students.

"You'll solve this puzzle. Maybe, write on the subject analytically? If things, weren't hidden from this world, I'd say incorporate it into the bandits. How the scientist found a way to mutate them. Perhaps it was from an Indian legend that they got their idea. Stranger things have happened," he said, stopping at our destination.

"You know Jones will expect more than one measly article. I don't want to change my theme. There isn't a lot of time left," I whined.

"It's only a legend. There are a lot of them," Owl acknowledged.

"I'm swimming in deep Jello," I admitted.

"This may have nothing to do with the black wolf following you," whispered Molly.

"True, but it's possible. There's no way I can do a report on the wolf tied to me." I put the article in my notebook.

"You're not even going to look at it?" asked Jenson.

"What good will it do? I can't apply it. At least not for this paper. I thought, it being, an Indian legend, there would be more information on the wolf of the night." I grumbled leaning back into the hard plastic chair. Jenson placed his arm around me. I rested my head on his shoulder. Too bad I couldn't go to sleep and forget about this.

"You could compose an essay on the meaning of wolves in the Native American culture. It would be extensive. Then include the Winnebago's in it," suggested Molly.

Owl slammed his fist on the table. "I got it! What about tribes that branched off of the Winnebago tribe? What about their beliefs or thoughts about wolves. Narrow it down, pick three and write about how they differ from each other. It might work."

I lifted my head up from Jenson's shoulder to see Maine. She'd been rifling through some books near us. She finished what she was doing and came over to where we sat.

"Did you know wolves, are sometimes associated with witchcraft in Northern Europe and some Native American cultures?"

"Um, aren't you angry with me," Molly interrupted her.

"Well, I"m trying to help Starla. I overheard the group, making suggestions for this paper. I was only here to borrow some art books." She held them up for us to see. "I found three that will work. My art teacher won't let me off the hook. I'll leave if you want," she offered and turned to leave.

"No, wait. We need to talk, not here, though," said Molly. She got up gathering her things. "If you have the time?"

"Um, what about dinner? We can meet at The Sunshine Cafe at say... six O'clock?" asked Maine.

"Ah, OoK..." Molly stammered.

"There will be other people there. It's only to talk, I promise," Maine reassured her.

Molly bit her bottom lip. Then nodded at Maine.

"OK, I'll see you tonight then."

"This evening," answered Molly turning back to us.

I took my hand resting on the table and set it on top of Molly's. "Call for backup if you need me. I'm not sure, what I'm doing tonight. No plans I presume. I'll probably stress over homework."

"Same goes for me," answered Jenson.

"Owl? Any exciting plans? You don't suppose Melina will call to apologize?" I asked.

"Not sure. I've got this thing to do for my parents. Du-Vance is gone so I've been wondering if perhaps, I should be the one to step in as the next Ranger. I haven't discussed it with Mike."

"What about your folks? They set you up with the tribe. They've always been supportive of you. Since the day we met you haven't discussed them much with us," I remarked.

"I'm barely home, between college and the tribe. I'm there to sleep and eat. I've cooked a few times for mom. She loves that!" He grinned. Then began to pack up his bag.

Jenson tapped my arm. "You ready to go?"

"Are you offering me a ride?" I asked, putting my books in my bag.

"Of course. I brought you here, didn't I? Are you OK?"

"Yes, just worn out I suppose."

"Come on, I'll take you home."

"Molly?" I asked.

"Mom's picking me up. We're going to get smoothies. There's a great deal to discuss."

"Are you going to tell her?"

"Oh, about Maine and I. She already knows."

"Okay," I answered, forcing myself not to make a snarky Starla comment. It seemed that Molly and her mom had gotten closer since she'd come out.

"I'll see you tomorrow? Jenson and I will pick you up at your house at nine-thirty. Will that work?"

"Sure, I told my mom I'd be out with you all day. We're good," she replied.

"Molly, if you need anything..."

"Okay, thanks," she answered.

Chapter 42

(Dan)

Earlier that morning.

I pushed the covers off of my feet to the end of the bed. My wife had stolen most of them in the night. I'd forgotten how cold, she claimed to get. I sat up placing my hand on her arm. "Wake up, what time do you have to be to work today?" I muttered.

She pulled me into her arms and kissed me aggressively on the mouth. I lingered in her embrace for a few moments. Then turned away to look at the clock, 7:48 a.m.

"Hey, we have a few more minutes," she grumbled gently taking my face in her hands. She brushed her fingertips over my cheeks. A smile spread a crossed my lips.

"I'm tempted to stay here all day. You could call into work," I teased. Then tickled her. She busted out with a loud snorty-laugh before pushing my hands away.

"Stop, come on now! You know I hate being tickled," she snickered. "Plus, you'd never call into work yourself. Hasn't anyone other than the clan contacted you for their services?" she asked between giggles. "What about the police office?"

I stopped tickling her allowing my hands to rest at her sides. "I'm scheduled to go there, Monday. I'll be reviewing several cold cases. Nothing exciting. I'm supposed to make sure the evidence is in order, should they choose to reopen any of the investigations. They haven't had a lot of anything since Du-Vance's death. That was all cleared up according to them," I replied, sitting up.

Tri scooted up beside me resting her hand on my shoulder. "I should make breakfast. Eggs and bacon or Oatmeal raisin muffins?"

"Either one," I shrugged, swinging my legs over the bed.

Tri got up. She grabbed her robe off of the back of the bedroom door. "If Megan isn't up yet, I'll wake her. Starla's either left already or eating cereal."

"You don't know what time your own, daughter works?"

"I do, it's usually eight or nine in the morning. Those are the shorter shifts. Don worked it out that way due to Jone's class."

I nodded as she put on her bathrobe. Then stood up and stretched. "I'm going to take a shower. I'm meeting Jones at four. Rascal showed up momentarily to the meeting last night. I didn't get a chance to speak with him. Care if I do that today?"

"Knock yourself out! I'll be re-shelving books our interns are leaving early for spring break. They won't be back until the 15th."

"Fun, fun!"

"Not really, but I'll survive," she admitted shutting the door behind her.

I wiped the fog off of the bathroom mirror. Old, but still not too shabby for my age, I reflected. Touching my face I realized, I needed a shave. Tri hadn't commented on it this morning. One of her pet peeves. I chuckled to myself. Soon Jenson and Starla would either want to move in together or get married.

If, it was meant to be. He seemed right for her, but it was too soon to tell. I reached for my razor when the door opened.

"I got a call from work. There's some sort, of inventory emergency. Help yourself to food. In fact, take some to Rascal. He'd probably appreciate it," Tri said.

"Sure," I answered, picking up the can of foaming gel.

"Ah, I was going to mention that to you."

"Shaving?"

"Yes."

I leaned over the sink and quickly kissed her. "Be safe out there. I'll see you later tonight. We should have dinner this evening all of us. Man, before this trial. We need a family dinner."

"OK, call Starla, Megan will be home after school. If you can pick her up, that would be great! If not call her, she'll take the bus," Tri answered.

"I thought you were against cell phones?"

Tri shuffled to the door. "I am, but I have to keep in touch with them. Don't worry. I got this!" she exclaimed, and shut the door.

She was right. She'd been mothering them for years while I'd been in and out of their lives. That is until now. I finished shaving. Then washed out the sink with the hand towel, replaced it and tossed the used one in the hamper. I went to the kitchen and put the muffins in a basket. That should keep them warm on the way to Rascals. What would we discuss? When I saw him at the meeting, he'd acted like the whole trial was a joke. A fiasco! It made me think he thought the case was useless. Du-Vance was his son. Didn't he want justice?

I had managed to put the basket of muffins over my arm. That way I could carry the gallon of orange juice in my hand, leaving my right hand free. I shut the car door, making my way up the porch steps. Then stopped to knock on the door. It wasn't long before I heard him inside. He rambled toward the door. Then peered out of the small square window.

"Give me a minute I need to grab my robe!" he hollered.

The orange juice grew heavy on my arm, to elevate it, I placed the muffin basket in my right hand. Then carefully maneuvered it into my left. By that time Rascal had opened the door.

"What have you got there?"

"Tri told me to bring over some breakfast. She thought you might appreciate it," I answered.

"Ah, well come in. It's still a bit chilly. Only a few more weeks til this cold blast disappears. Let's go into the kitchen. Do you want to hang your coat up?"

"Nah, I'll leave it on," I replied.

"That's fine. It does get awfully drafty sometimes. Old house, but you know, that already."

"I sure do," I answered trailing him. He turned towards me and held out his hand for the orange juice.

"Thanks. I'll put the muffins on the table," I said taking a seat.

Rascal nodded to me. Then moseyed over to the counter placing the orange juice container on it. He brought out two cups, then poured us juice. He came over and set them down. Then chose a place beside me. "I suppose you've stopped by to see if I'll be at the trial tomorrow."

"I did. The appearance you made the other night was brief. Didn't you believe it was important to be there?"

"Ah, Cavin can handle it. I often enjoy being a background observer. That way he asks me fewer questions. I was grilled enough by the sergeants during the investigation."

"True enough," I said, taking a muffin out of the basket, I pushed it over to him.

"Blueberry! Your wife is amazing. Not sure how she knew these are my favorite." He began unwrapping it. Then took a large bite.

I grinned, "Yeah. Things are working out well."

"Really?" He chided me, his mouth still half full of food.

"Yeah, how about you and Nuria since you're changing the subject?" Rascal finished chewing and then answered me.

"She's been busy helping Cal. Also, poor Minder."

"What's going on with her?" I asked. Then bit into my muffin. Wow, these are better than I remember. I chewed slowly and swallowed. Then took a drink of my juice.

Rascal smiled, "See I told you they were awesome. Now, Minder, she's just frazzled about the bandits. She hasn't gone near the containment area since Sika injured her."

"I can't say I blame her. I assume Cavin's bringing them in for questioning in cuffs. It doesn't seem safe to leave them able to fight."

"Obviously, he's in no mood for mischief as you've discovered. I'll definitely, be there. I don't plan on testifying. I wasn't there when..." Rascal paused, then looked at me. "Bad enough that I thought I had lost Nuria forever."

"I can relate to that, a bit. It's not entirely the same, though," I replied.

"You got that right. At least you knew where your wife was."

"Definitely," I acknowledge, grabbing another muffin.

"If all you came for was to see about me going. I have some things to tend to."

"Do you need any help while I'm here?" I volunteered.

"No, just tell Tri thanks for the muffins. She can have you drop em off anytime. I'd sure enjoy a visit from Starla and Molly too! It's been a while. I guess the next time I see em will be in court. Gah, poor girls. Cavin though always has to be fair."

"He sure does," I said, standing up from my seat. I pushed it in grabbing one more muffin for the road.

"You can take em home if you want," offered Rascal.

"No, you finish them. Tri would want you to. She can bake them for me whenever. I'll try not to be a stranger."

"Certainly, as long as you bring me goodies, I'm teasing," he jested.

"I'll let myself out then. I have to meet Jones at four today."

"Ah, well tell him hello for me. Make sure to thank Tri," he reminded me again.

I assured him I would, then left with an urgency to set things in motion for the hearing.

Chapter 43

(Starla, Thursday evening.)

Jenson stopped the car near the steps to our apartment door. "Are you sure, you're going to be OK?"

"I'm drained you get it right? Going from Denny's to talking to Molly about her dilemma, our assignment for Jones, and the trial. Maybe I should go in and lay down for a while," I said, unclipping my safety belt. After I was free, I leaned over to him and pulled him into a hug. Then gently gave him a kiss, leaving a smile on his lips.

"Call me tomorrow?"

He nodded to me, then pulled away. I reached for the car door, pushing it open.

"See ya," I said, shutting it behind me. I turned back for a second and waved goodbye.

Standing on the sidewalk, I bit my lip agitated at the thought of Jone's paper. Then strolled towards our entrance. I'd have to make due with what I had. There must be a way to be analytical about it without revealing the clan to the human world. I dug into my pocket for my keys. Odd, I swear they were there. Well, maybe someone will be home. I peered in the window. My keys sat on the side table where I'd forgotten them. Darn! I lifted my hand now in a fist and knocked several times. Fritz started barking wildly. He advanced to the door and jumped up on it with a huge smile on his face. My sister came bouncing down the stairs. Then opened the door. Fritz sniffed me and ran into the kitchen.

"Thanks! Ah, not sure how I forgot my keys this morning," I said.

Megan rolled her eyes at me. Afterward, she stepped aside to let me into the hall. I set down my knapsack. Then took a deep breath.

"Is mom cooking spaghetti? It's only five O'clock."

"Dad's at a meeting with Jones or was it, Cavin? He left the house about four fifteen. Mom's been pacing about ever since. Do you want to watch the news? It's that or PBS. So lame," she commented.

"I'm sure we'll find something. Anything new going on?" I asked. We passed the kitchen turning to the living room on the right. I flopped down on the couch, grabbed the controller and handed it to her as she sat down beside me.

"Hey, check the weather," hollered Tri.

Megan groaned switching on the television. She tuned into channel nine. Then took her shoes off throwing them beside the couch. She lifted her feet up sprawling out.

"Do you have to do that? You're invading my space," I complained.

"I have to relax. I'm hyped up, and not fond of mom hearing. You don't want her getting her hopes up for me or upset that she has to deal with another one of us having a boyfriend," Megan remarked sarcastically.

"So, tell me!"

"Chaz and that chic hit rock bottom. They were holding a shouting match in the hallway after bio. Mrs. Kurt came out of her classroom to find out what the trouble was. She told them they'd better get to class."

"Did you see anything else?"

"Nah," she shrugged, then leaned back into the pillows near the armrest.

"It certainly does sound promising," I added, turning back to the television.

"You're really, going to watch this?"

"Shhh, we might be getting rain! I'm so over snow," I commented.

"Well, I liked going ice skating the other week. After all, the chaos, you've been involved in," complained Megan.

I gave her an annoyed look. Then turned back to the television.

"Hey, girls," said my mother as she held onto the door frame and leaned into the room. She glanced at the T.V., then joined us on the sofa.

"We're looking at some warm weather! Can you believe it! Friday we'll see some rain and snow mix. Then Saturday we'll have a high of 35 degrees," said the newscaster. His name was Frank.

I hoped he was right. I'd had enough of Eskimo land. Not that I'd been there. I'd only seen them on PBS. My mom nudged me with her elbow.

"Yeah, what's up?" I asked, leaning my head against her shoulder. I stared at Frank. He was kind of cute but old. Ugh, did I just think that? I shuddered.

"Nayla wants you to meet with Minder for a quick reprise on training in the morning. Cal will be there. I'll get you up around 5 a.m. You need to be there at 8."

"What! When did you talk to her?" I asked, sitting up.

"I went over there, briefly after work today, she wasn't happy. I decided to run over, fox form you know." Mom winked at me.

"Jez, Mom! It's been how long since Nayla let me transform outside of training. You said yourself it wasn't safe with Fern and Earl around," I grumbled.

"At least you two have something in common," whined Megan.

My mom placed her arm around my sister, drawing her near. She pulled away but didn't get up and run to her room like I assumed she would.

245

"What about planting that garden we talked about?" Tri suggested lifting an eyebrow.

"Can we even have a garden here?"

"Yes, I talked to Fern the other day. She said, if you wanted to, she would help us plant some seedlings. She offered to buy some tulips," said Tri.

"I guess it might be fun, not as exciting as solving mysteries," she commented.

"How much do you know about what's going on?" I asked her.

"You're attempting to find out who killed Martin Du-Vance. It's not only that you've shared most of this with me, but Dad left his notebooks on the kitchen table," said Megan.

"You didn't!"

"I read them, so what? It's not like I'm not a part of this. I may not be a fox, superhuman, or hybrid but I am someone!" Megan shouted.

She ran out of the living room. Mom and I listened to her stomped up the stairs. "Dad, left his paperwork out? That isn't like him. When was it?"

"Not sure, if he did, it was picked up in the morning. It probably happened the night he moved in," Tri answered.

"I know you don't want to lose both of us to the clan. Still, we should introduce her after the trial. Then she'll see there's more work to being, a part of this than she knows. Plus, she was talking about that boy she liked today."

"What boy?"

"His name is Chaz mom. Mums, the word. You're not supposed to know. It's not like they're dating," I pressed.

"OK, let's get the table ready for dinner. Your dad should be home any minute now."

Chapter 44

(Dan)

I turned right into Hunter's Park and took the first parking spot available. Afterward, I glanced around to see if anyone was visiting. It appeared deserted. No Jones in sight. Would this meeting be as uneventful as the one with Rascal? It didn't seem as, if anything, could be done before tomorrow. I pulled the keys out of the ignition taking off my safety belt. The clock on the dashboard read, 4:35 pm. I was late! Besides that Tri wanted me home for dinner. I'd better make this meeting, brief. I turned to open the door and saw Kaya. I grabbed the handle and pushed it open, then stood to shut it behind me.

"Hey, I wanted to go out for a stroll. It's been forever since I've been outside of the woods," she said, glancing round. Then smoothed out her long skirt. A white shawl covered her shoulders.

"Aren't you cold," I commented while the door slammed shut.

"Nah, I'm used to the weather. It's pretty quiet today."

"I noticed driving in. Are the prisoner's still in place. Minder OK? Star? Nothing's out of order, is it? I was going to meet Jones," I stated, rambling over to where she stood.

Kaya smiled and patted me on the back. Then placed her hands underneath her shawl. "Let's walk and talk."

"OK," I replied.

We wandered towards the pine trees. She raised her head to indicate Ranger Mike's station to the right of us. "Owl's been considering taking over the park. He told me so today. I ran into him while he was on his way home from class. Jones has them doing a paper for the last project. He was a bit frazzled, said that

Starla's struggling with it. That hopefully the wolf would appear again?"

I shook my head, frowning. "Yeah, not sure on that one. Especially if it is, truly being held magically by someone."

We turned into the pines leading in the direction of the huts. Kaya must be taking me here for a reason. With any luck. Jones wouldn't be ticked, I'd left him hanging.

"Look, the kits are out training. Star's with them," said Kaya. We jogged ahead to see them.

When we'd stopped Kaya stepped back, letting me observe what was happening. The two young foxes appeared to be chasing something near a bush. They crept on all fours towards whatever they were hunting. Perhaps it was too small for me to see. Abruptly they leaped out of the wooded area and pounced! A tail hung out of one of their mouths, and it crunched the creature in its jaws. I immediately turned away.

"It's merely a field mouse," said Star, coming towards us.

"What about the other kit?" I asked.

"Oh, he already caught a mouse. I had to press him to let his sister give it a shot. Did you hear? Sika's been ranting and raving about how he needs to be let out. He's going mad!" exclaimed Star. She threw her paws into the air. Then let them fall to her sides.

Kaya's face began to turn a beet red. Her lips tightened and nostrils flared. "Shhh! Gosh, let the cat out of the bag," she shouted, slamming her fists at her sides in frustration. "I'm taking him to meet with Cavin."

"Sorry," she commented, turning back to the kits. Without a word, Star ran off with them deeper into the woods. We continued walking towards the huts.

"So, Sika is upset about, what?" I asked.

"Not sure, Gavin and the Gladiator have been trying to settle him down. It only upsets him more. They are his cronies so them giving him orders would be irritating. If you think about it."

I stopped a few feet away from the huts ahead of us, rolled my shoulders back, then stretched out my arms to the sky. I brought my hands back to my sides.

"You OK?"

"Yeah. I'm getting old," I answered.

Kaya laughed, slapping me on the back gently. "Come on, Cavin's probably stewing," she said, opening the door to the hut. She closed it behind us. Then motioned with her hand for me to go ahead.

I paused at the dining hall door and placed my hand on the knob. Then twisted the handle pushing it open. I couldn't see a thing! It was pitch black in here! Advancing cautiously, I called out, "Hello?"

I tried to adjust my eyes to the darkness. Evidently, no one was here. Perhaps they were in the reflection room? Where was Jones? If I was correct, it was usually only used by the women for meditation. The men inhabited the gym unless it happened to be a co-ed meditation or workout session. I wasn't on the up and up on everything nevertheless I'd been working with the clan for a time. I knew some things. Wrapped up in my thoughts I turned to leave.

"Ah, ha! You're here!"

"Jones! I was hoping I'd run into you."

"If I remember correctly, you were supposed to be meeting me today," he commented.

"Yes, but Kaya came. She brought me here."

"It's alright. There's a lot, going on. I've been attempting to pinpoint the problems surrounding this entire case. Cavin's caught me up on the details. Now, if we can get Sika to calm down enough for tomorrow's trial."

"He's here? Cavin let him out of his cage!"

"Come on. I'll bring you to the reflection room. Sika's in handcuffs and sedated. He's not going to hurt anyone. I imagine he's beyond that."

"Does this mean there will be no trial?" I asked.

"No, there will be. Oh, I can assure you of that. I don't think the immunity Nayla spoke of will be a possibility. I anticipate there will be a punishment of some type.

"But?"

"It can't be left as is. Afterward, we'll need to sort out this black wolf," he admitted.

"Minder is she with them?"

"Yes, so are Shellena and Lance."

"OK, What about Kaya? I thought she was right behind me? I'm not sure what happened to her," I said, turning back to look. "It's fine. She most likely ran into Nayla. We would've brought Tri and Starla in, but-"

"But?"

"It wouldn't have been a good idea," said Nayla trotting up to me. "Starla is going to have to be awake at the crack of dawn. I can hear her complaining now," she muttered.

Out of nowhere, Kaya ran up to Nayla almost knocking her over. She skidded to a halt a few inches from her nose.

"Nice of you to join us," Nayla commented raising an eyebrow.

"We're on our way to the reflection room," I admitted. Then started walking again.

"I see that, so they aren't in the dining hall now?" asked Kaya, continuing on with us.

"Nah, Cavin didn't want Sika messing it up," answered Jones as we passed pictures of past clan members.

Down the hall, a door creaked open. Lance peeked his head out into the hallway. "You need to get in here! You're going to want to hear what Sika has to say," he said, holding the door open.

We filed in and took our places in the circle with the other members. Shellena and Cavin, nodded to us. Sika was in the middle of the circle seemingly-calm for the description given earlier.

"So," I said, turning to Shellena. "What now?"

Sika let out a low growl, but simply stood there staring at us. It looked like he'd been placed, in a trance.

"I went out to give them their evening meal. Sika was yelling crazy phrases. He wouldn't stop talking about a shadow," said Shellena.

"That's what I told you! It's trying to smash through the force field you placed around our cage. It's been stalking us for two days now," Sika stated in a groggy tone.

Minder broke the circle. She stepped back over to stand near him. "Why did you wait this long to tell us? Weren't you concerned for the clan's safety?"

"I'm more concerned about our well being than yours," he admitted. Then brought his handcuffed hands to his forehead head. He massaged his frontal lobe for a few minutes, and let them fall back down in front of him. He slowly bent his knees and sat down.

"Well?" I demanded.

"I wasn't alarmed, till it began voicing threats. Well, they did," he started ringing his paws. "There's more than one of them. It spooked Gladiator pretty badly. He's one of my best sidekicks," he responded.

"Sika, you've been threatening members of our clan since your capture. Now you expect us to believe you when you cry wolf!" shouted, Shellena. It was more of a statement than a question.

Cavin raised his eyebrow, "she has a point," he added.

"While I agree, we should take precautions. I'll see if I can get the Trinity pack to monitor our parameters this evening," Jones suggested.

"It would certainly take the pressure off of Mike," said Lance. He stepped up to Sika, crouched down, and looked him directly in the eyes. "You'd better not be lying about this! Tomorrow, I'll be ready to step up if needed during the interrogation."

Sika snickered, "Whatever. You're not the one that worries me."

Nayla trotted up to Lance, grabbed one end of his T-shirt with her mouth and tugged till he rejoined the circle.

"What are you doing?" he howled.

"We'll be doing the grilling tomorrow," she stated, standing next to him.

"I can't believe you trust him," Lance grumbled, frowning in Sika's direction.

"I don't, but we have to be cautious."

"Nayla's, right. We can't assume anything at this point. We must keep our guard up," I answered.

"Good call, Dan. Jones, please inform the Trinity pack. Ask them to take turns monitoring our area until the trial."

"Okay, Cavin. Should I meet you back here afterward?" asked Jones.

"It's not necessary, unless Sika has any other information to give us, that is," he said, glaring at him.

"You're not going to make me go back in there! I won't, not tonight!" he yowled.

Cavin shook his head. "You're not staying here. We can't trust you!"

"River Rouge, Kidnapping, and perhaps Du-Vance's death! Do you think we're fools!" he yelled, throwing up his hands.

"Lance please take him back to the cage. Shellena, help him," suggested Kaya.

They marched over to Sika. He struggled a bit as they each grabbed an elbow. He must still be highly sedated still verbally, he put up a fight. Shellena and Lance dragged him towards the door. He made ill attempts to flee, kicking the whole way. I staggered to the exit. Jones followed me. Once there, I held the door open for them.

"You still have the entity contained in that necklace, right?" I asked Cavin, shutting the door as they left.

"Yes, it's stored in our vault. There's no way anyone could have triggered an escape," he replied.

"Okay, well, that's one we can check off the list," I commented glancing down at my watch.

"Is there someplace you need to be?" asked Cavin.

"Dinner with Tri."

"Ah, Then you should go."

I hesitated, "Jones has things handled then. The Trinity is securing the park?"

"It's fine, we have it under control," Nayla responded.

"Have a good night. We'll see you in the morning," Cavin reminded me. He joined Kaya's side, and Nayla trotted up to them. I turned the door knob and let myself out.

Chapter 45

(Starla)

I drained the noodles, poured them back into the pot on the stove and mixed in the tomato basil sauce. Yum, that should be just the right amount, I thought. Afterward, I placed the burner setting, on low. That way it wouldn't boil over. I reached up and grabbed the plates out of the cupboard plopping them down on the counter. Then twisted my body around to find my mom pinching garlic salt onto the bread.

"Can you skedaddle? I need to get this into the stove."

"No, problem," I answered, moving out of the way.

Once she finished, I went back to stirring the spaghetti. I hoped Megan wasn't too angry. Last I had known, she was OK with not taking part in our clan. Then again, she looked up to me. Which meant, she wanted to be like me.

"So, your father should be home any minute. Why don't you check on your sister? I'll finish this up. Then we'll eat."

I wanted to tell her Megan was mad at me. That she wouldn't listen to anything I had to say. Instead, I just nodded and headed out of the kitchen, pausing at the front door. Did I hear knocking? I pulled the door open. Nothing, but the headlights of cars in the parking lot. I shrugged, slamming the door closed and ran upstairs.

"Megan, it's almost time to eat," I shouted leaning against her bedroom door.

"I'll be down in a minute. Leave me alone!"

"Come on, earlier today you were telling me about Chaz. What happened? Why am I the bad Fox all of a sudden?"

I stood there, waiting for a response until she opened the door.

"Might as well come in," she offered.

I shimmied past her sitting myself down on a chair at her desk.

"Would you like to come to a clan meeting?"

She shrugged. "What could I do there? I don't have any magical super powers," she clarified. Then slide across the floor in her stocking feet to her bed. She sat down, slouching.

"Well, I'm sure Kaya could find something. One of the main worries is your keeping it all hush hush. I haven't done too well myself."

"What do you mean?" she asked.

"Maine's on board. She's studying Wicca. She and Molly, are experiencing technical difficulties at the moment. It has me concerned."

Megan sat up straight, her eyes wide-open." And you trust me with this information?"

"Sisters are supposed to share secrets and be able to rely on each other," I admitted.

"I could use it against you," she taunted.

"Yeah, you could, or we could form an alliance. I have a gut feeling that there's going to be another mission. Mom and dad. They aren't going to..."

"Starla, and Megan! Dinner," Mom hollered from downstairs.

I got up from the chair as Megan jumped off the bed.

"We'll continue this conversation another time," I said.

"Sure thing, race ya downstairs?"

I grinned, "why not?"

We sat down at the table ready to eat dinner. I picked up my fork and dug in. Yum! Lots of oregano too! I must have been more famished than I thought. I slowed down a bit to enjoy each savory bite. Megan reached for the Parmesan cheese. She practically covered her spaghetti in it!

"You girls sure made a racket running down those stairs. I don't know what it is about you two, and competition," said my mom looking up from her spaghetti.

I swirled my bread into the sauce. Then took a bite, chewing in silence. Faint footsteps approached the back door. I bolted upright in my chair, and Fritz dashed out of the laundry room. He paused at the back door. A low growl emerged from his throat, which turned into a bark.

I laughed at myself, "It's probably Dad."

The back door swung open. "Hey, girls. Sorry, I'm late. The meeting ran longer than I'd expected. The spaghetti looks good," he said, gesturing towards the table. "I'm starving." Dan took a deep breath, then exhaled. "Um, I have news.".

"Why don't you come sit down? Everything's set up at the dining table. Then you can fill us in," suggested Tri.

He nodded, closing the door, then bent down to pet Fritz. "Has anyone fed him yet?"

"No, I hadn't even thought of it," I answered.

"Poor Fritz," said Megan, pushing her chair back to stand up.

"I'll take care of it, girls," he said. Then, stood, grabbing Fritz's food off of the counter.

He leaned down to his bowl and poured the Dog-Chow into it. "Good boy, did those ladies forget to feed you?"

As I stifled a laugh at the dinner table, Megan elbowed me to shut up. I gave her an angry look. Dad pulled out a chair next to mom. He kissed her cheek and sat down.

"OK, what happened?" she asked.

"Sika has gone from a bully to a coward. It hasn't changed his ability to taunt us, though. Shellena went to take them their evening meal. He was talking crazy. I guess, for a few days, two to be exact. According to him, they're being threatened by shadows."

"Shadows," I said, putting my fork on my plate.

"That's what he says. Jones is having the Trinity watch over the park this evening. They're monitoring it."

"Logical," answered Tri.

"I guess, everyone assumes it's the black wolf," I groaned.

"No, actually it wasn't even brought up. These spirits did not show themselves. If they are spirits," said Dan.

I picked up my fork and began to eat. My head felt funny. Shadows, had I seen them before? How could they be anything but harmless? Perhaps some water would help? My hand wobbled as I grabbed the glass nearly dropping it. Then took a sip of water. Afterward, I carefully set it down. Mom and dad ate for a moment in peace. When they'd finished, I stood to clear the table.

"Starla, I want to show you how to use those cards I gave you this evening," said Tri.

"Okay, I'll just put these in the sink."

"That's fine. Megan, you can join us if you'd like."

"Um, me? You're going to let me into your gang now?" she asked.

"Megan," I scolded filling the sink with water.

"Move over, Starla. I'll finish this up. You gals should go with your mom."

257

I moved, letting my dad take over. He turned on the water before rinsing the plates. Megan got up from her seat at the table ready to make her great escape.

"Let's go. I'll teach you the basics of Tarot," said Tri.

"Mom, I hate to tell you this, but Starla already knows how to use those."

My mom's eyes widened in awe. She turned to me with her hands on her hips, "Starla, is this true?"

"In my defense, I saw it on Buffy," I replied holding up my hands. Then brushed my hair away from my face. "I had em stashed in my locker in L.A. I'm sad to report there still there." I stumbled backward towards the hall stopping in the doorway. My mom lowered her hands to her waist. I grabbed the door frame.

"Megan, you don't know how to use them, do you?" asked Tri.

"No mom, I'm the good one," she replied, joining me at the entrance.

"Come on, I'll race you upstairs," I said pushing my sister. We took off, and mom followed behind us.

Megan pushed open the door with a grin on her face. She'd beat me upstairs. I shook my head as I walked into the room. Then flicked on the light. Mom slipped into the room between us. Nothing was out of place. I stared up at the fox poster then at Buffy. Should I redecorate? No time to consider that. Tarot cards, I told myself.

"Care if I make myself comfortable?" Megan asked.

I raised my eyebrows at her. "Knock yourself out," I answered, shutting the door.

"The cards I gave you hold special meaning. Star gave them to me long ago. Where did you stash them?" Tri asked, sitting down on my bed.

"I'll get them. They're in my nightstand drawer."

"This one?" asked my mom touching the nightstand next to her.

"Yep, that's the one," I answered.

She opened it, pulling out the cards she'd given me. "Are you going to stand there all night? You're not afraid of the cards are you?"

I shuffled over to the bed and stood beside her. "No, not especially. What are you planning to ask the cards? If I remember correctly, the responses are vague."

"Sometimes, but not always. It's been ages since I've done this. I'll be a bit rusty. Why don't we have your sister start? I only want to familiarize her with the process. Then I'll let you ask a question."

"I want to know about Chaz! Oops. Apple bits! I spilled the beans," announced Megan.

"We're not playing that game," I grumbled, sitting down next to my mom.

"Girls, let's be serious! Star and I've successfully used tarot in the past. Megan, if you want to be a part of the clan, it's important."

"I didn't think, it was, what you wanted," Megan stuttered.

"No, but this is, what it's come down to the trial with the bandits, followed by the search for the scientists."

I put my hand on my mom's shoulder, then took the cards from her.

"What are you doing?" she asked.

"A reading for you. The Celtic cross is our best bet," I replied.

"Okay. I'll need to shuffle them first. Also, you'll need this."

She handed me a small booklet. I took it and quickly looked through it.

"What about Chaz?" Megan complained.

"If we have time, we'll find out about him. I don't know why you're so interested in me. Everything is currently surrounding you."

My mom shuffled the cards. Then handed them over to me.

"So, I'm going to lay them out. After that read them to you as they lay."

"Okay, that's good."

"Right, so you were thinking of a question when you shuffled? What was it?" I asked.

"How do I deal with what's to come?"

"Okay," I placed the cards on the bed in the form of the Celtic cross. Then uncovered them while I read each importance.

1. **Seven of cups**: "Mom, this represents your hopes and fears. You might not recognize what your best move is. It's a struggle for you to determine your place in the clan. You're feeling it out."

"Right, go on," she urged.

"**The Magician:** represents a strong positive man, entering your life. It's most likely Dad. He moved back in with us. He'll inspire you even when you face obstacles. Are you worried about him? It says here that this card represents something the inquirer is concerned about," I stated, looking up at her.

"I always worry about your father," she replied. Then reached over me, to reveal the next card.

"**The king of pentacles**. It's reversed."

"This one makes no sense at all. What get rich quick schemes are you interested in mom!"

"Starla it could signify something else. Are you certain that's what it says?" she asked, leaning towards me to view the booklet.

"Of course. It discusses financial situations. It says be leery of get rich quick idea's that are offered to you," I answered.

She pressed her lips together in frustration. "Well, I'll keep that in mind. It may mean being leery of being misled by someone. Let's move forward."

I turned over the next card. "**The Page of Pentacles**, there will be good news. Maybe things will work out. We'll find out who killed Du-Vance. You'll find your place with the clan."

"Perhaps," she responded.

Megan got up, taking out one of my magazines. I could tell she was already bored. Mom grabbed it from her, setting it aside. Megan glowered at her, sighed, and I continued the reading.

The Page of Rods, "Ah, this is me! I'm under 25, fun, spirited, and, enthusiastic. Not sure what it has to do with you, mom." I almost threw down the cards. It seemed pointless. I didn't recall them being this dysfunctional.

"Hey, it could be me!" Megan piped up. "How do you know it's you?"

Mom laughed, " It could be either of you."

I turned over the sixth card. My mom took it from me, "**The Queen of pentacles**, It could represent myself or a friend. So I'm supposed to listen to myself, or him or her?"

"Apparently. Have you talked to Cal's mom lately?"

"Not recently, I'll see her at the trial. I'm sure."

"This is taking forever," Megan groaned, throwing herself on my bed to stare at the fake stars on the ceiling.

"We've got four more to go. Do you want to ask about your past, present, and future with Chaz?"

"For sure," she announced, as I turned over another card. It revealed **The Page of Cups**.

"You're seeking emotional happiness. It could represent a social gathering of family and friends. Hence the trial. We'll all be there, except Megan."

"Exclude me again," she murmured.

"I don't think you want to be near the Bandits. They aren't much fun," I retorted, turning over the next three cards. **The Fool, Reversed-Eight of Rods**, and **Two of Pentacles**.

My mom touched the cards delicately in an inquisitive manner. "I must be careful of those in my inner circle. This is, what the Fool warns me. The Rod tells me to slow down. I need to take my time. The last cards the outcome. Well, it could be. If I choose, to stay with the clan. Which I'm sure, I have. I'll be juggling two lives, jobs pretty much."

My jaw nearly hit the ground. Megan was still staring at the stars on the ceiling.

"Cool, mom! You're with us?" I asked.

She laid her hand on my back, then leaned her chin on my shoulder. First, she looked at me, then at Megan. "Pretty positive. For now, let's keep my decision between us. I hope, I don't change my mind."

"Me too. That was exhausting. It's been months, since I've done a reading. It didn't tell us anything about the wolf or the outcome of the trial."

"It wasn't supposed to. It was guiding me to make the right choice, to select a path." Mom looked at her wrist watch. "It's late. Chaz Tarot will have to wait. I'm sorry Megan."

"I guess it's Okay," she grumbled. "I'm worn out. Sis? You'll eventually show me how to use those?"

"Okay, later. I have to be awake at six in the morning. I guess, we're not going on that foxtrot tonight."

"Who told you I was considering it?" Tri asked.

"No one, just a gut feeling I had," I answered picking up the cards. I put them back in the box, grabbed the book, and shoved them into my nightstand. Megan bounced off the bed. Afterward, heading to the door.

I started to stand, but my mom reached over pulling me into a hug. I squeezed her back. Then she let go of me.

"Night mom."

"Night," she answered following my sister out into the hallway.

Chapter 46

(Dan)

I pulled back the curtains that concealed the outside world and stared out into the night. There wasn't a soul in sight. The parking lot was nearly full. What was our visitor's policy? Oh, why did I care? I drew my hand away from the window. The curtain dropped back into place upon hearing the bedroom door creak open. Tri quietly slipped into the room.

"How did it go? Did Megan learn about Tarot?" I asked.

"Megan wanted to find out about Chaz. He's a boy in her class. Starla though had other plans," she stated, wandering over to our bed. She plopped down and took off her shoes.

"She did, did she?" I asked, joining her. I laid my hand on her shoulder. Then propped myself, up behind her placing my hands on her back. I began to give her a massage.

"Thanks. Yes, our daughter decided I ought to have a tarot reading. It was a pretty good one too. Out there mind you, but well performed. Megan wasn't kidding when she said Starla had used them before. How did she hide it under our noses?"

"Let me remind you how we hid things. Or you hid things for years to protect the girls. Starla's, always been independent. Yeah, she prefers to live at home. In spite of that, you can't take the wild out of the Fox. Clearly, the two of you need bonding time." I began chopping her back lightly with my hands. After minutes had passed. She pushed them aside, turning to face me.

"The cards were spot on tonight. Everything's still here," she said, patting her chest area to indicate her heart. "My confusion with the clan, the strong man in my life who helps me face, and overcome obstacles. You know I love to admit that," she chided, getting up to get her nightgown out of the closet.

"True, did the cards tell you anything you didn't know?"

"That I should be leery of get-rich-quick schemes. Although I think it has more to do with watching out for people misleading me. The fool was in the set," she admitted. Then turned away from me opening the closet door. She reached in and pulled out a long purple shirt. Then shuffled back to the bed. She set down the nightgown and thought better of it.

"What's up?"

"Maybe I should take a shower. It's been a long day."

"Can I join you?" I asked.

"I'd like to be alone, think over everything. Right now I'm mulling over obstacles."

"Tri, what kind of problem are you trying to solve?"

"Whether or not I should swim, or fall back. Starla's last training sessions tomorrow. You should get to bed. Get some sleep. I may wake our daughter for a midnight run. Bonding as you were saying. Not sure yet," she acknowledged, grabbing the nightgown off of the bed.

I stood up, pulling her to me. Then traced her cheek with my fingertip, leaning in to kiss her. It was quick and so, sweet. We parted, and she turned to leave. "Do what you need to, Okay. Just try not to wake me when you come to bed."

"Okay," she said, closing the door behind her.

Chapter 47

(Starla)

About an hour later I woke up. Somebody was banging on my door. Who could it possibly be? If it was mom, wouldn't she just march-in? I threw off my covers sliding off the bed. Cautiously, I inched to the bedroom door.

"Who's there? Mom? Megan is that you?"

Suddenly the door flew open. There in the hallway, a fox stood grinning at me. Startled, I jumped back and hit the floor. It trotted into my room. It wasn't Nayla, could it be? I stood up carefully approaching it.

"Mom? Is that, really you?"

"We're going for a midnight run," she stated.

"Nayla isn't going to be happy." I cast my eyes downward on the floor and started to pace. Mom darted underneath my hand, and I grazed her fur.

"Come on, you constantly say, I'm too rigid. I don't let loose enough. You kept talking about us doing this. Why are you so reluctant?" asked Tri.

"Because, I have to be up in six hours!" Who was I kidding? My mom was opening up to me. Why did I want to shut her out? I walked over and sat back down on the bed.

"Tomorrow, everything could change. Meet me out back? I can leave if you want to transition alone."

I shook my head no. "It's Okay mom. Where exactly are we going? You know Fern and Earl are on the look out," I reminded her.

"Yeah, I didn't think about that," she remarked. I turned to look out the window. Satisfied. She looked back at me. "I'm attempting to be spontaneous. Go me!"

I snickered. Then took my stance to begin my transformation. I was about to close my eyes when a shadow arose inches from my mother. My eyes widened. "Act fast-Mom, run!" I cried.

She sprang in the opposite direction of where she stood, stumbling against me. I tried to push her through the doorway into the hall. Instead, we fell in a heap on the wood floor together. What am I doing? A shadow couldn't harm anyone, could it?

"What's going on?" Megan demanded, standing in the doorway, her hands rested on her hips. "I heard yelling, then a thud. Mom, what are you doing in Fox form?"

"Something was here. A shadow! Sika was telling the truth," she announced, ignoring Megan's question. I brushed against her as I stood up.

"It was right there!" I pointed near the window where it had materialized. Something red lay on the floor, but nothing else.

"What's that?" asked Megan. She took a few steps, then a few more.

"Don't, leave it!" I shouted, grabbing her shirt. I yanked her back near mom and me. "We don't know what it is," I scolded her. Then let go of her nightshirt, allowing her to stand next to me.

"Yeah, but it could be a tracking device," she whispered.

"Leave it, for now," I replied.

Mom nudged me with her nose. "Starla, try to contact Nayla."

"Definitely, should I buzz them using my birthmark or mind speak?"

"Either," she instructed.

I positioned myself on the floor, breathing in, then out bringing my mind into solace. Then built a protective wall around myself hoping nothing could enter. I pushed an immediate buzz out to Nayla. I was going to attempt Shellena when seconds later a loud stomping sound came closer and closer. Abruptly, it stopped. I jolted upright before contact. My dad stood in the doorway.

"Way to go, dad!" I exclaimed, slamming my fist into the floor.

"What?" he asked as he stepped into the room. "Is this what happens when I allow you to run rapid as a fox," he joked.

"No time for jokes. This is serious. I was trying to contact Shellena. I may have reached Nayla. I'm not sure," I answered.

"I thought you were going on a midnight run. What the heck happened?"

"A shadow, maybe Sika's," Megan fretted. She pulled her nightshirt tightly around herself.

"Tri, did you actually, see this shadow?"

I rolled my eyes at my father. Why would we lie to him? It's not as if I had a reason to try to gain his attention.

"Of course, we did!" exclaimed Tri.

Megan pointed to the floor where the unknown object lay. My dad nodded to her. Then cautiously moved towards it. He was almost there.

"Don't touch it! It's evidence," a voice spoke.

Dan stopped.

Where had that voice come from, Nayla? I thought looking around. She emerged in front of him as if she'd come out of nowhere. Was she projecting herself? How did she do that?

"Whatever occurred, we cannot compromise evidence. Was it the black wolf?"

I stepped towards her. "No, it was a shadow. I'm uncertain if it was the same one Sika was ranting about," I added.

"I see. What are you doing in fox form Tri?"

My mom looked around as if she didn't know what to say. She'd been caught red-handed. Nayla didn't wait for her to answer.

"Well, If you still sense you require this midnight run. I'll join you. It's not safe to go alone." Nayla stepped aside and proceeded to examine the object from a distance. She backed up and sat on her hind quarters. "Dan, grab your gloves, and a kit. It appears to be cloth of some kind. Bag it. We'll take it to Cavin."

"But I thought you said you'd go on a run with us?" I interrupted.

"You'll follow us to the park. That should be a long enough jaunt for you to let off some steam. We might as well stay in the reflection room. There are blankets in the closet there. Also, those pillows we use for meditation," Nayla commented.

Megan, who'd been standing in the middle of my room finally spoke up. "If everyone leaves, I'll be alone. Alone! And what if that shadow comes back?" She squeaked. She sounded like a mouse.

"You'll come with us. If that's Okay with Nayla," Tri suggested.

"I don't imagine we have any other choice at this point. Dan, grab your things. Then carefully collect the evidence. I can't touch anything in this form."

My dad nodded to Nayla, slipped out of the room, and we waited for him to return.

"Shouldn't you go back to your body? How is it we can see you?" I inquired.

"It's sort of like a ghost, residual."

"Freaky," Megan commented, leaning against the wall.

"What about Fern and Earl? What if they see us?"

"We'll take our chances. It's not as if foxes don't exist in Springfield. Just don't put on a show. Starla, you should shift. Megan, grab your sister some clothes and put them in her knapsack. Then get dressed. Starla, you'll have to contact Jenson and Molly tomorrow."

I heard my dad stomp up the stairs. He was out of breath. Swiftly he moved with gloved hands retrieving the evidence. Afterwards giving Nayla a thumps up.

"Dan, get in touch with Owl. He should bring Molly and Jenson to the trial," Tri instructed.

"Will do! I'll meet everyone later at the park," he said turning to go. He gave my mom a quick kiss before departing.

"Mom, did you just read my mind? No, this is so not cool!" I groaned. Buffy's mother never had any super powers! I glared at my sister annoyed that she was taking things so lightly.

A sly smirk formed on Nayla's lips. "So you're back for good?"

My mom took a deep breath, then shook alleviating the stress from her body. A slight radiance of confidence was emitting off of her. "I'm not sure," she laughed. "That's the first time, I've done that, in a long time."

Great, my Mom could read my mind! How was I going to handle this? What about my intimate thoughts!? I began to panic. Yeah, I wasn't supposed to change this way, but it was happening!

Nayla tapped me with her paw. My head felt as if someone had hit me with a baseball bat. Groggily, I stood up on all fours. Then stretched my body forward, then backward. I sat down facing her.

"Mom, can't read my mind all the time, can she? I can't live like this. I can't. There's already so much going on! It makes my head spin! I feel like Linda Blair in *The Exorcist*."

"Calm down dear. It's going to be Okay. Tri isn't going to invade your mind every second of the day. It's activated through fear. Granted, she used to be able to control it. Come now, everyone's downstairs. Dan's collected the evidence. We have to go." She bounced up shoving me towards the hallway.

"Megan has my clothes? I'm all set for tomorrow?" I asked, looking back at her.

"That you are."

I trotted to the door, then stopped. "Are you alright?"

"I'm okay. After this trial, I'll be leaving. I can't stay here much longer. I'm hoping this black wolf. The one claiming he's a protector of sorts. I'm praying to the gods, he takes over." Nayla trotted to me, then pushed me from behind. I nearly fell flat on my face.

"Come, Tri is waiting. Dan's probably already at Hunter's Park by now. We need to get you and your sister tucked in. Ah, you're making me sound like a mother."

I chuckled, "Were you ever?"

"No, dear, I can't have kits."

I gave Nayla a sympathetic look. Then raced down the stairs as she trailed behind me. Fritz dashed out of the kitchen at us. My eyes grew wide. I backed up trying to get away from him. "Fritz!" I hollered

"Let him be."

He leapt up at me. Then began his examination. Once he finished, he scampered down the hall into the living room. Nayla and I dove into the kitchen, heading for the back door. Out the doggie door we went. I spotted my mom in her fox form near a bush. Hidden to detour Fern and Earl from suspicion.

Chapter 48

(Dan)

I entered the kitchen switching on the light. Then made my way to the counter. I'd been reluctant to leave everyone upstairs, especially after Megan had freaked out about being left alone. Maybe I should have stayed? Before Starla, changed into fox form, I'd gathered up the evidence. Then left. I glanced down at it in my hand. I'd stored it first in a zip-lock bag. Then I'd put it in a box. It should be safe I thought and placed it under my arm. Now, should I go to Ranger Mikes first? Do I take the car, or walk? What would be the least suspicious? I felt in my pocket for my keys and pulled them out. I probably looked awful. My hair was a mess, and I'd grabbed jeans and a T-shirt out of the hamper. Darn it! I hope I had a coat in the car.

Well, I should go. My family would join me shortly, I thought reluctantly. I grabbed the door handle, opening it. Fritz ran out of the laundry room barking. He knew something was wrong. "No, no Fritz. You have to stay here," I said, shutting the back door. I stood there examining the parking lot. No one in sight, best to leave now. At least I wasn't a fox. I didn't have to worry about Earl and Fern fussing about that. However, leaving our apartment at one in the morning was a different story. I scrambled to the car. Then got in. Before putting the keys in the ignition my cell phone rang. It was Jones.

"This better be vital. I'm on my way to Hunter's Park. Tri and Starla were going to go on a spontaneous fox run when a shadow decided to appear," I informed him. Then put the keys in the ignition starting the car. It roared to life.

"Crap! The Trinity reported three of them, lurking around the park. This is, what I was afraid would happen. Where are Starla and Tri now?" he demanded.

"They're with Nayla," I stated, pulling out of the complex, and into traffic. If I'd been driving a squad car, I'd have put my lights on. I'd need to come up with an excuse if I was pulled over for speeding. At least I had my badge the officer's from the force had given me in case of emergencies.

"Are you still there?"

"Yeah, I'm here," I responded.

"All right. I'm with Ranger, Mike. Cavin was just here. He left to meet everyone in the dining hall."

"Is this trial happening tonight? Has it got that out of hand!" I blurted as I turned onto the road leading into the park.

"No, no. We're just going to lay low there for the night. It's better if everyone stays together. Cavin and Kaya believe it's safer that way."

"I don't blame them. What about the bandits? Are they attempting a breakout, or cowering in their cage?" I asked, pulling into Hunter's Park.

"There is a protective barrier encircling them. They cannot escape. The shadows should not be able to enter. Sika isn't thrilled with being forced to stay there this evening. He though has no choice."

"Right. I'm parking now. Are you at the station, or...?"

"Yes, meet us here. Then we'll go to the dining hall. Mike has flashlights."

"Is the power out?" I asked.

"Not yet, but we're preparing for the worst," he answered.

"I'd hope so," I said. Then hung up the phone. I parked the car and took the keys out of the ignition.

Should I call Tri? Nah, they were probably on their way here. She had mentioned contacting Owl, but I didn't have his number. If I called Rascal, he'd be pretty ticked I woke him up this late. What about Jenson? Yeah, he and Jenson were buddies. I'd just call him. I flipped my phone back open and dialed his number.

"Whoa, is everything Okay? Who is this! You know it's one-thirty in the morning!"

"Jenson, it's me. Dan. Can you do me a favor?"

"Well, it's pretty early in the morning to be doing favors," he muttered.

"I know, I know. I just need you to bring Molly and Owl to the dining hall tomorrow. There's been an emergency."

"Is Starla, alright? What happened?"

"It's okay. No-one's hurt. I don't want to discuss it on the phone. We've relocated to Hunter's Park. Please stay, putt!" Something fell on the floor. "Jenson, are you there? Are you Okay?"

"Yes, I knocked my alarm clock off of my nightstand. That's all. If Starla needs anything have her call me."

"Boy, it's late. Our clan will protect her. I promise they won't let any danger come to her. I have a hunched that if it did, that black wolf would be back. There's something about that spirit. I can't quite put my finger on it. It's an itch. You know the one you can't scratch, but when you do. You know you'll feel better," I added.

"Ah, Okay."

"I'll see you tomorrow," I said. Then hung up the phone and stuffed it into my pocket. My jacket! I turned to the back seat. Thank goodness it was there! I grabbed it, then pushed open the car door. I got out, shut it behind me and began to walk towards the Ranger's station.

Chapter 49

(Starla)

Mom and I darted in and out of traffic into suburbia. I glanced back to make sure Megan was still with Nayla. When we'd reached a safer area, I fell behind allowing mom to lead. I needed to collect my thoughts. They were more jumbled than before the mission of Thunderhead Bay. I had faith we would resolve some of the issues. What I wasn't anticipating in the mix, was a black wolf and shadows. I'd hoped trigger would show up again. Either giving me more clues or in actuality becoming my spirit-guide. I thought I already had one! I wrinkled my nose in confusion. Amare? I hadn't seen her in ages. Is it possible to have two spirit guides? Trigger said that's what he was. What if he was lying? I had a hunch that once we found out who Du-Vance's killer was Trigger would come to us. Who was holding him? Why couldn't he break free? Then there was Cal. I needed to introduce her to my friends. The clan couldn't keep her hidden forever.

"Starla, you're heading the wrong way! Stop."

My paws shot out in front of me, and I dug into the dirt with my nails. Then came to a skidding halt sinking to the ground. How had I been going the wrong way? I looked around at the trees and houses. We weren't too far from Hunters Park now. Nayla skipped up to me. My mom stood back observing us.

"So what's wrong? What did I do?" I asked Nayla. Megan stood beside her. Then sighed, placing her hands on her hips.

"It doesn't appear as if I'm off track. Hunters Parks close by," I pressed.

"Sis, I have to agree with our fox friend. You were heading the wrong way."

"How do you know? You've never been to the park before!"

"Uh huh, with Carol!"

"Girls, this is no time to argue! It's been rough kid, I recognize."

I scoffed at that. Nayla, trying to be cool. Then clamped my foxy mouth shut. She was an elder who was guiding me. Respect, I reminded my sassy self.

"Heres the issue. It's not quite over yet. You're going to need to support a lot of people. They, in turn, will help us. Our destination is to the left. You were heading that way." She pointed to a community of homes. I had no clue I'd been heading in that direction.

"I was? That's weird. Um, Okay. I guess I'll take your word for it," I answered.

"You should," whispered a voice.

I turned to see who had said that. No-one was there? Perhaps it was Trigger. Who else would it have been?

Mom trotted up to us. " We need to get moving. Star and Nuria are waiting for us in the reflection room. It's all set up. Dan's already at the park."

I gave my mom a strange look.

"What, it's not as if I asked to turn on this gift. I had no clue what you were contemplating," Tri complained.

"Really mom? You expect me to believe you?"

Megan waited off to the side while Nayla pushed me with her nose, urging me to stand. I stood up and began to run ahead of them to the left. Where Nayla had said, we needed to go. I listened to the trotting of fox feet behind me. Megan galloped along with them. I could hear the backpack she held on to swinging behind her. So much, for mother daughter bonding time. Maybe I just needed to get some sleep.

We worked our way down the corridor. Megan stared at the walls as we passed the pictures of our clan family. I slowed down, permitting her to examine one or two. She didn't stop to ask questions. I managed to catch a few inquisitive looks, though.

"Ah, here we are," said Nayla, opening the door to the reflection room. Everything had been, set up as she said it would be.

Candles? I was hoping I'd be allowed to rest. My sister stared in awe. She'd been floored ever since she saw the huts. How had they built them? What tools, were used? Nayla answered some of her questions. A lot of her inquiries had to do with our mix breed.

"Don't worry about the candles," said Star.

"Are you?"

"Reading your mind. No, I immediately knew you'd be curious and on your guard," she answered.

I sat down on the makeshift bed that was set up. I choose the blue pillow. I laid down in my fox form barely able to keep my eyes opened. Mom had trotted off with Star. It sounded like my dad would be here soon. At least to make sure we were alright.

"Where should I sleep?" asked Megan.

"Right here by me. You like pink," I volunteered.

Megan shivered, then pretty much obeyed me. She seldom listened to me. It usually ended in a sarcastic fight. I saw her remove the pillow and fluff it up. Afterward, she pulled her blankets closer to me.

"Hey, it's going to be fine," I told her.

"I suppose your right. Mom and dad have kept us safe this long. I'm sorry about complaining earlier. Now that I'm here, I'm involved." There was a hesitation in her voice. I could tell she was trying to sound cheerful. She quivered ever so slightly. I reached over placing my paw on her back.

"Change back into human form. It creeps me out seeing you this way," she admitted. At that moment she inched back a bit as if I was going to bite her.

My paw fell to the floor. I lifted my head up off of the pillow. "I get it. I can also talk. That must amplify it," I snickered.

"Turning, what's it like, does it hurt?"

"It did the first time I switched. Weren't you at all curious to ask, then?"

"I was wrapped up in school, Chaz, and *Great Expectations*," she answered snuggling down into the blankets.

"Hey, after all, this is over. I'll read your cards. As long as mom doesn't try to stop me," I offered.

"Why would she?"

"Mom said those cards are special. She didn't tell us why."

"She will," said Megan. Then let out a long yawn. "If your friends are getting us up, in what 3 hours? I'm going to get some sleep. I'll see you then."

"Night sis," I answered, closing my eyes to join her.

Chapter 50

(Dan)

Ranger, Mike had met us at the station. From there Jones and I left. We hiked through the dark forest in silence. I listened to the animals scurrying back to their homes. Then looked up to see an Owl perched in a tree. It blinked its beady eyes at me. I pointed it out to Jones. He smiled and nodded knowingly. There was nothing new to discuss that we hadn't already. From time to time Jones scanned the perimeter to ensure our safety. I'd hoped Tri and Starla had made it to Hunter's Park unharmed. I pulled my cell phone out of my pocket, flipping it open. Nope, no calls, or texts. Afterward, I closed it placing it back into my pocket.

"Where's the Trinity pack? Shouldn't they be monitoring these woods?" I asked.

"Yes. They're here, not out in the open of course. When we arrive, check in with Tri. Then meet me in the dining hall. I'm sure Starla will already be fast asleep."

"She's usually up late," I replied. We moved closer to our destination traipsing through what was left of the snow. I turned sideways to avoid colliding with a bush.

"Perhaps she'll get more sleep knowing what's to come tomorrow. It's hard to tell with teenagers. I never had any myself. I only teach them."

I chuckled, then cleared my throat. My eyes had adjusted to the night fairly well. We rambled on enjoying the vast amount of stars in the sky. Without warning, a bat swooped low nearly missing my head. Instinctively, I ducked down. I stayed there for several minutes not knowing if I should get back up or not.

"Come on. It's gone."

I took my hands off of my head, then stood. It had landed in a nearby tree.

Jones gestured towards it as we continued to hike. "That one has almost clipped me a few times while I was out here. Sometimes I run at night, haven't in a while. The last time I heard strange noises. I never saw anything. On one occasion Shellena and Lance played a prank on me. They attacked me with water balloons. They thought it was a total riot. I warned them if they did it again, I'd make them clean the gym. They decided it wasn't worth the risk,"

Each step we took brought us closer to the huts. I could see the string of lights in the trees illuminating them. As we walked, I turned to face Jones. "That isn't the worst job. I've done it before," I answered.

"No," he replied. "The worst would be cleaning up the kitchen after a clan party. That's what I've heard."

"You've never been invited to one of them? I thought I saw you there a few years ago," I responded.

"I was only attending for security reasons. Ah, look, Come on! There are Shellena and Lance."

We jogged the rest of the way to the hut containing the dining hall and reflection room.

"Here we are. Shellena and I are going to search for the bed rolls. We'll see you a little later. If not tomorrow," said Lance. He turned away from us, and Shellena followed him out the door.

Jones and I stepped into the dining hall foyer. I took off my jacket and held it in my arms. It was a good thing I'd had it in my car.

"Aren't you going to check in with your family?" he asked.

"Sure. I only want to see what's happening. In fact, I'll probably squat there for the night. So, if you see Cavin let him know, Okay?"

"Yeah, I'll check in with the Trinity," he answered.

"Let someone know. I wouldn't want you to vanish," I replied.

Jones gave me a cockeyed look.

"I'm serious."

"I've got my phone. I can take care of myself," he answered..

"Alright." I sighed, turning back to the dining hall. It was bustling with half-breeds. Amer was here. I didn't see Sensi or Jun. The large table which had been set up for Cavin for the trial now had a small spread of appetizers. What was this? A party? Mango, an elder, strolled up to me.

"Hello, there. I thought I'd drop by and see what all the fuss was. I kept hearing how we'd caught the bandits!" A grin formed on her face. "Is Starla here?" She turned, scanning the room, assuming she was in the area somewhere. "The last time I saw her, she was only a kit! She kept transforming back and forth. That is until you insisted on isolating her from the clan. I suppose now, though she's on track."

"Yes, she is. Tri and I had our reasons. We wanted to keep her safe." I glanced towards the exit leading into the hall. "I have to go."

"Well, tell her I said hi. I'd like to see her again. If I may after all this is over with." With that, she turned around the room as if she was looking for someone. She spotted Lance, pushing open the kitchen door.

The bed rolls covered the front of his face. I bet he could barely see what he was doing. Shellena was right behind him. Better run, I thought. Mango liked to chat. She was harmless, sweet, and giving. Unfortunately, this was not the time. I managed to slip out of the dining hall into the mud room. Then peeked into the hallway. Star stood near the pictures of our ancestors. Why? She'd seen them a million times. She turned and saw me standing there.

"Megan and Starla are asleep. I'll be waking them in a few hours. Tri is out like a light too. Nayla, on the other hand, decided to join everyone in the dining area," she added.

"I must have just missed her. It sounds like a party in there. Not a meeting. Mango already grilled me about Starla," I said, leaning against the door frame.

"Sounds like Mango. She only wants to be a part of the action. Are you going back to the hall?"

I stopped leaning and stood up. "I'd like to stay with my family. At least til morning."

"I understand. There are blankets set up. I believe there's a spot left. I had planned on staying with them, but I can reside in the dining hall. It's not a biggie." She shrugged gesturing for me to go ahead. "When Minder gets here in the morning with Eva and Cal you'll join the men in the dining hall. I'll go let them know." Star trotted away.

I drifted down the hall. Then paused at the door of the reflection room, placing one of my hands on it. I hesitated before turning the door handle. Then, reluctantly pushed it opened, peering in. Starla, Megan, and Tri were fast asleep. Without a sound, I shut the door behind me. Awkwardly, I shuffled myself around them spotting a blanket on the floor. I picked it up. Then reached for the pillow beside it. I stumbled over to the farthest wall. I leaned myself against it and drew the blanket over myself. I'd watch over them til I fell asleep.

Friday Morning, April 2nd

Was I on a highway? A beautiful landscape lay before my eyes. Lush trees, flowers, and a waterfall with the pavement, in-between them. Did this place exist? Had I seen this before? Where was I? I stirred in my sleep, rolling over. What was I witnessing? Wasn't it my daughter who had lucid dreams? I heard a low growl. The wolf! Where was it? If I was on the highway, I was either driving or riding in a vehicle of some type. I looked in front of me. Sure enough, I was driving. No one was in the passenger's seat beside me. I pulled over to the side of the road to explore my surroundings. Not bothering to look at the car's make or model, I got out. Then headed to a cluster of trees. The growling persisted.

How had I heard it in the car? I shook off my fear entering a wooded area. Then stopped in the middle of the road. There the black wolf stood smiling at me.

"I knew you would come. This is where they're hiding. It's nothing fancy. A small drive through, recreational park found in Grandville, Illinois. What frightens me is there are residences along the path. I've guarded them. As long, as the scientists are left alone, no-harm will come to them. The army of shadows are protecting the scientists. Sika isn't aware of any of this. He's too terrified of the shadows."

"Are they not a part of this?" I demanded.

"Yes, they were created by the scientists. Their first task was to help them locate our dwelling. Find out who killed Du-Vance. Then move forward. We cannot waste any time. Inform Jones, he'll know what to do.

283

"He comes from a line of semi Immortals. He won't live forever, but his existence is prolonged."

"So he has people who can help us?" I asked again.

"I'm not aware if he does. I'll keep in contact with you. After the trial, I'll give you more details. As of now, I don't know when they'll attack."

"Okay, so it's going to happen tomorrow? The shadows know where we are! Can they harm us?"

"It doesn't appear that way. If they could, it would have already happened. Oh, and do not tell Cavin. He needs to focus on the trial."

"Before I wake up, where am I exactly? What park again?"

"It's off the highway, near the water. The camps, hidden. That's all I can disclose. Once you catch..."

Was I waking up? No!!!

A loud rapping came from the door. Someone leaned over me shaking me awake. I opened my eyes. "Megan?"

"Wake up Dad! You were talking in your sleep. Minder's bringing us breakfast."

She moved out of my way as I sat up to stretch. Light shone into the room through the tiny window off to the side. A small coffee table had been brought in. Who was knocking on the door? I pushed myself up off of the floor and stood. Megan skipped over to the exit as the door opened.

"Hey, I come bearing food," said Minder. She held a tray in her hand of toast, eggs, bacon, and fruit. Cal held a gallon of orange juice in her right hand. Then a roll of paper towels in the other. Starla still lay fast asleep.

Megan pointed to her sister slumbering on the floor. "Someone is going to have to wake her up, and it's not going to be me."

Cal snorted, "I'll do it. She needs to eat, then train. Megan, you can hang out and watch if you want. Afterward, you'll sit in on the court hearing." Cal pushed past Minder setting the orange juice down on the table. She waltzed over to Starla to shake her. Instead, Starla sat up, looking around bewildered.

"What's going on? Is it morning already? I swore I heard a wolf growling," she admitted.

"Not unless you were in my dream realm," I added.

Minder closed the door behind her. Starla quickly got up from where she sat noticing she was still in fox form.

"I'm going to transform in the bathroom. Megan, can you please put my clothes in there. It's near that back wall," she said, pointing to it with her right paw.

"Sure, let me grab it." Swiftly she dashed to the other side of the room, opening the door for Starla. I watched her rush into change. Then turned to help Minder with the food.

Chapter 51

(Starla)

I rushed in ready to change. I'd most likely be repeating the process after food. Oh, Buffy, you had it easy, girl. I wish, my only job was to kill vamps. Instead, I shift forms, read dreams, and so much more. Megan shut the door behind me, but before I shifted I swear I saw an image of the black wolf in the mirror hanging over the sink.

I ignored it. Then rummaged through the bag my sister had packed for me pulling out a pair of jeans. She'd also selected a white T-shirt along with a multi-colored low slung sweatshirt. Ah! Classic 80's. What was she doing? Digging through the back of my closet? At least Cal might get a kick out of it. I smirked, then put on the clothes. I attempted to fix my hair. What a mess. Hadn't she considered packing me a brush? I turned to the sink. Water might help. I could use it to smooth out some of the frizz. I turned on the warm water. Then placed my hands under it. After that, I ran my fingers through my hair. There that would have to do. Satisfied, I shut it off. Then turned around little by little so I wouldn't knock into the sink or the toilet. I grabbed my backpack and pushed open the door. I almost fell sprinting towards where everyone sat. I looked up to see Eva, Cal, and Star had joined us.

"Sis, you need to be more careful," Megan advised as I sat down next to her.

"You're right," I replied, grabbing a paper plate off of the table. I filled it up with fruit, bacon, and a piece of dry toast. Cal was already munching happily away next to her Mom. I contemplated what Nayla had in mind for this morning's lesson.

Would we be doing something different? I put my fruit on my toast and took a big bite.

"Dad, what were you dreaming about when I woke you?" asked Megan.

My dad cleared his throat, and Mom moved closer to him. She put her arm in his drawing him near.

"I had a visit from the black wolf regarding the shadows. It's not essential at the moment. We need to focus on today," said Dan.

That was probably the growling I heard, I thought. Then put a piece of bacon into my mouth. I chewed then swallowed. I was about to address my dad, but Megan beat me to it.

"But!" added Megan.

Eva gave her a stern look. "There are no butts here! I agree with him. Now, Everyone finish eating. Nayla will be here soon."

Minder nodded to Eva setting down her empty plate on the table. She stood up and motioned for Cal and me, to follow her. Cal stuffed the last bit of toast into her mouth. Then finished her orange juice. I drank mine too quickly causing me to cough a little. It seemed like an eternity before I finally stopped.

"Where are we going?" I asked.

"Come, we'll meditate before Nayla arrives. You two are not to depart from your bodies, or to leave in this meditation. It's to calm you."

Cal and I hastily joined her on the floor.

"Now, close your eyes. Relieve your stress, find inner peace. When Nayla arrives, I will advise you on the next step. For now, concentrate," said Minder.

Okay, did I need this to do some Buffy like move or would I be learning a new skill to defeat an enemy? One where Minder would connect with Cal and me? Nayla had to be preparing us for the attack on the scientists, or the shadows. This preparation was not a current affair. Did dad know what she was planning?

Rascal must be a bit upset not having been included in all this. Du-Vance was his son. Should I have gone to see him instead of letting my father run the show? I put my hands up to my temples and rubbed gently. I needed to let go of rambling thoughts.

"Starla, stop, you'll get us in trouble," Cal mind spoke to me.

I sighed, then released the questions clouding my brain.

"Starla Araina," said Nayla nudging my arm. I opened my eyes. The room seemed awfully bright. She trotted into the center of our circle. Then sat on her hind legs facing us. "Where's everyone else?" I asked.

"Dan went to see Cavin in the dining hall. I sure hope Jones shows up! Tri and Megan are with Mango," Nayla answered.

Who was Mango? I tried to conjure up a picture in my head. Hadn't I seen any photos of her? I'd have to ask mom later.

"Ah, and Eva?" said Cal concerned.

"Also in the dining hall, ah ha jury room. Please, let's not worry. Shall we begin?"

Cal and I nodded. Minder blinked a few times but stayed silent.

"This exercise will not only ensure safety but are tactics you can use as a team. After this trial, we'll be facing our worst enemies. It's not going to be as easy as Thunder Head Bay. In fact, after the hearing. We'll be facing unusual demons."

Cal looked over at me. I glanced away for an instant. Minder shivered, then regained her composure.

"I'm not sure what happened at Thunder Head Bay. I don't know why I couldn't escape from Sika. Before I'd always been able to outrun my enemies. I picked up large logs in the woods when traveling with Cal. I even made us a makeshift hut to stay in on our journey."

Nayla shook her head. "Well, we'll need to resolve this. I'd like you on the defense line during the next mission. Eventually, Jenson and Molly will be joining us. I wasn't going to press this issue, but with the black wolfs appearances along with messages given. I'm troubled."

"I agree. I'm willing to do what it takes. Is it possible that I could be cursed?" asked Minder.

Nayla laughed, "That's highly unlikely. It could have been nerves or fear. We need to work on that. Fear can freeze you up. It isn't good. It's the reason I had you meditate first. This being said I want Minder to start by attempting to lift both Cal and Starla Araina. It also might sound silly, but I will have you dash from one end of the room to another. I need to see how you perform when you're not under pressure."

Cal's jaw dropped open in shock. "What if she drops us?"

"I won't. I promise," Minder chuckled standing up. She approached me first.

"What? I'm the guinea pig?"

Minder winked at Cal. Then reached out to me with her right arm. She swung it around my waist rapidly lifting me over her shoulder effortlessly. Maybe I shouldn't have eaten so much. I felt a gurgle in my stomach. Then a shot up to my throat. Hold it in! Hold it in! These were my only clothes. I gulped it down before it came back up. Gross!

"Are you Okay? You look kind of sick," said Cal.

I gave her a thumbs up forcing myself to grin. Then returned to my relaxed pout as soon as she turned to Minder.

"Are you prepared?"

"I am, you've managed to pick up Starla Araina. I should be fine," Cal admitted.

Minder rambled in the direction of Cal as she held me tightly on the right side of her back over her shoulder. Slowly, she knelt down, scooping her up using her left arm. She'd used the same technique but had taken it slower. Why couldn't she have done that with me? Perhaps I wouldn't have almost vomited all over the floor.

"Now run with them in your arms," instructed Nayla.

"What! You didn't say anything about running," I blurted.

"Oh, you'll be just fine," said Nayla. She swished her tail back and forth in an annoyed manner waiting. "Go to the other side of the room. I want you to move as swiftly as you're able. Stop once you near the window. Stop fast. Do not hold back."

"Alright, I don't suppose you want me to break through the wall," Minder added.

"No, but as fast as you're able," Nayla replied.

Geez. Minder's bony-shoulder dug into my stomach. She needed to eat more. Didn't wolves eat a lot of meat? I shot Cal, a fleeting look. What was she pondering? She had her face all scrunched up, and her eyes were closed.

"Okay, I'm going to give this my best blast. Understand that I might leave marks on this carpet," she warned her. Then carried Cal and me to the other side of the room as instructed. Minder turned on her heel back around to face Nayla.

"Take your stance, breath in, and out. Now visualize your goal, movements, and abilities. Go!" Nayla shouted.

My face felt as if it was being, flattened! Were her huge wolf feet even touching the floor? Would we go through the window pane?

"No!" shouted Nayla. She dove towards the window, reaching underneath it with her paws. She tried to open it. Minder ducked. Then dug her claws into the carpet to slow herself down. She skidded against the wall. Instinctively, I reached up placing my hands over my head in case of emergency. Plaster fell from the wall hitting me on the head. We crashed grinding the carpet further into our bodies.

"I warned you," Minder snarled.

Nayla backed up defensively. I guess she hadn't expected that type of reaction. Minder kept us close to her torso. She cautiously moved her arms out from underneath us. "Are you two ok?"

"I'll be fine. Except for the small bump on my head." I rubbed it, then sat up. Cal repositioned herself on the floor. She pushed her hand into her pocket and pulled out an object inspecting it.

"Did you finally get a cell phone?"

"Yeah, making sure the darn thing didn't break," she said showing it to me.

"Cool, you'll have to give me your digits."

"Sure, so Minder. It seems like everything's fine concerning your abilities. Do you think it was fear that held you back that night?" asked Cal. She handed her phone to me. I proceeded to put my number in it for her. Then, handed it back.

"I presume we'll find out during the next mission. Unless Nayla has any idea's on how to prepare me for unexpected fear," she replied.

"I'll set something up after the trial. Once it's settled, we should be able to form a plan to infiltrate the scientists. Leave your things here. Cavin should have everyone prepared and waiting."

"Okay, that was fast!"

"Yes, this was to help Minder not everything's about you Starla Araina. Let's go."

Minder stood up, and we followed her to the exit. Had I been arrogant or was she just on edge? No one even spoke of the evidence found last night or what had occurred.

Today focus on today. Then you can voice your concerns I told myself silently following the leader.

Chapter 52

(Dan)

Before I'd left Starla in the middle of her meditation Nayla had promised, it would be brief. Tri and Megan had gone to see Mango. Tri was supposed to be reassuring her of our safety. I turned to the dining hall door, then swung back around. I thought I'd heard a noise. Nothing. Maybe I should contact Jones. He was supposed to be here by now. I took my phone out of my pocket and dialed. It rang several times before going to voicemail.

"Jones, I need to talk to you before the bandits are brought in. Get here as soon as you're able. If not, we'll discuss it later," I stated. Then hung up.

Had Cavin gotten a chance to decipher the evidence? I'd handed it over to him as soon as I'd arrived. He'd taken it into his chambers. A little corner room I'd never been in before. I didn't ask to enter. Instead, I'd stayed out here to mull things over. Cavin peeked his head out of the doorway.

"Please get everyone in the dining hall. Shellena and Lance are on their way. I contacted Nayla. She's bringing Minder, Cal, and Starla Ariana," he informed me. Then shuffled back into his chambers, leaving the door ajar.

Impending footsteps came from around the corner. I heard Molly's voice. "This is going to be creepy. We haven't seen these monsters since the mission."

"We're safe here," said Owl, his voice echoed throughout the hall. Jenson swiftly turned to the entrance nearly running into me.

"Ah, sorry. We made it here safely. Can I see Starla?" he asked.

I could tell Jenson was nervous. Before I could answer him, Cavin came outside to join us.

"They should be here shortly. Why don't you go inside? Kaya will show you to your seats. Don't be frightened," he said, holding the door open for them. Then nodded, before shutting it.

"This is it," said Jones.

"You have to stop appearing out of nowhere. Is there something you aren't telling me!" I demanded.

"No, no. I slipped in behind the crew. I got your message. What is it?"

I glanced up and down the hallway. Then turned to Jones. "The shadows are close. We have to be careful!"

"And you know this how?"

"This morning I had a vision-dream. I figured it was Starla's thing. The wolf contacted me once more. Weird, if you ask me."

"Go on with it," urged Jones.

"They're located in Grandville, Illinois. It's a strange park, a drive through. Residential living is on one side, and the other is vast parkland. The shadow army is in that location. The wolf didn't confirm regarding the scientists."

Jones shoulder's stiffened as Shellena and Lance came upon us. They held the bandits firmly in their grasp. Gladiator and Gavin remained silent. Sika huffed all the way to the entryway glaring at us. Avoiding contact with them, I opened the door.

"Thanks," Lance muttered.

"Come along, we're going to have to deal with this, after the trial," Jones stated.

"The girls," I pronounced, pointing to Nayla, Cal, and Starla. Minder strutted behind them.

"I see, come along! Hurry now. There's no time to waste. Cavin will want to start right away!" said Jones.

I ushered Starla and Cal over to their seats. I wasn't too concerned about Tri. Megan was probably bored out of her mind. Either that or asking Mango a ton of questions. When Mango started talking about the past, it was hard to shut her up.

Chapter 53

(Starla)

I'd taken my seat, but Cal decided she'd sit with Eva and Star. I stared at the notebook she grasped in her hands. What was in it? I hadn't thought about it since the meeting. It felt like ages ago. She hadn't mentioned any new information. I took a deep breath in and exhaled rubbing my sweaty palms on my jeans. Megan and Mom hadn't come back yet. Why was Mango keeping her? I fidgeted next to Jenson. He took my hand squeezing it to calm me. Molly and Owl sat on the other side of me. I leaned over her to whisper to him. "Where's Rascal? He's coming isn't he?"

"Nuria's bringing him. They'll be here," he assured me. I sat upright scanning the courtroom for faces I knew. Cavin sat in front at the judge's table with my father to his right. Nayla was on his left. Where did that leave Kaya? I turned around to see her sitting behind us with Rascal and Nuria. They must have snuck in undetected. Shellena and Lance had the bandits in a corner box of seats to the right of my dad. Cavin stood to address us.

"First and foremost the Bandits are on trial for attempted manslaughter of Rascal's son Martin Du-Vance. Today we'll establish which one murdered him or if they hired someone else to do it!"

I heard chattering behind me. Jenson and I turned around to find out who it was. Kaya and Nuria were discussing some of Cal's schoolwork. Rascal sat in silence. Jones was there with them. I moved away from Jenson and leaned to my left. Mom, Mango, and Megan straggled into the room. You couldn't miss Mango. She was a brilliant orange. I noticed she had white paws, and the tip of her tail was black.

"Hey, Starla. I met Mango. At first, I was scared. She's pretty chill, though. Those bandits up there though are eerie."

"Yeah, they are," I admitted.

"Hey there, youngster. I knew you, before you knew yourself," Mango joked.

"Um, Okay, fill me in later."

Mango smiled, then winked at me. Odd, Mango didn't seem fazed. Didn't she know this was serious? I turned back to pay attention to Cavin. Out of the corner of my eye, I thought I saw something move.

"Jenson, did you see that?" I whispered.

"No, nothing. Why? What did you see?" he demanded.

"Movement, I couldn't see a figure or outline of anyone. Never mind. It must have been my imagination," I answered.

"It's most likely nerves. We've been anticipating this."

"Order! Order in the court! Everyone needs to remain quiet during our interegation. That's final! I'd like to call Sika to the stand," said Cavin.

Shellena and Lance stood. Sika looked uncomfortable in cuffs. The expression on his face was similar to Gavin's when he couldn't break through our force field at Thunder Head Bay. What did he think, that he wasn't supposed to be here? Shellena and Lance led him over for questioning. He twisted away from them roughly then sat down. Lance shot him a stern look as he strutted to his seat next to the other prisoners. Shellena nodded to Cavin and sat beside him.

"Go ahead Dan. Address the people in the court. Then question the defendant," Jones instructed.

Dan got up, and pushed in his chair, gazing at Sika. "We're here today to determine whether or not the bandits killed Martin Du-Vance. Cavin may I approach the defendant."

"You may," he replied.

296

"Sika, where were you on February 19th, the night Du-Vance was killed?"

Sika sat blinking his eyes. He turned up his paws rubbing them almost raw against the cuffs appearing agitated.

"Sika! Answer Dan!" howled Lance.

"Order, badgering the defendant! Let him answer," urged Cavin.

"My boys and I were out hunting. We were about to call it a night. I hollered at Gavin and Gladiator to come back to me. I thought I'd heard a cry in the woods. It could have been an Owl. I went to look, but nothing was there. So then we all went back to camp. I had Minder guarding Cal."

"Can Minder, or anyone in your group, verify this?" Dan asked.

"Gavin, and the Gladiator. I don't have any paperwork if that's what your after."

I held my breath for a moment. "I wouldn't expect you to. I'll be calling them into question on the stand."

Sika glared at the jury. He looked down at his cuffed hands. "Minder also. She isn't too good with dates. That's why she hasn't come forth."

Minder glared at Sika from her seat.

"If this is true, then can you tell me the date she left? How long was it after the death of Du-Vance?"

"February 20th. We had an argument over Cal. She'd wanted to see her folks. The kid was always complaining about that! I didn't stop hearing it in all the years we'd kept her. It was right after we got messed up with that entity," he answered.

"My reasoning was you'd hired the creature to capture Cal and Starla. It was a trap wasn't it?" Dan asked.

"Grr..." Sika slammed his fists on an arm of the chair. Lance stood up ready to jolt to the front of the room.

I nearly leapt out of my chair. I stopped, then looked at Jenson. He put his arm around my shoulders. I eased back into my seat and turned to observe the trial.

"Did you?" asked Dan.

Sika exposed his claws clenching them in and out. "Yes," he snarled. I sank further into my seat. He could have easily ripped into Martin with them. Wouldn't there have been evidence left, unless he ate him? I shuddered.

"All right then. But you didn't have anything to do with Du-Vance's death?" Dan asked again.

"No, and I'm not aware of who decided the boy had to go!" he shouted. In his anger, he dug into the chair.

"Enough. Is that all Dan?" asked Cavin.

"No."

"Proceed then," he answered.

"If the entity did not kill Du-Vance, who did?"

"How should I know? All I'm aware of is that we wanted Starla and Cal's powers. We got a hold of the entity to do that. But it never happened thanks to you!" He spat literally, right in my dad's face.

Lance hurtled out of his seat like a bullet out of a shotgun. Jones was faster stepping in front of Lance. He put his hand out stopping him.

"Let me handle this I'll cross-examine the bonehead! He doesn't know what's going to hit him!"

Sika shifted his body in the chair. He took a deep breath, then exhaled out.

What was he doing yoga? I thought. Gradually his claws retracted into his paws. My dad stepped back from Sika whispering something to Jones. Cavin nodded to them both while Nayla sat silent. Dan went to his seat, allowing Jones to take his place.

"Okay, so we're clear that you sought Starla and Cal's powers. Once you had them what was the plan? Who created this monster for you? Did you hire someone?"

Sika ground his teeth in irritation. He held on to the arm of the chair rocking back and forth. It looked like he was about to fly out of it.

"Answer the question!"

"I can't," he stuttered.

"You can," said Rascal, standing up from his stool. He marched to the front of the room joining Jones.

"My son was killed. Mutilated! If you can identify someone, any of your sidekicks. We want to know. Either clear your names, or we'll banish you," Rascal threatened.

I found it surprisingly odd that Sika had put away his claws. Was there something in the room, he couldn't attack? Sika tightened his grip on the chair. Suddenly he stopped rocking. I was hoping he wouldn't pass out. I looked at Rascal, then Jones. The chicken bone in my throat rose. Outside the window, a few shadows lingered. No one else noticed. I wasn't about to cause a scene when there was one currently taking place. Sweat dripped from Sika's brow onto his face. He'd begun to perspire tremendously.

"You say you saw nothing. Answer our question, or we'll call someone else to the stand." Jones paused, waiting for a response. "No problem, you can sweat it out while we grill Gladiator."

"All right, all right! We were going to take over your clan. Finally get rid of each and every one of you! Then go after the scientists. We screwed it up assuming Starla was a novice. We knew she'd come looking for her friend. We didn't imagine you'd be tagging along," he grumbled.

Gavin stood up from the bench. He glowered at Sika, afterward turning to face Jones. "He's lying, don't believe a word he says! We were never going to attack you. We were going to use their powers to defeat the scientists!" he admitted.

They what? Wanted to attack the scientists? This whole thing kept getting twisted around. I wasn't sure what was happening anymore. The trial for the bandits, the black wolf, shadows, and scientists. I couldn't wrap my mind around it all. Were the scientists after the Bandits too? Had they been bystanders in this all along? Even though, they were killers. After all, we couldn't dismiss River Rogue.

Jenson grabbed my hand. He squeezed it, reassuringly. Molly muttered to herself, "What the fudge is going on?" Owl sat in his seat with a look of disbelief.

"Gavin! Shut up. I'm the boss. You and Gladiator will follow my orders," he demanded.

I jumped but managed to stay seated, trying not to panic. Megan held on to Mango. She was terrified, yet had not raced out of the room. I hadn't heard a peep from my mother. Mango, however, held her views.

"Well, well, this is interesting," she bantered loudly to herself.

Eva and Cal whispered amongst themselves, and a door slammed shut. Sensi rushed into the room, taking the nearest chair. I didn't see Amer or Jun with her.

Cavin banged his gavel on the desk. "Order, Order in the court!"

Jones and Rascal stepped up to the desk to deliberate with Cavin. They waved my dad over to them. Quietly I got up to peer out a nearby window. I was so scared I couldn't breathe. Outside shadows hovered over our hut. I couldn't count them all. They'd almost completely covered it. I shivered and shook uncontrollably. What the hell were we going to do? I held the curtain open whirling back around to face my father almost unable to speak.

"D.. da.. da... Dad? Something is happening. I don't know what to do," I whispered.

"They're here! I have to get out of here!" shouted Sika. Gladiator and Gavin stood up and ran over to huddle next to Sika.

"You fools! I'm not going to protect you. You need to guard me!" he cried.

I rolled my eyes, letting the curtain fall back into place. Sika floored me. He wouldn't even protect his own. That was just sad. I let out a sigh, blowing hair out of my face and faltered towards the front of the room near the judge's bench.

No matter how frightened I was, this needed to end. I am the so-called guardian. I let the rush of adrenaline enter my body turning my fear into courage. "No-one's leaving until you tell us who killed Martin Du-Vance. Who did it! Why? If not out you go!"

"Starla, this is my interrogation. What are you doing?" asked Dan.

"Finding answers dad. Maybe if we threaten them with 'The Shadows', they'll listen for once. I've had enough of these games. Haven't you?"

"The shadows did it," answered Gavin in a calm voice.

I laughed, "That's hysterical, no way. The black wolf said they aren't able to hurt us. He wouldn't lie," I exploded.

I twisted round to find Sensi inches from me. Nayla trotted to where I stood. She didn't even acknowledge Sensi.

"Starla we don't even know who this black wolf is."

"I know, but he knows Jones," Dan interrupted.

"What? How?" I asked, turning to my dad.

"My dreams the wolf told me in my REM cycle. In a vision, he claimed Jones would know what to do."

Jones appeared troubled. He placed his hands on his forehead trembling. "He may know me, but I do not know him, directly at least."

301

"Ok, one thing at a time. Starla Araina. You're right. No one is leaving here until someone comes forth admitting their guilt. Now we'll just sit here until they do. I hope the Trinity pack is safe. They were supposed to be monitoring us," said Cavin.

"I... I saw them! Amer and Jun are with the Trinity. We put up a barrier block, but It won't hold them for long. Once it dissipates I'm not sure what will happen," Sensi stuttered.

"All right, then. We'll need to settle this quickly."

"Sika didn't answer the question. Who created the entity? After that, I want to know about Du-Vance. No more question-dodging!" I stated.

"Right on," shouted Lance standing up. Shellena hit him on the back hard. He fell into his chair and swiveled around. Jenson tried not to laugh cupping his hands over his mouth.

Cal got up from her seat looking around at all of us. She'd been a mouse all day. I watched her swallow, then take a few steps towards Sika.

"I might know. I'm starting to remember more and more. Small details. The night I wanted to tell you about, the orders. The scientists consist of two women and three men. That's what you said." She pointed to The Bandits. "Why are you so scared of the shadows? I don't get it?" she whispered, backing up into Star who had joined us.

"We have no choice but to tell them. We need their help. Who else will protect us? Certainly not the scientists who are after Starla's clan," admitted Gladiator.

Ah, he was the smart one. Would he tell us what was going on?" I pondered.

Sika began to beat his head with his cuffed hands. "No, no, no this was never the plan! Have you not learned anything from me?" he asked.

"Apparently not," offered Gavin.

302

Chapter 54

(Dan)

Minder managed to calm Sika down. We were all worried he might try to hurt her. Although with the clan there maybe he was afraid to be his evil self. Gladiator had taken the stand. Sika sat off to the side. Everyone gathered their seats around the witness stand. I stood ready to listen to what he had to say.

"The shadows created the entity we hired. At the time we did not know they were developed by the same scientists whom we'd planned to eliminate. Now they have located your clan and are after us. I'm assuming they will observe your behaviors. Then try to find a way to enter Hunter's Park. In order, to gain control of everyone here," announced Gladiator shaking his head.

"You're sure of this?" I asked him.

"Yes. Sika isn't lying about Du-Vance. We don't know who murdered him. We did, however, want him dead. I won't lie about that."

I scoffed, "Well, thanks for not lying. Cavin, have you gone over the evidence I gave to you?"

"I have, the cloth had been dyed with what seems to be blood. It's a much larger piece than those we took from the crime scene. If we had up to date equipment, we could process the evidence faster to find out who's DNA is on it."

"So you presume this will establish who the killer is? I don't believe it's our best option to rely solely on this," I pressed.

"True, I had Mike send it over to be analyzed. They should have it to us by tomorrow. I had them put a rush on it. Don't worry, under the radar," Cavin admitted.

"Who did you manage to get to do that?"

Cavin put his paw to his lips to indicate he wasn't going to voice the man or woman's name.

"Dad's right. This cloth was left at our house last night. It could be anyone's blood. If a shadow left it, the material could be something else entirely," Starla interjected.

"Do you suppose it has anything to do with the red streak I saw in the forest? Maybe it's part of a cape. How do you know it's blood?" asked Sensi.

"We don't know for sure. While we wait, I want to know the details on these Shadows. How much do you know about them? Is it true, do you believe they killed Du-Vance?"

"Dad?"

"What Starla! I'm attempting to figure this out."

"When I received the vision of Du-Vance's death. There were shadows. How could I have forgotten? Maybe it's because of Trigger."

"Who's he?" I demanded.

Crap, I wasn't supposed to use his name! "The wolf-spirit who's been visiting me, us. What if these Shadows can manipulate animals or people. What if, they killed him but used someone else to do it?" Starla asked.

"What would bring you to that kind of conclusion," challenged Star.

"It seemed that the animal was being shadowed or was a shadow. Maybe that's why I couldn't make it out. If one of the bandits was controlled by it or another wolf, who do we blame?"

"The one controlling it of course," Nayla concluded.

"Yes, I need Gavin to the stand immediately. He clearly stated the shadows killed Rascal's son. How, why, and if he saw it happen, who were they controlling?"

"Hey, I'm right here! I don't even have to take the stand. I can answer you from here!" he exclaimed.

Gladiator snickered into his paws. "Gavin isn't going to tell you anything. He's useless."

"Let me be the judge of that. Shellena, please bring him here."

Sika pushed Gavin into the circle. "Go ahead. You've already ruined the whole thing! And after all, we've been through."

Shellena, grabbed Gavin before he tumbled over on top of me.

"Are you Okay?"

"I ah, guess so," I answered steadying myself.

"I'll just go sit down. I'm ready to answer your questions. If I do, though what do I get?" Gavin inquired.

"Oh gosh," mumbled Sika, rolling his eyes in Gavin's direction. He seemed not to care what happened anymore. Would he not acknowledge it was coming to an end?

Nayla trotted up to our suspect. She gave me the I got this look. Really? I was supposed to be interrogating them. She stood in front of him staring him in the eyes. "For once in your life you'll be doing the right thing. Just as Gladiator has done thus far. You didn't ask to be this. It is understandable you crave revenge. What happened to Du-Vance?"

"Well, duh!" exclaimed Sika.

Gladiator interlocked his hands still held in cuffs. He brought them down on Sika, who slumped deeper into his chair. "That ought to shut him up. Go ahead."

I turned to Gladiator startled by his actions. "Why are you helping us? Should I even ask?"

"It's out of control. The shadows came after us when we couldn't provide them with the payment for the entity. Sika thinks we're fools. Well then, how come he assumed we'd be able to deceive you? Now, it appears we have no choice but to raise the white flag."

"What else, are we gonna do?" asked Gavin.

"Tell the truth. Then go from there. We'll probably still be banished. River Rogue was not an accident. I don't regret it. This fox clan has caused us nothing but trouble! Unfortunately, to preserve ourselves, we must comply with them."

Nayla jumped out in front of Gladiator, "Enough! Gavin, Dan will be questioning you. You'll answer him. Then we'll make a decision. Gladiator, sit down!"

Whoa Okay, time to go into battle. I nodded to Cavin. Shellena and Lance escorted Gavin to the stand.

"What happened in the forest the night you were hunting? Did you see anything unusual?" I prodded.

"Sika led us on the hunt. He ah kept telling me to stay back. I'd scare away the prey. He always said things like that." Gavin shook his head and went on. "Thinks I've got rocks in my noggin. But I know, what I know! He raced to the front of us spotting a kill. There was a deer up ahead on the path. Of course, he pushed me behind, told me that he was going to kill it. That's when I saw it!"

"What did you see? I want details."

Gavin looked over at Sika still cowering from the shadows outside. A sneer remained on his face. Even in his terror, he appeared pissed off, but what could he do? He was pretty much trapped. His clan was about to tell all.

"I stopped while Sika moved in for the kill. A man rambled through the forest muttering to himself. I couldn't make out the words. I sat there, not sure what to do. I didn't know where I was. Hell, didn't think we were that far from home. Maybe he was?"

Gavin gave me a questioning look. I turned to Cavin shrugging.

"It's Okay, just have him continue," he responded.

"All Right," I answered peering at the audience. Those who sat in the jury seats remained silent. The door to dining hall swung open. Amer and Jun stepped into the room unannounced.

"We got away! The shadows were right on our heels," panted Jun. Amer stood next to him stunned unable to stop shivering.

"I told you!" shouted Sika banging his hands on his knees.

"Silence in the court! You both should take a seat unless you have anything to add pertaining to the case," interrupted Cavin.

Nervously they sat in the back. I turned to Gavin. "Please state for the court what you saw."

"I... It happened so fast. Out of the wooded lot to the left of me, a wolf shot out after a rabbit. It went to go grab it."

"Yes, and?"

"It stopped sniffing the air. Then sat on its hind quarters. It seemed to be looking for something. A shadow moved on the ground slowly inching towards the wolf. The animal didn't suspect a thing. It attached itself to it. The wolf went mad. It moved through the trees towards the man I'd seen talking to himself."

"Did you see anything that might identify who this wolf was, or is?" I asked.

"It's ear had a chunk missing out of it. The markings it held were normal, grayish. After the attack occurred, it limped away confused. The wolf practically devoured the boy!"

"Gavin, are you sure this is what you saw? It sounds far fetched to me," I sighed, and shook my head in doubt.

"No, it happened! I'm not lying." He banged his cuffed hands on his head several times. Then let his hands fall into his lap. "Maybe Sika would lie, but I wouldn't."

Sika let out a howl from his seat. Then hid behind Gladiator. He was acting pretty cowardly compared to earlier in the evening.

Star clenched her jaw tight, then bit her bottom lip, letting her front incisors show. "It... it can't be! Why? How? He's hardly

307

ever around. Granted, he tried to chat up Spark. He has a thing for, that kid. I don't understand it?"

"Do you know who it is? I mean several of our wolves have been involved in fights. How do we confirm an identity?" I asked.

"Jinx has a torn ear. He's the only one who does," Star spoke.

A hush came upon the dining hall. Everyone looked at one another in utter silence. What would happen to Jinx? We couldn't punish him. If the scientists had this power, then why hadn't they annihilated our clan? Why were we still here?

A fog like substance formed in the middle of the room. I backed up, confused at what was occurring. Jones wasn't as startled. Did he know what was coming? The black wolf, Trigger materialized. He nodded to us, then spoke.

"The shadows were only in their experimental-form at the time of Du-Vance's death. I was with him when it took place. I couldn't make out who they were controlling nor could I divulge this information to you. I had to let you figure it out yourself. I can only appear to you now because I've escaped my tether for the moment."

"How were you captured if you're a spirit?" I asked.

"When Du-Vance died, I had nowhere to go. I was set free. That's usually a good thing. Afterward, I'm supposed to wait until instructed by the head wolf spirit for the next attachment. The shadows sensor's picked up on me. Trapping a spirit is tricky. I didn't know they had that kind of power. All I knew is that Du-Vance was dead, I'd failed him. Soon after I'd hid, I felt a pull. I fought against it trying to disappear, run, or transport. I couldn't stop it. The Shadows pulled me into a vacuum. Since I am a spirit, I move where the shadows move. I'm not sure how much longer til they pull me back in."

Blasted! We were dealing with something much greater than the entity. This mission would take all we had. Spirit guide?

Perhaps Starla would now receive two. It couldn't hurt. She and Cal could protect each other. But if a spirit-guide, could be caught that meant these shadows were deadly.

"You were Du-Vance's spirit animal? His guide? Did he not know you were there with him?" asked Owl standing up from his seat.

"Ah, the best friend. I guess you could say I too had been a shadow in the darkness. A few weeks before Martin began contemplating changing his plan of a peace treaty to that of infiltrating the scientists. His father had taken him to a pow-wow. At this gathering he told him that coming of age, he'd gain a spirit guide. There they held a ceremony where I attached myself to him. I wandered beside him for a few weeks. By the time I'd planned on revealing myself, it was too late. That night on his walk while he muttered to himself. That's when I was going to do it! Then I saw this figure overtake a wolf. I shuddered at it, then backed away into the forest. I hid like a fool instead of protecting him. I was supposed to guard him!"

"Why couldn't you?" asked Nayla. She'd begun to pace back and forth.

"Fear, they had used another of my kind. They could easily have found a way to pin the crime on me. It's another reason I had to lead you to the answers. I only knew what I'd seen. I've been following Starla and her father. I wanted to make sure they were safe. I may not have been able to shield your son, Rascal but I didn't want to let down the clan. That's when I decided I should help Starla Ariana as a spirit-guide."

"I see. That does make sense. You would have been the prime suspect. No one, though, even knew you existed until recently. I presume you'll assist us?" asked Nayla.

"Yes. I projected my spirit from Grandville, Illinois. Recently I've been moved wherever the shadows move. I'm almost free. I need you to meet me half way. Once done, we'll form a team to go in after them," said Trigger.

Rascal exhaled noisily, as he shook his head. He looked like he didn't know what to say. How to respond to what this black wolf had told us. There was no reason not to believe him. Where did we go from here? How could we escape what was outside of this hut? Would they leave, or would we have to dive right into another mystery? How would we protect ourselves? Was this another dead end.

"And Jinx, he wouldn't remember killing Du-Vance at all?" Rascal asked, standing up.

"No, he won't be able to give you details. Helping him remember might cause more damage. It's important to take that into consideration prior to doing so. A Wiccan might be helpful. One who would know how to initiate complex spells. I've been unable to locate anyone of that level nearby," Trigger replied.

"Star has various Shamen abilities," I admitted.

"That will be useful. Now, calling on spirits to protect us will only last for a short time," Nayla interjected.

"That's accurate," Star commented, maneuvering around chairs to the front of the room.

"Now you need to send them away. The shadows have a more difficult time appearing in well-lit areas. Call the sun goddess, Igaehindivo to illuminate the park it will keep them at bay. However, those in this clan, including individuals involved might want to remain here in the evenings. During the day be on guard. This is until we can move on to infiltrate the scientists as a team," suggested Trigger.

"What? My mom, will freak? What am I going to tell her!?" exclaimed Molly out of the blue.

"My old apartment has not yet been leased. I'll speak to your folks and see about you moving closer to the college. You should be relatively safe there. It's close by," I added.

Owl placed his hand on Molly's shoulder. Starla stood up, "You told me not to involve Maine. She's barely begun to practice Wicca. She's not even a full fledged witch, but it would help wouldn't it?"

I gave my daughter a stern look. What choice did we have? I didn't know any other witches in town. Star's the closest thing we had.

"She's right. I'll look into it. Check her out if you don't mind. She'll never know. Afterward, I'll give you an update," answered Trigger.

"No! What if it's not safe? Maine and I may have our differences, but I don't want her in harm's way. How would you feel if it was Jenson," argued Molly, turning to Starla.

"She has a point," Jenson stated.

"I realize this, but we have to do something! If she can help us, we should let her," Starla snapped.

"Enough," shouted Cavin. "Star will lead us in a prayer to the sun god. We'll ask her to illuminate the forest until we go on our journey. Jones, how much longer will you need to be free, for the college?"

"I could end the semester early. The dean won't like it," he said, raising an eyebrow. "Starla, Jenson, Owl," he nodded at them. "The assignment must be completed by the end of next week. I'll notify the other students by e-mail. Then the dean of my 'family' emergency."

"Thank you, Jones. Where's Trigger?" asked Cavin.

"Vanished, he has a habit of saying what needs to be said then parting," I acknowledged.

"We'll deal with him later. I want the bandit's in their quarters. Everyone else, if you've been milling about please join us."

"I.. I don't want to go back out with the shadows!" Gavin howled. "Bonehead, you're going back to the bench," snapped Gladiator.

Chapter 55

(Starla)

That evening...

Jenson sat beside me while I fixed my shoelaces.

"How are you holding up?"

I managed a weak smile. Then looked over at Megan astonished she hadn't freaked out. I almost had a gut feeling that somehow she was fitting in better than me. I shrugged it off.

"Starla?" said Tri.

"Yeah, I'm Okay. Megan doesn't appear shocked by any of this. It's kind of, creepy."

Jenson chuckled. I lay my head on his shoulder. My eyes wandered across the circle. Mango, now sat near Eva. Molly and Owl situated themselves next to us on the floor. I noticed Ranger, Mike lean over to Jones. He had a few words with him and then exited. He must have left to check the park. Before I could turn my head, I felt a hand rest on my right shoulder. Mom lowered herself down to the floor and sat between Molly and me.

The circle we had formed took up the entire area free of chairs and tables. Star placed herself in the middle. My dad? Where was he? My heart raced. My eyes darted back and forth across the room. Calm down Starla, calm down, I told myself. My eyes discovered my dad beside Cavin. Jenson took my hand in his. My heart rate lowered a bit. Glancing at Molly, I could tell she wasn't happy about our need to include Maine. I let the thought pass. My concern was finding a way to free Trigger from his hold. Would we have to defeat the shadows before we could free him?

Trigger hadn't explained himself. Star cleared her throat. Then stood in the middle of the ring.

"Listen carefully. I need everyone to take caution. When out walking, or if you're away from Hunter's Park, try avoiding places of shade. Open areas are the most desirable at this point. I don't believe they'll attack there. If you can't, please take an alternative form. If you run into a shadow, you'll most likely be able to outwit or outrun them. Do not hesitate to call for help! Starla, this means you. Tri, you too!"

My mom let out a loud gekkering sound! I imagine you didn't have to be in fox form to produce it in her case. She wasn't happy regarding this. I'd be walking on pins and needles until the mission.

"Now bow your heads, a minute of reflection, create a picture of serene light." Star paused, allowing us time to conjure our images. Then began to speak, "I call upon the sun to arise! Take over the night, let our moon rest until we complete our purpose. Hear us, now," she stated.

Was that it? I peeked out into the room. Everyone else's eyes remained closed. Shadows drifted back and forth watching us through the windows. Minutes passed, I patted my mom on the shoulder. She pushed me back opening her eyes. Star had positioned herself in an odd stance with her hands to the sky motioning for the sun to overtake the moon. Jenson gripped my hand. Gradually a light emerged out of nothingness. I was in awe. How long would it last? Would it give us enough time to sort this out? I closed my eyes fast before Star saw mine opened. I"m not certain if she'd seen mom gazing outside the window either.

"Open your eyes. This condition will last less-than-two-weeks. In these Starla, you and your friends will complete your college classes. Molly, we're going to want Maine on board. You'll have to trust us to keep her safe. Rascal, we will be informing Jinx of his involvement. He'll be under the watchful eye of Cavin. We need to make sure he doesn't go into shock. You know what a softie he is, this will be difficult for him," Star admitted.

"You're right everyone, be on guard. Stay close with family, friends, and the clan. Molly, you should discuss the apartment Dan spoke of with your parents. It's a lot to ask, but we need you," Cavin confessed.

"I know, I have been considering moving out. I've worried about my mom being alone," she replied.

"You'd still be close." Star reminded her.

"True, I'll look into it."

"Alright then. The shadows have moved out of the way. Everyone should be safe to leave if you wish. Star, thank you for leading us in the prayer," said Cavin.

"This takes the Cake! Funnel Cake! I can't believe all the excitement in one night," hollered Mango.

"Mango, calm down. We'll need you to help the elders with preparations. You have two weeks."

"What for?"

"Those incredible mirage tricks, your gift. They'll come in handy when we're away. If the sun goddess fails us we might need you sooner," Cavin suggested.

"That's great! I mean, yes sir. I'm on it." Mango leapt to her feet. Then hurried out the door.

"What about us?" asked Gavin.

"They're going to use us," grumbled Sika.

Star and Nayla trotted to them.

"Of course we are boys! You owe us after killing our family members and kidnapping. I'm not certain if you were involved in more than Cal's disappearance. There were others," stated Nayla.

"Others, what others?" asked Sika.

I shook my head in dismay. The punishment didn't seem to fit the crime. We knew where the scientists were hiding. So why did we need the bandits?

"Because we will," said a voice. I turned around looking behind me. No one there. Had it been Trigger? I glanced at Lance, who picked himself up off of the floor. He shook his body in a frenzy and howled. Shellena joined him.

"Stop! You're going to whip these monsters into shape. If they do not obey. We'll take it to the last resort," announced Cavin.

"Aren't we going to testify?" I asked in a shaky voice.

"Under the circumstances no. Unless you have anything to add we're not already aware of," said Nayla.

Cal's face was red with anger. She dug her fists into her thighs. "Cal?" I asked.

Eva placed her hand on her daughter's shoulder as she whispered in her ear. Then pulled away.

"I don't trust The Bandits. I'm not certain they'll be useful to us at all. This Trigger seems trustworthy. Cavin, why would we train the enemy? Shellena and Lance are correct We cannot place any trust in them," she spat, tears streaming down her cheeks.

"What if we used them as bait? We could lure the shadows and scientists out of hiding. We'd need back up. Dad? You'd have to ask for reinforcements. That means involving humans. There must be a way to destroy the shadows. The scientists won't get a trial, will they? We can't eliminate."

"No, not by death. I'll begin the paperwork to take those on board who worked Du-Vance's case," Dan answered.

Cal smirked slightly. "An idea I agree with, it's better than training them, bringing them along, and expecting compliance with us."

I observed my mother nod in agreement with my father. She took my hand and squeezed it, then let it go.

"While I identify with your anger. The Bandits did not kill Du-Vance. On the other hand, they do not seem at all remorseful regarding River Rogue. I'm going to agree with your proposal Starla," said Cavin.

My dad gave me a thumbs up sign.

"Shellena and Lance, please take the accused back to their chambers. They'll remain there until needed."

"What! We gave you all of that information, and now we're just cattle to you!" Gavin exclaimed.

Sika spat at him. "I told you, nothing good comes from us, nor them."

What an awful attitude to have about yourself and others," I thought. Whatever had led them, to hate us, and themselves, must have been pretty awful.

After we'd departed, dad drove us home. Megan wouldn't keep quiet about all that she was learning regarding our clan. I sat in the back seat watching the street lights fly by. Jenson had offered to take Molly home. Owl had come with Rascal. No one, actually got to say goodbye. I wouldn't say Molly hated me, exactly. Nothing was the same, and now we'd be going on another mission. I loved them, though, didn't I? Mysteries, the brilliance of bettering the world, the excitement? So why did this feel different? I slumped down in my seat, closing my eyes.

"Starla it's going to be Okay. Nayla's going to hold a few more meetings with you before we leave on this operation. Then she has to go back to her home. You and Cal, are almost ready. There's nothing to be afraid of," said my dad.

"I want to believe that everything will come together, and the nasties will get it in the end. A nice clean shot similar to a stake through a vampire's heart."

"Where does she come up with these things?" asked Dan.

"Buffy, remember?" Mom coached nudging him with her elbow.

Megan giggled to herself. I quickly sat up peering out the car window. Maine was heading towards the bookstore also known for supplying herbs. It was fairly late. I smiled to myself, definitely a Willow. I wondered what kind of family, she came from.

"Everything Okay, back there?" asked my Mom.

"Yes, I thought I saw Maine is all," I answered.

"Well, you'll have to speak to her soon, work things out with Molly. Things are good with Jenson?"

"Things are great with him," I admitted. Then sighed wrapping my arms around myself trying to keep out the chill.

Dad pulled into the apartment complex and parked. Then opened the car door getting out. "Are you girls coming?" Tri asked.

"Yeah, mom give us a minute," said Megan.

What could Megan possibly want? I eyed her curiously. Then immediately unbuckled my seat belt.

"Sis, it's going to be okay. We know Jinx killed Du-Vance. We have to get Maine in on this. I can help. We're a team."

Megan was already tearing up. She started to choke attempting not to cry.

"Sorry, I'm just happy, emotional. Gah, sometimes I hate being a girl sis."

I grabbed my sister in a bear hug.

She pulled away from me, then turned to exit the car, but before she did, she turned back to me.

"It's going to be all right. We'll get through this."

It almost resembled a promise, and I believed her.

Author's Note:

Thank you for reading Spirit-Guide, book 2 in the Myth series. I'm currently working on book 3. Writing brings me a lot of joy. It's where my passion lies. It is my hope that these books will encourage the reader to think outside of the box. The one each of us often lives in. If you liked this book, please leave a review @ amazon.com or the site where this book was purchased. Outside of my day job and writing, I enjoy taking walks with my dog, Butters. I also have two cute kitties who keep me company while I'm busy at my computer.

www.ingramcontent.com/pod-product-compliance
Lightning Source LLC
Chambersburg PA
CBHW031543240626
47153CB00002B/363